DEAD

A

LONG

TIME

By Tim Mahoney

ISBN: 978-0-9908974-1-5

Other books by this author:
If the Dead Could Speak
Secret Partners
Jack's Boy
Ghost Patrol
We're Not Here
Halloran's World War

This one's for
Kathy,
Russ,
Vicki
and Emily

This novel is based on real crimes of the Gangster Era. The Barker-Karpis gang committed its most notorious crimes from its base in Saint Paul, Minnesota. The gang had a secret partnership with certain politicians and policemen in that city.

The two most powerful figures in that underworld were Jack Peifer and Harry Sawyer, as depicted in this novel. Their sidekicks Sam Tanaka and Pat Reilly are also historical characters.

The accounts of Ma Barker, Alvin Karpis, Fred Barker and others associated with the gang are based on historical research.

CHAPTER ONE

"Well," said Myrtle "that's the last of the bacon."

She held a strip of crispy bacon in front of her bright red lips, as if it were a sacrament.

"You don't want it?" she asked. "You sure?"

"Gout, remember?" I said.

"We're perfect together," she said. "You lug home the bacon and I eat it." She chewed and said: "Don't look so mournful, sport."

"I don't want to go back," I said.

"You got no choice," said Myrtle, wiping her lips with a red-checkered napkin. "Guys can't just disappear. Let me be your counselor, sport. Trust in old Myrtle. She's smarter than any lawyer ever donned a pin-striped suit."

"Counsel me, oh wise one."

She pushed her chair away from the kitchen table, stood, wagged a finger in my face.

"There's one guy for you, and that's all. Harry. Go with Harry. He'll be boss for a hundred years. He's got the firepower and he knows the right cops."

I couldn't tell Myrtle everything. I couldn't tell her that my last job for Harry was to drive Pop Anderson to meet his executioners. Harry had tricked me into it. Harry had told me I was driving the old man to a sanitarium so he could dry out.

I felt sick, low and miserable whenever I recalled that rainy afternoon in May. Pop's body had been found on a muddy lakeshore the next morning, clothes ripped off, bullet in the head. Pop, he was just a hard-drinking blabbermouth who'd never hurt anyone.

"We could hide out here," I said. "If I could find some way to make a living."

"Winter's coming, sport," she said. "I ain't one of those people loves to ski. The only way I get through winter is steam heat and fur coats. Besides, the only jobs up here is lumberjack. I've seen you swing an axe. You're no Paul Bunyan."

"Lucky me," I said. "Go for a last swim?"

"Ah, you're all wet."

I shuffled into the bedroom, worked into a bathing suit, and whistled for the dogs.

Snowflake was a pure white fluffy German spitz. He was usually aloof. Maybe he understood he was high-bred. Hula Girl was a border collie mutt, black with a white stripe on her chest, the friendliest, happiest dog I ever met. Both of them knew the path to the lake better than I did. We breezed across the mowed yard, past the big collapsing red barn, down the crooked path in glorious dappled sunlight, then into the dark fragrant forest of birch and pine. Just past Cousin Cindy's cottage, we climbed a mound and spilled over to a sandy beach. The lake water was clear. Gentle waves lapped in, spooking Snowflake, who never trusted anything wet. Hula Girl splashed along the reedy shore, then swam like a little black crocodile.

A feeling came over me of peace and solitude. Sitting on a log on that lakeshore, I was just another animal admiring this world of quiet beauty. Atop a pine tree across the cove, a bald eagle flapped its wings, hovering above its sprawling nest, feeding fish to its eaglets. Time? There was no such thing as time.

When that magic spell broke, I went for a swim in water that was almost tropical warm. I floated on my back, staring up at puffy clouds, blue sky. Dragonflies hovered, considering me for a landing field. I'd spent my summers here as a boy, and it was just this glorious: warm, lazy, peaceful, and ending, on a lucky day, with a thrilling thunderstorm.

When I paddled in and dried off, I hung my towel from the branch of a birch tree. When this tree was a sapling and I was too, I got a BB gun for my birthday. I brought it to this lakeshore, and shot a bird that was resting on a branch. I was proud of my marksmanship until I walked up to the base of the tree and saw the little dead bird. Something, I don't what, something deep inside me asked the question: *Now what did you do that for?*

Thirty years have passed, and I still don't know the answer.

I walked back toward the farmhouse along a wide gravel driveway. Snowflake and Hula Girl raced into the forest on expeditions of their own. As I began to cross the meadow, out of the forest walked a white buck.

He'd been grazing and he lifted his head. We stared at each other. It seemed like a look of mutual curiosity. Snowflake scampered out of the woods and plowed to a stop. He too merely stared at the deer.

It was a holy moment in dappled sunshine, pure silence until the buck coughed, turned and ambled into the woods. He didn't bound or run, but merely disappeared behind the tangled undergrowth. Snowflake stared in awe. Hula Girl ran up and began sniffing the spot where the white buck had stood.

As a boy, I had spotted this buck's great-great-grandmother at the edge of the woods. These white deer had become a legend around Eagle River. They were not pink-eyed albinos but healthy, white-coated freaks of nature. As I saw the last flash of that white buck, I got goose bumps. I felt I had been granted a privilege, sent a message, but from whom, or what that message said, I might never know.

I walked through the knee-high grass of the meadow. Here Uncle Joe once planted potatoes, before whiskey and despair killed him. From that meadow I could see the white farmhouse, surrounded by red outbuildings: barn, chicken coop, woodshed, outhouse, shower room. Even if I could make a life out here, I couldn't live without Myrtle. Her life was urban: the clang of streetcars, the wail of police sirens, the shouts of newsboys, the scrambling pedestrians, the butcher, the baker and the cocktail shaker, those were the sights and sounds of Myrtle's world.

For the two weeks we'd been out here, Myrtle had dressed every day in pearl necklace, off-the-shoulder dress, full makeup, as if we were going out to hear the Ben Pollock Orchestra. Then she sat around the farmhouse, paging through magazines, restless and bored, getting into the whiskey sours before noon. The shabbiness, isolation, peace and silence of an overgrown potato farm drove her crazy.

I often drove Myrtle to downtown Eagle River, where we'd dine at The Black Forest supper club and see a movie. Loaded up on prime rib and baked potato, Myrtle dozed through the films. But those outings lifted Myrtle's mood. In the sweaty quiet night, we clung to each other after sex until we could stand the heat no more, then walked naked to the outdoor shower. There, we were tender with each other, like children, playing under starlight with soap and water.

Now, with the nights turning chilly, with Labor Day behind us, the gangster city of Saint Paul was pulling us back like it had gravity. I couldn't think about Saint Paul without remembering I was short the September rent.

It was a five-hour drive back to the city. Myrtle fiddled with the radio, trying to extract waves of civilization out of the forests of Wisconsin. She got mostly static. The tourist town of Minoqua, and the railroad town of Ladysmith, both displayed signs at their borders warning off job seekers. A hand-lettered sign along Minocqua's main street advised:

WE DON'T HAVE ENOUGH WORK FOR OUR OWN

One of many signs at Ladysmith declared:

HOBOS, KEEP GOING, THERE'S NO WORK HERE.

When we reached Saint Paul, I dropped Myrtle at her apartment. This was a three-story palace of luxury brick and marble on a prestige street. Myrtle was a professional shoplifter who'd walked out of many a swank shop pregnant with fur stoles. For full-size coats, she had perfected "the switch," where she walked in with a cheap imitation mink and exited in the real thing. Shoplifting was an income sport for Myrtle. Grand Avenue was lined with merchants from whom she could filch this and snatch that. She was banned from half the stores, and suspect in all of them.

"Don't call me for a while, Mick," she said, when I unloaded her suitcases from the trunk. "I'm feeling low-down. You know how I am. Don't waste your time on me. I'm an awful person, empty, hollow, I don't take no joy in things no more."

I said: "You're a wounded bird, that's all."

She kissed my cheek.

"You're a sweet man. Go find a girl who wants to play farmer's wife for you."

Two at a time, I carried all six suitcases to her front door, as if I were her bellboy. She put her key in the lock and swung open the door to her apartment.

"I hope I ain't been burgled," she said.

Her apartment, royally appointed with rugs and vases, pots of ferns and lush curtains, seemed dark and dusty.

"I'd invite you in," she said. "But you got things to do."

"Like…?"

"Like making nice with Harry. He's going to wonder where you been. Mick, you can't just walk out on these guys."

I kissed her on the lips. I was in love with Myrtle, even if I dared not mention that word in her presence. Myrtle in the daylight was tough, cynical and cold. In the dark she was warm, soft, loving, and sweet. A spectacular, but guarded, warmth shone from this woman's eyes. She was a beautiful child imprisoned in a stone-cold castle.

Usually I took Myrtle's advice seriously, but I had no intention of checking in with Harry Sawyer. Harry ran Saint Paul's underworld from a dank room in back of the Green Lantern tavern. He was a giant spider, with a web that stretched from the Black Hills to the Illinois border.

Lucrative and bloodless bank robberies had made Harry's reputation as a mastermind. Even notorious, hardened criminals begged for an audience at the Green Lantern. But Harry was a user, and I was tired of being used. I was determined to come back from vacation as my own man.

I drove up the slippery streetcar tracks of Grand Avenue to my tobacconist. Most of the "cigar shops" in this town were fronts for speakeasies or gambling parlors, but Victory Tobacco was an honest business. It had a glass humidor the size of a small garage, and was run by a Purple Heart veteran. In a damp room that smelled like an enchanted tobacco forest, I selected an ounce of

Havana Gold, scraped it into my leather zip pouch, paid the owner, and crossed the street to the Rosedale Pharmacy.

The Rosedale was typical of drug stores in the wealthy districts. It was a neighborhood hangout as well as a pharmacy. It had a green Formica lunch counter. Six matching booths lined the windows. Placards above the soda fountain announced "specials" that never changed: Grilled Cheese and Ham Sandwich, 19 cents. Root Beer float, a dime. Coffee 5 cents and Dutch Apple Pie with whipped cream, 12 cents. The entire back wall displayed magazines and dime novels. The lurid ones had disappeared, probably after a visit from the Legion of Decency.

Between the booths and the magazines stood two pinball machines and a sign that proclaimed: NO LOITERING.

Five teenaged boys loitered around it.

I told the pharmacist that my gout was acting up, and he recommended Sal Hepatica and colchicine tablets. He sold me a bottle of each and warned me to expect nausea. But what really made me sick was when he opened the cash register. It was a giant 19th-century thing made of wood and brass, the money slots crammed with bills. It was enough dough to see a man through a winter of unemployment.

I walked around the block, past a dry cleaners, an insurance agent who'd boarded up his storefront, and a German butcher shop. I began to study the Rosedale Pharmacy.

I nixed the idea of a daylight robbery. Too many people. Two waitresses, two pharmacists, three clerks and a delivery boy. At any given moment, there were 10 or 12 citizens in here, half of them buying "medicinal alcohol" prescribed by their doctor.

You would need a gang to hold this place up. It would be like a bank job. You'd need a "sweeper" to get the cash, a getaway driver parked with the engine running, a snarling "inside man" for crowd control, and a brazen "outside man" to watch for cops. Even so, the risks were high. Down at the Green Lantern, I'd heard the stories of holdup guys. On every job, something went wrong, some crazy thing happened.

I walked around to the parking lot, burglary in mind, although I don't have the tools or experience. The windows had been bricked in and the door looked like solid steel. Perched above was a spotlight and the speakers of a burglar alarm.

I didn't want to be noticed marking the joint, so after a few minutes I took the lurching, stinky streetcar home and returned to the pharmacy after dark.

One careless neighbor across the alley had left his two-tone Chrysler open, so I waited inside it in the darkness. Just after ten o'clock, the drugstore's back door opened as clerks and druggists finished their shift. About ten-fifteen a young man peeked out. He walked out under a spotlight: A gawky, six-foot-tall string bean, mid-twenties, carrying a money pouch. He hustled to a black Ford and drove off, headlights bouncing.

No way, I muttered, does that bag have less than $200.

CHAPTER TWO

In the morning I awoke with doubts, nausea from the gout medicine, and a throbbing toe. I limped around the apartment, cursing. Now I had both the side-effects and the disease. Even if I got up the nerve to rob the Rosedale, I wondered if I could limp away fast enough.

And did I have the nerve? I had begun ten years ago as a freelance bootlegger, then graduated to broker of shady deals. For a while, I was in good with both of Saint Paul's master criminals, Harry Sawyer and Jack Peifer. But I wasn't a brazen thug. I wasn't intimidating. I was an Army veteran, but had never fired my M-1 after basic training. Back home on bootleg runs, I had been hijacked at gunpoint once. I'd been in two brief duck-and-fire shootouts. But I had never pulled an armed robbery.

Catholics aren't supposed to believe in Fate, but I was beginning to wonder if my destiny involved a bedroll and a soup line. It wouldn't take my landlords more than a month to evict me. Once you're thrown out on the street, things go downhill fast. And in Saint Paul, that was downhill literally. At night from my apartment on Cathedral Hill, I could see the hobo campfires. There were tent cities lining the river, and winter was coming. In Minnesota, winter is always coming. Two months from now, Doc Ingerson's boys would be escorting the corpses of frozen hobos to their frosty graves.

I knew I couldn't keep Harry from finding me, so I cornered

his main man Pat Reilly in the muddy parking lot behind the Royal Cigar Store.

It wasn't really a cigar store. Overhead, eight black wires connected the shop to the telephone pole. What cigar store needed eight phone lines?

"Pat," I said.

"Where you been?"

"Out of town."

"You're limping."

"Just an old war wound," I lied.

"You're kidding, right? Who do you like today?"

"Haven't read the Form in a month," I said. "Missed the whole Saratoga meet."

"Still smarting over the Derby?"

I had lost $500 on the Kentucky Derby, four months back. Of course I felt like a fool now. But I'd had 14-1 on that horse. I was a few strides away from a life-changing score. The winnings would have supported me for years in Eagle River, even if the farm never sprouted another potato.

Pat lit a Lucky Strike. He was a little guy with stained, crooked, broken teeth, a hint of platinum hair around the edges of his flat cap. When you looked at Pat, you either saw a bobbing lit Lucky or rotten teeth.

"Pat," I said, "I'm a little low on cash."

"So's the whole country." He blew smoke. "Why do you think I'm here working a second job? For my health?"

"You know anybody who needs help?"

"Jeez," said Reilly. "Not these days."

"Harry's not mad at me, is he?"

Reilly gripped the door handle like he wanted to get away.

"If Harry thinks you need to know," he said, "You'll get the message."

He blew smoke. "You're a horse player, Mick. What are the

odds against a sure thing?"

He opened that steel door. Built to withstand a police battering ram, it closed on Reilly with a thud.

I began to convince myself I could pull off a robbery. The Rosedale wasn't in my neighborhood. They didn't know me. I could walk in, flash a weapon, solve my problems in one courageous moment.

Working in Harry's gang could be lucrative, but you never knew what hand he'd deal you. One day you'd be negotiating a simple protection deal with a grocer running numbers in Rondo. The next day you'd be driving a drunken old man to meet his killers. If I set up and pulled off my own jobs, I could call the shots. And in my gang of one, there'd be no shots at all. I'm not God. I don't decide who lives and who dies. A couple of months rent isn't worth a fella's life. If I want to live, so does the other guy.

Harry had no job for me right now, which was bad news for my finances but good news for my peace of mind. In a better world I would have quit Harry's gang after Pop Anderson's murder. But Harry's soldiers were alive only so long as they were loyal, and there was no backing out of his gang. Knowledge of Harry's crimes put you in serious company. Harry feared two things: betrayal, and the federal government. The recent imprisonment of Al Capone had only made Harry's paranoia worse. No matter what it said in the newspapers, Harry was convinced that Capone was betrayed by his underlings. Harry, Saint Paul's Capone, doubled down on his drinking the day the Feds slapped Scarface in prison.

So I couldn't outright quit, but I intended to tell Harry, if I could get to him, that I'd be interested in jug marking. My half-hatched plan to make a living as a lone stickup guy was shaky and desperate, and in thoughtful moments I knew that. There's less risk and plenty of reward in jug marking. I'd be one of Harry's boys, but avoid any murderous assignments.

The jug marker was the brains behind every bank job. In a way, it was an echo of my dad's profession. He made up railroad timetables. I would do the same thing for bank robberies. I'd select the target bank based on how much money it handled. After weeks of intricate planning, I'd finish by drawing the "git maps" which showed escape routes and alternatives. I practiced the speech I would make for Harry. *I'm a numbers man, Harry, you've got plenty of guys for the rough stuff.*

In the meantime there was rent to pay, so I watched the Rosedale Pharmacy. Saturday would be the big bag. I dressed in my best gray suit and fedora, complete with red tie and shined shoes. I had learned this from notorious robbers: dress up. Look like an insurance salesman, and take 'em by surprise.

The guy with the two-tone Chrysler apparently never locked it, so I waited in there. The drugstore lights dimmed at ten, and all but the young delivery man exited by the back door. I pinched open the cylinder of my shiny little revolver. I shook it to confirm it contained no ammo. I looked through every one of those five cylinders, pointing the pistol at the streetlamp. I fidgeted, sick to my stomach from gout medicine or nerves or both. I sat sweating, cursing the gawky clerk as each excruciating second went by. I began to wonder if I'd missed him. Then the door opened a cautious crack.

The clerk peeked out into the parking lot.

Quiet, I opened the Chrysler door. I fought the urge to take a wicked piss. I forced myself to cross the street, legs feeling like concrete stilts, mouth dry. The clerk pushed into the spotlight, money bag jammed under his arm. He turned around and I was twenty paces from him.

I opened my mouth to shout orders, but the words jammed in my throat. I may have said something like *gaaa gaaa.* I pointed my pistol at the clerk. His face lost what little color it had, his eyes seemed to expand to big blue marbles, his Adams apple throbbed. He bolted for his Ford. Door flapping open, his car spun out on squealing wheels, spitting dirt and pebbles that stung my face.

I stood like I'd been struck by lightning, a spot-lit failed gangster with a gleaming unloaded revolver in his left hand. I snapped to when I realized the neighbors would be on the phone with the cops. I pocketed my gun, tilted my fedora low, and double-timed it down a dark alley.

CHAPTER THREE

On Monday morning, I walked from my apartment to the streetcar stop at the Selby tunnel. Across the tracks, the Saint Paul Police, their green uniforms blending in with the bushes, were clearing out a hobo camp on the hillside. Broken, dirty men, carrying satchels, bedrolls and hobo sacks, stumbled along the rocky cliff face desperate to escape the swinging nightsticks. A long stairway ran up the hill, connecting the Cathedral with the vice district at Seven Corners. The hobos stumbled down or clawed up, knocking each other aside in frantic escape. I felt bad for these men. Was this what we had come to as a nation? That a man's only worth was his job? What would these poor souls do in two months when it turned freezing? Some might ride the rails to Florida, others would freeze to death, and be scooped up like trash and buried with only a stranger's blessing. All because they couldn't find a job.

The streetcar clanged out of the tunnel and blocked my view of the rousting. I paid my nickel, climbed in among the gawking passengers, and watched out the dirty windows as the cops regrouped at the bottom of the hill. Saint Paul Police, clueless at solving kidnappings and murders, were brilliant at inflicting misery on helpless hobos. Still, I knew most cops hated this duty. Bums with jobs, rousting bums without jobs, that's what this came down to.

I got off the streetcar at the police station, and climbed to the third floor to see Sergeant Billy McAmbly, the one-man Bertillion squad. Billy had been my teammate, the catcher during our championship year at Sacred Heart. He'd gained a lot of beer weight since.

Billy sat on a stainless-steel stool behind his counter, his back turned to me, gazing out a dirty window.

"Who let you in here?" he said.

"How did you know it was me?"

"Eyes in the back of me head." He lifted a bottle of Hamm's beer to his lips. I walked to the window and stood beside him.

"What are you staring at?" I asked.

"You see Charley Bragg killed himself?" he said.

"Yeah, it was all over the papers, how well did you know him?"

"Drinking buddy, family man. Right in the bank lobby, Jesus." Billy put a finger-gun to his head and dropped the thumb-hammer. "The brass stationed him in the bank lobby to humiliate him. That's how bad it is around here. Cops shooting themselves in public places. Blood all over the bank windows. Big crowd of gawkers. Jesus, it's indecent."

I patted him on the shoulder. "Billy, Billy, you've got family, you've got a job."

He grunted. "So did Bragg."

He drank. "He's got my kids thinking: Oh. Daddy's a cop. Is Daddy going to shoot himself? Jesus, it's too late for me to get another job."

"Which is what I came to see you about," I said.

The view out those grimy windows was blocks of slums and the gleaming white state Capitol, crowned by four golden horses.

I said, "Anybody hiring. City? County? State?"

"Don't you read the newspapers?"

"Sure," I said. "But somebody's always handing out a favor. I'd take street sweeper, I really would."

"Maureen is sick. They don't know what's wrong with her."

"Oh God, Billy, I'm sorry to hear that. What is it?"

He shrugged. "Kidneys? They don't know." He swirled the last of that beer and drank it. His beer belly bulged so much that he couldn't button his brassy green police tunic. He lay the empty bottle on the dusty window sill and stood hands on hips, staring out.

"She's in the hospital?" I asked.

"They want to take her to Mayo. I can't sleep it's killing me, and then there's the goddamn doctor bills."

I put a hand on his broad shoulders. "Wish I could help you."

"Try Minnesota Mining," he said. "I hear sandpaper's selling like hotcakes."

"They want a science diploma, Billy."

"Because the city, we're on short pay now. Every time you think it's gonna get better, it gets worse. Swift? Armour? I know the work is bloody but..."

"Packing houses laying off."

"Ford?"

"I've been trying there all year."

"The breweries?"

"I'm on Papa Alt's list of Commies and malcontents."

"The railroads? Doesn't anybody on the Northern remember your old man?"

"Dead clerks have no friends," I said.

"Newspapers?"

"They hire college grads now. College boys! In the newsroom! Are they kidding? I'm hoping Reilly can get me a job selling daily doubles at the Royal. Tips are okay but you've got to pay up front for that job, and I'm dead out of cash."

Billy turned from the window. Tacked to a cork board were Bertillion cards. A little bigger than baseball cards, they depicted Saint Paul's most wanted men: bank robbers and bootleggers mostly. Stuck in the cork board were six darts, every one having missed its target.

He collected the darts. "Quarter a hit," he said.

"I don't have a quarter to spare."

"Come on." He loosened his dark green tie, cast me an accusing glance. "You play the ponies, don't you?"

"Haven't placed a bet in months." I shook my head. "Maureen. Poor kid."

Billy puffed his red cheeks.

The Irish, renters for centuries in their own land, have a natural terror of dispossession. I kept imagining eviction notices posted on my apartment door as I took the streetcar to my sister Kelly's place. She lived in a bungalow on the blue-collar side of town. Kelly and I and Mona had grown up mostly in apartments. Sometimes, if my dad had a few consecutive years of healthy employment, we'd rent a small home. I remembered being evicted from two of them. I was nine years old the first time we were tossed out. It was a summer day. I was sitting on a brick wall, baseball glove on one hand. A sheriff's deputy stood by silent as Mom, Dad and Uncle Matt loaded our furniture into the back of a horse-drawn wagon. My Aunt Doris sat beside me, put her arm around me, and that's when I felt safe enough to sob. "You'll be okay, Mickey," she told me. "It's just one bad day."

Kelly was the only Powers kid who'd managed to buy a home, although it was mortgaged. It was over on Magnolia Avenue, where nobody fancy lived. It was a narrow, battleship gray bungalow, with a long driveway to a single-car garage in back. Attached to the front porch was its only frill, a tattered striped awning, faded to neutral colors.

Kelly was as tall as I was, five years younger, and with every mark of the Irish upon her: strawberry blond hair, freckles and blue eyes. She percolated coffee, served it with the a Danish pecan cake, and the moment she sat down I asked to borrow fifty bucks.

"You're kidding, right?" she said.

"For the rent," I said. "This is not gambling money. Pay you back by the end of the month."

She sighed. "I guess. We have it. We're lucky. I shouldn't complain. Gary has plenty of work, thank God."

She leaped up, returned with a damp sponge, began wiping the tablecloth of crumbs that were visible only to her.

"You know Saint Barbara's now," she said, "mandatory uniforms. It's a scam, I tell you. Between the Church and the uniform companies."

"Two girls in Catholic school, it's a big expense, I know."

She tossed the sponge into the sink. "Mona was over here for money too."

"How is she?"

"Twice in one month," Kelly complained. "Never see that money again. From her, are you kidding, queen of the tavern flappers?"

"She'll settle down," I said.

"She's almost twenty five! New guy every week, that one, I swear. One day she's going with a gray-haired banker, the next day it's a college boy."

"Mona, well, who knows about her, but I'll pay you back for sure."

"I know you will, Mick."

Kelly didn't trust the banks any more than the Church, and kept her savings in a coffee can. Her husband Gary was a coal and ice truck driver, a Teamster shop steward. He had mastered the art of creating overtime pay. If there wasn't a traffic jam on his route, he'd create one. His coffee breaks were legendary. There wasn't a tavern or lunch counter on the East Side where he wasn't known by name. He'd even been known to take in a ballgame at lunch. There was no figuring this world, really, where one guy gets time-and-a-half while a thousand others can't get the time of day.

When Kelly counted out my loan in fives and singles, I swore before all the Irish saints that I would repay her by October.

"I've got money coming in," I claimed.

"God knows where you get your money, because I don't," Kelly said. "How long's it been since you had a job?"

"I'm an entrepreneur," I said. "It's the American way."

On the way back home, I hopped off the streetcar at the Mother Mercy Rest Home to see Aunt Doris. I wanted to assure her that her farm house was still standing and tell her I'd had a good time. I wouldn't mention Myrtle. Aunt Doris had never met Myrtle. Aunt Doris, if she were healthy, would pick up a broom and drive a woman like Myrtle out of the house.

But Doris wasn't healthy. Her body was frail, her eyes were cloudy, her mind wandered. Barring a miracle, Aunt Doris would never see that farm again.

"Oh. Who are you?" she said.

"Michael, darling, your nephew."

She had been propped up in bed by the nuns. Doris was feisty, a solid, honest American. Her parents were rugged pioneers who had moved to Saint Paul not long after its founding. Doris married the affable immigrant Joe Finnerty and they had two children, but both died young. That tragedy, compounded by Joe's loss of his warehouse job, sent them in retreat to a Wisconsin potato farm. They had to escape a city where they had been wounded so badly. There wasn't much money in a potato crop, but Doris aced the civil service test and became chief tax clerk for the Vilas County government.

Doris's salary saved the farm. We Powers kids visited from the city every summer, keen to swim in Snipe Lake, but not so keen to dig potatoes. Doris was a big-hearted disciplinarian who would slap your face for cursing and make you an ice cream soda when you were feeling blue. Children never forget proper discipline and small kindnesses, and Aunt Doris, loony and decrepit now, was strong in my heart.

"Is Michael still alive?"

I held her bony hand.

"Yes, Aunt Doris, it's me, Michael and I'm right here for you."

"Good." She squeezed my hand. "Because you'll be dead a long time. Live your best life, Michael, because all of us … will be dead … for such a long time."

As if she were auditioning for the Great Beyond, Doris fell instantly into a sleep that didn't seem far short of death.

Back at my apartment building, the manager, Mrs. Holy Reardon, answered my knock on door. I'd never been inside her place, but from the hallway could see the sacred convention of statues, crucifixes, and holy pictures behind her. I paid $50 in crumpled bills, and promised never to be late with the rent again.

Fifty bucks was a hefty rent, but in return I lived in the swank part of town. My apartment was top floor of a building that overlooked downtown, and stood directly across from the magnificent Cathedral of Saint Paul. The apartment building had been put up about ten years ago, during the boom, and was top class, with cream brick outside and oak floors inside, and electric wiring built right into the walls.

Aunt Doris' warning chilled me as I climbed the stairs to my fourth-floor apartment. I had come to suspect that my ex-wife had been right. As our thirties slipped away Peggy complained that we'd been wasting our lives, hustling for money, partying in nightclubs, mistaking drinking buddies for true friends. The party's over, Mick, she said, I want my babies.

We tried. We consulted two doctors. One advised Peggy to stand on her head after sex. That didn't work. Nothing worked. We visited an adoption agency but neither Peggy nor I had a legitimate job, and we were turned down. I rescued Hula Girl and Snowflake from the police impound, figuring they would be substitute children. By then Peggy was lost to me.

Now I fed Hula Girl and Snowflake from a diminishing tub of sausage mixed with corn flakes. I let Charles and Ameila out of their cage for free flight. Both rewarded me by crapping on the couch.

Parakeets back in the cage, I opened the windows to let out the late summer heat. I went around the apartment gathering things I could hock: golf clubs, wedding ring, revolver, what was left of the family China. Altogether it might bring $20, and I needed $100 by the end of the month.

I changed my mind about that revolver. It was a handsome, nickel-plated Smith & Wesson five-shot revolver with a pearl handle and a shrouded hammer. It was meant to be carried in your pocket. It was given to me by Jack Peifer, master of the Hollyhocks casino, and prince of the vice rackets. He had shot off the tip of his pecker with this gun. He had been drunk, pulling it out of his pocket. It was a bad luck gun, and had almost cost him his manhood, and that's why he gave it away.

That revolver reminded me not just of Jack and his very personal accident, but of my former friend Sam Tanaka. Sam was Jack's top man, and Jack had jobs to give out.

Jack had once trusted me. Well, trusted me enough to give me black-bag jobs. That's just what I needed now, something simple and low-risk. Some job so quiet, so humble, that word of it would never get back to Harry. They were rivals, Harry and Jack. You had to walk a delicate line between them. So I felt a little shaky when I called over to the Hollyhocks. I didn't dare ask for Jack. Everything Jack had to go through Sam first.

I didn't know what to expect. Sam had quit talking to me after the Derby. The race had proved him right, and me disastrously wrong. Had Sam and I pooled our research and cash, and bet as he suggested, he might be on his way home to Japan by now. Sam was even more desperate to escape Saint Paul than I was. He had two children back in Japan, where war clouds were drifting over from China.

"Mister Tanaka," I said.

"Mick," Sam said, "I will do you a favor and hang up. Let's forget you called."

Click.

I dropped that phone receiver. I picked up the revolver. It glinted in the September sunlight. Was I a man, or a pathetic worm living on money borrowed from his sister?

CHAPTER FOUR

On Wednesday I saw in the Daily News exactly three jobs under Men Wanted. One of those jobs was apartment janitor, free rent, no pay, married man only. Another was a one-week factory job paying $12. There'd be a hundred guys lined up for that one job, and the man hired might well be stiffed on the pay. That's what it was coming to now, factories running short on payroll.

The third job required references. For the last decade, I had only worked for bootleggers.

The newspaper ads convinced me I needed to go into hock. In a city full of Germans, there were a lot of guys named Dutch. I went to see the most infamous one, Downtown Dutch, at Pawn Paradise. I took the streetcar, lugging an embarrassing assortment of worldly goods: golf clubs, typewriter, wedding ring, box of China.

"Powers," said Dutch, "what is it you prought me?"

Dutch had lost an arm in the War and was known around town as a human one-armed bandit. More than a decade had passed since the War, but anyone who spoke with a German accent was suspect. Dutch insisted that he'd lost an arm for Uncle Sam, although he was vague on the details of his patriotic service.

As if to show off that missing arm, Dutch's shirts were crisp from the laundry, the flopping sleeve doubled back with a giant gold pin.

When dealing with trusted guys, he emerged from his locked

steel cage.

"Golf season is pinished," he said, rattling the bag and clubs. "Too expensive. And who buys golf clubs in September?"

I shrugged. "Guys headed to Florida, maybe."

"Pica?" he said, tapping the typewriter keys, "or Elite?"

"Elite," I said.

"Elite don't sell," he said. "It's a girl's machine."

"What do you mean?" I challenged him. "Girls type. This belonged to my wife. You don't think I owned a typewriter, do you?"

"Please, Powers," he said, "I know what sells in my pawn shop."

"Pure gold," I said, and handed him the wedding ring.

"No such thing," he said. "Perhaps eighteen carats, Powers. My advice: keep it. Perhaps she'll come pack to you. Where did she run off to?"

"Pearl Harbor," I said.

"Where's that?"

"Far, far away."

He flipped the wedding ring in his palm.

"Two pucks," he said.

"Two dollars? For a pure gold ring? For the ruins of man's life, two dollars?"

"It's scrap, Powers."

"Give it to me," I said. "My bride slipped that onto my finger as we said our vows in front of God and the Priest. It is not scrap. We had ten good years, you know. Take a look at the China."

He dropped the ring on the glass countertop, which shielded a display of cigar lighters and gold cigarette cases. He peered into my cardboard box, turned over a dinner plate. It gleamed in the sun that streamed around the burglar bars.

"Padly chipped," he said.

"What's chipped?"

"The gravy poat, handle proken," he said. "Ten pucks for the lot."

"Without the ring," I said.

"Seven cash, eight pucks credit."

"Hard cash," I said. "No funny bills."

Rather than risk losing that ring carrying it in my pocket, I wore it, but on the right hand. That's where a divorced man wears it, so he can beat himself up about what he did wrong to drive his wife halfway around the world. Seven bucks? Or as Dutch would say, seven pucks? Those seven silver dollars might as well have been hockey pucks, for all the good they were going to do me.

I took the streetcar past the Rosedale Pharmacy. Through the big windows I could see that young man I'd tried to rob, stocking shelves with aspirin and cough medicine. I got off and rode the streetcar back, safe surveillance from my wooden seat among old ladies going downtown for shopping.

I was surprised to see my sister Mona, crossing the street, heading for the drugstore.

Last I'd heard, she was living near the Capitol with an appliance salesman from the Golden Rule department store. Mona was a sturdy-built, beautiful platinum blonde, with startling blue eyes and a loud, raucous personality. She wore a purple dress, mid calf-length, and high heels, like she was going to work, although she had never held any job for long.

She couldn't stand to have a boss, and no boss could stand her, either.

I'd been avoiding Mona. She was quite the person for accusations and fault finding. I had no desire to be apprised of my shortcomings. So on the streetcar, watching Mona, I sat low.

In the morning, my downstairs neighbor Janie knocked. She had just turned 23 and was chubby-cute, with curly red hair and freckles. Can you adopt an adult? I wanted her for a daughter. One

year out of college, Janie was learning the news game in the inky
offices of the Daily News.

I hadn't worried much about Janie during my Eagle River
vacation. She'd been called back to Waunakee, Wisconsin, to the
family dairy farm, by emergency. That was a relief for me. Janie,
ambitious to be a police reporter, had been asking dangerous
questions about the fiery demise of two prostitutes. I had warned
her about poking into the underworld's business, but she was
headstrong. When she took a leave of absence to go back to
Wisconsin, a part of me hoped she'd never return.

"So Powers," she said, as I poured coffee from a stainless-and-
glass French press. "How was your vacation?"

"No shortage of mosquitoes," I said. "How are things back on
the Vetter farm?"

She shrugged. "Mom's back."

"And healthy?"

Janie sighed. "There's no living with that woman. She's a
stubborn Dutcher. When her mind's made up it's made up. Thank
god, though. My dad's lost without her."

She sipped coffee from a chipped mug. "Did somebody steal
your China?" she said, looking at the empty hutch.

"No, I gave the China to my sister," I lied.

"Which one?"

"Kelly, the married one. I don't entertain. She does."

Janie tugged her skirt to cover her knees. They never lose it,
Catholic school girls, that sense of modesty. I had never seen Janie
in the clothes of temptation.

"It's good to be back," she said. "You don't know how much I
missed this city. And guess what, Powers, I'm off the women's
pages. They hired an intern to do weddings while I was gone, and
she's working out. I'm on the county beat now."

"Covering Ramsey County government?"

"It's a snore, I know, but you've got to start somewhere."

She rose to stand before the big painting in my living room. It was a copy of an English country scene by a famous landscape painter. I had forgotten who, exactly. My wife had picked it out, and said it gave the room class, hanging there over the beat-up sofa.

"Gainsborough," she said.

"Yeah, that's the guy."

"Landscape with a ruined castle."

She leaned in to examine the painting.

"Lovely," she said. "Bright, but at the same time gloomy. Sad, don't you think?"

"Janie, do you think they'd hire an old leg-man down there?"

"Where?"

"The Daily News."

"Powers, I thought you were some kind of gangster."

"Are they hiring or not?"

She scoffed. "Radio's killing us. Advertisers fleeing in droves. Hey, I thought bootleggers were immune to bad times. I mean, people are still drinking, right?"

"Yeah, well."

"Come on Powers, I sense a story."

I certainly couldn't tell her that, in service to my so-called friends in gangland, I'd unwittingly delivered a helpless old man to his executioners.

"Look," I said, "when I got into this game, twelve years ago, it was innocent. A guy motored up to Winnipeg, drove back with a few cases of hooch, doubled his money. It was too much money and too easy, that was the problem. The cops started taxing us. Then thugs began hijacking our loads. Soon the cops got jealous of the thugs, and they became hijackers too. Then the gangsters started shooting each other, fighting for territory, until only ruthless killers were left. Then the gangsters and cops made a pact to vacuum up all the money. What started as a joy ride degenerated into a murderous racket. This isn't 1922. You can't make an innocent run to Winnipeg anymore."

"Too bad," said Janie.

"The easy money is hard now."

"You must be desperate if you're thinking of the news business, Powers. How long's it been?"

"Just a thought."

"How long?"

"Before the War," I admitted. "Ancient history. Hell, when I started out, half the car crashes involved a horse-drawn wagon. How's Major Hoople treating you?"

"Well, he did give me the leave and he did take me back."

"And you're off the women's pages."

"And I got a five dollar a month raise. I know I've been lucky. It's just… I want more. I want Page One. That's not wrong is it? Ambition?"

She sipped.

"Powers, you should open a coffee house."

"With what money?"

"That's the problem, isn't it?"

She glanced at the wedding ring on my right hand.

I took the ring off and held it up.

"I won't be nosy, Powers," she said.

The ring gleamed in sunlight that bounced off the Cathedral's copper dome. I lay it on the white coffee cup saucer, where it rang a musical note.

"Took it in to get it appraised," I said.

"Oh, what's it worth?"

"Two dollars more than a sacred vow."

Janie pushed her chair back, walked around the table, and standing in back of me, rubbed my shoulders. I could see the red nails of her chubby fingers, feel the warmth of her breath as she whispered into my ear.

"You won't be happy, Powers," she said. "Until you let her go."

I shut my eyes. Her soothing hands came away from my shoulders, her shoes shuffled across my hardwood floor, the parakeets chirped in their cage, the dogs scrabbled, and I heard the door open and close. Only then did I raise my head.

And there I sat, before two drained coffee cups. Me, my dogs, my parakeets, and a ring that was made out of gold all right, except for the hole in the middle.

CHAPTER FIVE

All that sleepless, gout-painful night I replayed that failed drugstore robbery in my head. I dreamed up other joints I might stick up. It had to be a quick one-man job in the dark, and drug stores were the richest targets. I wasn't willing to do a daylight stick-up, even at a small store, because I didn't want to use a loaded gun. I didn't want to kill somebody over a few bucks and besides, an unloaded gun would get me a softer deal if I ended up in front of a judge. The Rosedale Pharmacy would be on high alert now, and so would others in the swell part of town. The thought of casing some nickel-and-dime joint in a crappy neighborhood threw me into a blue funk. If I was going to rob somebody, I wanted to rob the rich.

Who else had the money?

So I phoned Reilly at the Green Lantern, maybe my last call, since Tri-State Telephone was getting serious about collecting its bill. I was determined to get in to see Harry and convince him that I would make a good jug marker. Planning bank robberies was a low-risk, no-rough-stuff job, and paid good money, usually half a share. If I could plant in Harry's booze-addled mind the idea that I could mark a bank, I would no longer need these errand boy jobs that put me in service to every vicious thug out there.

"Patrick," I said. "Hail Caesar."

"Yeah?"

"So what do you say?"

"Eh," he said. "Nothing doing."

"What did ever I do to you, Pat?"

"Nothing."

"So?"

"Quiet as a Monday Mass down here."

"Come on, am I a rube now?"

"He's in a drinking mood," Pat said. "I'm not barging in there for no reason no how."

"I'll handicap a card for you."

Long pause.

"Patrick, I'll dutch the Wood. We'll go in together. I made a killing last year, the Wood."

"Okay, it's your funeral," he said. "The Wood Memorial, eh? The horses owe me. Win, place or show, I don't care anymore. I'm due." He put the phone down. Two minutes of static later, he said: "Get down here and say hello like you hate me."

Bess ushered me in to see Harry. As I followed her down the corridor, I wondered whether she was between men. She was a gorgeous slender redhead of thirty-some years, sober and smart. I'd have asked her to dinner, but she had a reputation as a gold-digger. I'd never known her to date a broke guy.

She opened the door and stood aside with a sick smile, as if to say: good luck, sucker.

"Harry," I said.

It was two o'clock on an afternoon that was eighty degrees and sunny. Except in here. Harry's office was illuminated by a tiny bulb, swaying by frayed cord from the ceiling. Underneath it lay a galvanized tub holding a block of ice. Covering that ice was a wet canvas tarp, topped by a whirling black Westinghouse Electric fan.

"Hey, isn't that dangerous?"

"What?" Harry barked.

"Electric and water don't mix."

"Thomas Edison now."

He was slurring drunk. I sat, the desk between us. The room's chill gave me goose bumps.

"What the fuck are *you* doing here?" he demanded. He pushed a sloshing bottle of Canadian Club across the desk.

"Reilly sent me," I said. "I'm looking for a career change, Harry."

"Have a drink."

His desktop was littered with glasses. I picked one I hoped was clean and poured a finger of whiskey.

"Okay to talk in here?" I asked.

"J. Edgar Hoover," he growled. "Fuck 'em."

"Harry," I said, "you should try me out as a marker."

"I already got the best guy in town."

"Well," I said, "there's always room for one more. Right?"

He pushed his chair back from the desk. He was a roly-poly man in shirtsleeves with dark curly hair. He had started out as a butcher in Nebraska, and looked like one now, meaty and crude.

"I wish I had something for you," he said. "You're a good boy. I like you."

Boy. That was how he referred to Reilly. To Harry you were either a level gangster or a boy, only tough enough to run errands.

"Keep me in mind, Harry, I'm behind in the rent."

"Something else came up about you," Harry said.

"Harry, I…"

"It's about a dame."

"Myrtle," I said. "We've been…"

"No the other dame," said Harry. "The news hound."

I felt like that whirling fan had electrified me.

Harry said: "The one lives downstairs in your joint."

"Yeah, the kid, I've … I've seen her around."

"Redhead. Works for the Daily News, that one."

I tried a bluff. "Yeah, I think she writes about weddings and baby showers."

"She's got a big mouth," Harry said. "I got no use for these people ask questions. You know this kid? Get to her. Shut her up. Okay? Do me that favor."

"Sure, Harry. If I could ask…"

"Nothing doing, no questions," he said. "On the way out, turn that fan to high, will you?"

I walked out into the bar room, my head buzzing. Harry's Green Lantern Tavern was like a factory, manufacturing crime: bootlegging, drug running, gambling, pimping, fencing, money laundering, bank robbery, hijacking and murder for hire.

Murder for hire, that's the phrase that whirled dizzy in my mind.

I wandered in the bar room like a man on dope. All around me, lively people were enjoying themselves. A Frenchman who'd lost a leg in the War limped around the kitchen making, oddly enough, fabulous garlicky Italian meals. Pat Reilly ran the bar with a generous pour, and his kegs oozed the freshest beer from Papa Alt's brewery. Bess guard-dogged the Blue Room, keeping the cops out and letting the gambling fools in. Rubes wandered in day and night, hoping to see Machine Gun Kelly, or Pretty Boy Floyd.

But I was probably the only gangster on display at the time. I leaned over the bar and called to Reilly for a ginger ale.

He slapped an iced glass on the bar and said, "No booze, no charge. How long you been off the sauce?

"Your first day of gout is your last day of heavy drinking," I said.

I tipped him a buck I could not afford.

"How long's Harry been boozing like that?" I asked.

"He'll drink himself into the grave, poor guy," Pat said.

"Or electrocute himself. Maybe the gout is doing me a favor, keeping me sober."

"I ain't seen you limping like this in a while."

"Well, too much meat. Barbecue season."

"Meat?"

"Yeah, bad for the gout."

"Jesus you got to go off meat and booze too?"

"It's rough," I said.

A Lucky bobbed in his lips when he said: "Next you'll tell me cigarettes are bad for you."

I sat on a bar stool near the coatroom. I liked this shadowy corner. You could see everyone, they could hardly see you. I glanced around to make sure Bess was out of earshot. She was known to hear gossip a half-mile away.

"The man's getting paranoid," I whispered to Pat. "He's afraid of girl newspaper reporters now."

I'd hoped that Pat would fill me in. I certainly wasn't going to mention Janie's name.

"The man's got his thoughts," Reilly said. "The man's got his ways. He knows things unknowable. He sees things invisible. If he sobered up, he'd be the greatest genius since Alvin Einstein."

Pat wiped the bar with a wet gray rag.

"In Harry we trust," he said. "If he's got a problem, somebody will take care of it, believe me."

"Yeah," I said. "You're right, Pat, somebody will take care of it. Hey, keep my name in front of him, okay?"

"What's it worth to me?"

"Ten percent."

"Of nothing is nothing," Pat said.

"But you know I'm a homer, I'm not on the next train for Chicago, skipping with your cut. So Patrick, go with the known. Mick Powers, he's a level guy, he's a local guy, he's a trustworthy guy, he's a loyal guy. He's plenty smart enough to mark a bank. Suggest that to Harry. Remind him who his friends are."

The back door opened and in walked Swede Fanlund and his buddy Rico. These were the thugs who had come gunning for me last spring, before Harry became my uncle and saved my life. Swede and Rico were the killers who had taken Pop Anderson out to the lake and shot him dead.

They were shadowy figures, Swede tall, Rico short and round. When Bess opened the door to let cigarette smoke out, I saw that Swede wore a leather jacket over a clean blue mechanic's uniform. Rico was dressed like a banker, gray suit and red tie.

I have a little round scar on my shoulder 26 years now. It was put there in high school by Swede Fanlund. The pain was nothing compared to the humiliation, a hundred witnesses in the schoolyard.

I stared into my icy soda as Swede hung up his leather jacket. Rico stood on the tiptoes of shiny shoes to look over the partition and into the barroom.

"No problem," whispered Pat, but I wasn't so sure. I wasn't so much worried about myself, since the Green Lantern was a sanctuary. But I was struck with the sudden fear that Harry called in these killers to deal with his Janie problem.

It was hard to know exactly what Harry wanted me to do with Janie. He usually issued vague orders, and waited to see how you carried them out. This served the purpose of constantly testing and evaluating his men. I was guessing it was up to me to silence Janie, and Harry didn't care how, as long as the job was done. Harry chose me, I reasoned, because a warning would be the safest way to get the job done. No blood, no police inquiry, no outcry in the newspapers, no chance of a stool pigeon.

I told myself Harry would allow time for a warning to work. It would be too soon to engage his most vicious hit men. Swede and Rico had probably just stopped in for spaghetti.

But as my mind was engaged in cold, comforting reason, my heart was pumping out urgent warnings.

Rico passed behind my barstool and grunted. Swede patted me on the back.

"Nice to see you, Shaky," Swede said.

My index finger twitched. That was all the greeting I had for Swede. Rico held open the kitchen door and peered in. There's nobody as paranoid as an assassin.

"Easy," whispered Pat.

"They did try to erase me," I said. "Last Saint Patrick's Day. Hard to forget that."

Pat shrugged. "Nothing personal. They was employed."

"Yeah," I whispered, "by who exactly? I want a name."

"Even on a sunny day," Pat said, "it gets foggy in this town."

Bess unlocked the dutch door and let the two killers in to the Blue Room.

"They're not after you, believe me," Pat said.

"Why should I believe you?"

"Because I'm too ignorant to lie."

"What? Make sense, Pat, will you?"

"Mick, Harry's your uncle I'm telling you, the man loves you to death."

"What did you just say?"

"Harry's got a heart as big as the moon," Pat said. "You done something for him last May, remember? Like a drunken elephant, he never forgets. He figures you deserve another birthday. Loyalty, see? What did you learn in Catholic school, Mick, about the Seventeen Cardinal Virtues, right? Well around here, there's only one virtue. Loyalty."

He smiled, a mouth full of broken, nicotine-stained teeth.

"You got no worries, Mick, with Uncle Harry. You're untouchable. Not by Swede and Rico, not by nobody."

Bess leaned, elbows on the bar. She blew red curls away from her face, looked at me with penetrating green eyes. "Swede Fanlund wants to buy you a drink, Mick."

Pat raised his eyebrows. "See?" he said. "Everybody's friends in here. It's like Saint Valentine's Day."

"You mean the Massacre?" I said to Pat.

He rolled his eyes.

I said: "Tell Swede I've quit drinking."

CHAPTER SIX

In Minnesota, the trees surrender in early September. The maples and elms of Mears Park in downtown Saint Paul were already shriveling. Maple seeds and gold-tipped leaves littered the park's walk. Squirrels hid their winter stashes from rival squirrels. Birds fattened up for the long, sensible flight south. Mears Park is a grassy urban block, overshadowed by warehouses and office buildings, and surrounded by speakeasies, lunch counters, barber shops, travel agents and three busy shoeshine stands. There were way too many shoeshine guys in this town, because they handled more than one kind of boot.

The Saint Paul Daily News occupied a brownstone on one corner. Taking a break from her scribe duties, Janie Vetter was eating lunch, alone, on a park bench. Between bites of a hot dago sandwich, she turned pages of the rival Saint Paul Dispatch.

I stood behind that bench. She was so absorbed in the news she didn't notice me. A hot dago was a mess of sausage, cheese and tomato sauce on Italian bread. Janie held that sandwich in wax paper. A bottle of Coca Cola sat on the bench, straw poking out. A streetcar clanged behind me. A bum approached Janie with his filthy hand out, and she reached into her purse for a dime. When the bum walked off muttering, I sat beside Janie.

"How's it going on the county beat?"

"Hmm," she said, trying to manage that sloppy sandwich.

"Talk to the Irishman much?" I meant Irish Kinkead, the

prosecutor who ran county government. He ran it the Irish way, for the benefit of his bank account and his drinking buddies.

"Sure," she said. "His door is always open to me. So he says."

I put my arm around her, but without actually touching her, just resting it on the backbench, friendly. She wore a white blouse and a string of fake pearls that descended into her bosom. Her short-cut red hair flicked in the breeze. There was a red lipstick stain on the white straw poking out of her Coca Cola.

"Be careful what you say in Kinkead's office," I said.

"What do you mean?"

"He's a dangerous man."

She sputtered. "He's the county attorney."

"Janie, he's so much more."

"Powers, if you mean he goes easy on our city's vices, I already know that."

"What kind of questions are you asking him?"

"The ones that come up during the course of my work. What is this, Powers, the Inquisition?"

"How about the Burned Ladies."

"What about them?"

The Burned Ladies were Sadie Carmacher and Rose Perry, who had been murdered and incinerated by Saint Paul gangsters, back in March. No one had been arrested for these gruesome murders. Janie had been preparing an article on them for the national detective magazines.

This was exactly the murder case Harry didn't want solved.

I said: "Have you been asking any county officials, directly or indirectly, about the Burned Ladies?"

"Maybe," Janie said and wiped her fingers with a napkin.

"Well, stop," I said.

A rude breeze whipped up a little tornado of hot dog wrappers, cigarette butts and grit. A lady walking her Dachshund glared at us, as if we had kicked up the whirlwind ourselves.

"I take orders from my editors," she said. "And that's bad enough. I don't need you, Boss Powers."

She picked up her green leather purse, rooted in it, came up with a skinny reporter's notebook.

"Look me in the eyes, Janie. If you pursue this case, the gangsters will come after you and kill you. Just like they did to the Burned Ladies. KILL YOU. Is that plain enough?"

"Powers, I don't like that look in your eyes. You're scaring the hell out of me right now."

"You are one wrong question away from being murdered, do you understand?"

"Powers, stay away from me."

She snatched up her purse.

"Stay out of Kinkead's office," I said. "Forget the Burned Ladies."

"They wouldn't hurt a reporter, Powers, it's never been done."

"They will shoot you in the head."

"Thornton has been writing police stories for years."

"Did Thornton pester people about the Burned Ladies? No! He did a single follow up story and dropped it. Because he knows better."

Janie looked around for help.

A horse-drawn ice wagon clomped by. Across the street, a policeman, wearing Saint Paul's distinctive green uniform, was getting his shoes shined, probably for free.

"The bad guys know we're friends," I said. "They told me to warn you. There won't be a second warning and I won't be able to stop them if they come for you. And neither will the police. Move your lips. Tell me you understand."

"I understand you're a monster, Powers."

"The underworld is bigger than you and me, Janie. You must know I'm half in love with you. And because I'm fond of you I'm advising you, very seriously, to quit asking questions and lay low. If

I were you I'd pack up and get out of town."

She looked down to see a tomato sauce spatter on her white blouse.

"Oh, why did I ..." she said and dabbed at it. "It's a new blouse."

She finally engaged me with those green eyes.

"Red sauce," she said. "It stains."

CHAPTER SEVEN

When Myrtle says don't call me, it's a loyalty test. It usually means she'd love to hear from you. At the very least, she wants the opportunity to turn you down.

"Dinner at the Lowry?" I said into the phone.

"The way to a girl's heart is through your wallet," she said.

Dinner with Myrtle set me back three bucks, potato casserole for me, fried chicken and cocktails for her. This sumptuous occasion took place at the Lowry Hotel's Terrace Cafe, just the kind of place I should avoid until my cash flow improves.

I could not seem to flatten my life-style to fit my wallet. My old man, God bless him, did the best he could, but he was sick a lot, and we were raised humble on uncertain salary. There was no sick pay on the railroads then. Office workers weren't covered by the Brotherhood. But my old man hated the Brotherhood. The Irish were a race of mules, he said, and he was determined to make a living with his pencil and his brain. Half the world's ditches were dug by the Irish, he used to say, and I'll be damned to hell before I take up the shovel.

So our family moved a lot. Over to the West Side when he got healthy, into the downtown slums when he fell sick again. The slums is where we lived during my high school years, with Aunt Doris paying my Sacred Heart tuition, and me selling newspapers on the street corners. My parents needed my newsboy's earnings, that's how bad it got sometimes.

So now I love my top-floor luxury apartment with its sweeping views. The better nightclubs, with orchestras and dancing, appeal to me. Dirty speakeasies do not. It sometimes seems I was born with a Racing Form in my hand, and $2 bets are okay, but I can't wait to get back to the $10 window.

"Why the hell are you so quiet tonight?" Myrtle asked over Jell-O and whipped cream.

"They serve it in silver, so it's fifteen cents," I said.

She madly scooped desert past her glistening lips.

"Money this, money that," she said. "Money money money with you."

"I'm scraping around," I admitted.

"Don't hit me up."

"Wouldn't think of it," I said.

"I'm down three animals. I was counting on them, you know, for hard times."

She pushed the empty dessert cup across the white linen.

"Don't feel bad, Mick. I stole them furs from somebody and somebody stole 'em from you. I guess that's square all the way around. Come on."

"Yeah, I just saw those assholes, Swede and Rico. I think they're the ones who tossed my apartment."

"Nah," said Myrtle, "It wasn't them. It was cops. It was Crumley and the Bulldog took my furs out of your closet. They're the greatest break-in artists this town has ever seen."

I was only half listening. I imagined Swede and Rico, looming in the night outside Janie's apartment. With a sick feeling, I envisioned Janie turning off the light, and never seeing anything again.

I shook that dark vision off. I took Myrtle by the arm and led her out into a beautiful Saint Paul sunset. The city seemed like a living thing, glowing in soft light. The traffic, the streetcars, the swells headed for the theater, the bums panhandling in the park, the fellas and gals knocking at the speakeasy doors, all dressed fancy for Saturday night. The swellest of them clogged the doorway of the Crystal Room, where tonight Kay Kyser's band was beginning its week in Saint Paul. The college kids lined up outside the Eagles dance hall. The sporting girls, dressed sexy, laughed at the cops. A guy in tuxedo drove a white one-horse carriage, bride and groom snuggling in back.

"Ain't love sweet, Mick? I give 'em a year until they hate each other."

Janie's face flashed in my imagination, her eyes rolled up, dead cold. She was lying on a steel table, under a white sheet, in Doc Ingerson's morgue. And maybe that corpse lying next to her was me.

The big spoked wheels of the wedding carriage rolled away.

"Let's splurge on a taxi," I said.

I handed a hobo a quarter. Then I hailed an expensive cab.

"Life is short," I told Myrtle. "And when we're dead …"

"They'd better dress swell," said Myrtle, "if they show up at my funeral."

In the alley behind Myrtle's apartment, weeds had grown up around Flyboy's popsicle stick grave. As Myrtle stuck her key in the door, I said: "Are you over Flyboy? Are you ready for Charles and Amelia?"

"I'll never be over Flyboy," she said. "Easter! I find the holidays depressing."

Myrtle's apartment was expensive in a mixed-up Oriental way, with Persian rugs, Chinese lamps, and Japanese prints of the Kama Sutra variety. She undressed casually, as if stripping for the shower at the YWCA. She was cute rather than beautiful, well held together for thirty-five, stocky, small-breasted and dark-skinned. She was naked by the time I had my shoes off. She spent a lot of time naked, and maybe that accounted for the drawn shades. She used to open the shades for Flyboy, but since he died, she's been living in the shadows.

"New guy," she said, examining her face in the dresser mirror. "Maybe you know him. Andrew Stockwell."

"Oh yeah that uh…"

"Martini joint."

"How's that doing?"

Myrtle shrugged her strong shoulders.

"He's got money," she said.

"Who's he paying off, Jack or Harry?"

Myrtle spread her lips, patted off lipstick with a tissue and finally said, "I don't make payoffs my business. Some things, it ain't healthy to know."

"Maybe Andrew will help you get over the Professor."

She frowned at me through the mirror.

"Don't be a bastard. Andrew doesn't know about the Professor."

I was sitting on her huge, fluffy bed and she came at me full naked. I lay back, half clothed, and she hung over me like a wrestler pinning her foe.

"He's kind of a sucker, Andrew," she said, "but I like him. He's in tight with the Alt family. He opened with Papa Alt's money so you know he's working the rich side of town."

She lay on me, lovely warm. She stared at me with those soft, vulnerable, mysterious eyes. She said into my ear: "So if my stall is occupied some nights, you'll understand right?"

"Sure," I said, my arms around her for a kiss.

"You're an understanding guy, Mick, that's why we get along like oil and water."

"Oil and water don't mix," I said.

"If you say so," said Myrtle. "You're the one who finished high school."

I never met a woman who needed sex like Myrtle did. Her

orgasms were loud, and brought sweaty pleasure to her face. For a few minutes she went to Myrtle heaven, and it didn't matter who was her escort.

When she bit her lips, I knew her pleasure had turned to something else, and I, briefly her lover, had become an inconvenience. "Enough?" I said. She, sweating like a marathon runner, nodded.

I rolled away from her and sat naked on the edge of the bed. I lit my pipe, its fly ashes landing harmless on my thigh. I smoked, then with Myrtle snoring, took a shower. While I dried off in her white-tiled bathroom with a Hotel Saint Francis towel, a knock came at the door.

I was afraid it was Crumley or the Bulldog. They especially among Saint Paul's cops loved to pester Myrtle.

But I heard a soft male voice call out, unfamiliar to me. Then came Myrtle's footsteps. The bathroom door opened. Myrtle was in her bathrobe. She dug into its pocket and handed me a brass key.

"It's Andrew," she whispered. "I made him wait in the hall. Let me get dressed. When I'm gone, let yourself out, Mick, okay?"

She rubbed my cheek with her rough hands.

"Your mama raised a good boy."

CHAPTER EIGHT

Maybe it should have tormented me when Myrtle dated other men, but it troubled me only a little. Myrtle didn't love them. This was business. She had a living to get. Like me, Myrtle had no job prospects whatever. And a shoplifter whose picture has been in all the newspapers? She's reaching the end of her criminal career.

So Myrtle had learned another game: how to squeeze a money guy. I know she truly cared for me, because she never put a cash squeeze on me. This Andrew guy would buy her jewelry, pay the rent, deliver sacks of groceries and then he, or maybe his wife, would wise up, and Myrtle would come back to me.

When I arrived home from Myrtle's, I had a more immediate problem. Snowflake hadn't eaten yesterday, Little Elmer told me. My dog curled his lips when I held a lump of bratwurst under his nose. I drove to the vet, Snowflake limp across the front seat. The vet said Snowflake would be "under observation" until a blood test came back from the lab. Exploratory surgery might be called for, he warned, at a cost $50. He also quoted a price, $2, for euthanasia.

I fired up the Chevy coupe I had borrowed from Filben's bootlegger fleet and drove it down Selby to its home: Herb's Garage, a block from my apartment. Herb kept sloppy records, had a collection of bogus license plates, and shut his mouth in the presence of a badge. So his ramshackle building had become gangland's favorite garage.

Uphill I walked and at the big oak tree outside our apartment,

Janie played catch with Little Elmer. He wore a leg brace and used one crutch. One hand was covered by an oily, almost black, hand-me-down baseball mitt. Because of that crutch he couldn't use two hands, so he caught the ball, removed the glove, tucked it under his arm, and threw the ball back in a weak, high arc. The boy wore white shorts down to his knees, a pitiful, unnatural curve to his steel-encased polio leg.

"Hey, how's Snowflake?" he shouted.

"He's staying in the hospital tonight," I said.

"Oh." A look of misery took over the boy's pale face. Elmer, too, had been in the hospital lately. "You think he ate bad food?"

"Don't know," I said. "He might need surgery. Don't worry, Elmer, I'll get the money somewhere and Snowflake will be fine."

Janie walked toward her basement hovel and I tried to soothe Elmer by talking baseball. He loved the Saints and hated the Millers. The season was barely over and he was convinced that the coming March would somehow transport him to Hot Springs for spring training. His mama had promised him that trip, once he got stronger.

Janie returned and said, "Michael, can I see you in the lobby?"

When the lobby door closed on us she handed me two crisp $20 bills. "My kitchen savings," she said. "In case you need it for Snowflake."

"Couldn't take it," I said.

"You must," she said. "I insist. I have faith in you, Powers. I know you'll pay me back."

"I'll let you know. If I really need it … I won't forget you for this, Janie Vetter."

"Whatever it takes," she said.

"I thought you hated me now."

"Well, I don't hate your dogs." She put a finger to her lips. "Actually, I don't hate you, Powers. I feel sorry for you. You've given in. You've given in to gangsters."

I stared her down. Those big green eyes seemed as deep as mineshafts.

"I talked with my editor," she said.

"Oh no."

"I told him I was threatened by a gangster. That would be you, by the way. And my editor offered to put me back on the women's pages. I said no. I've worked too hard to get a real beat, and I'm not giving it up."

"I'm going to have to shoot Swede and Rico," I said.

"What did you say?"

"Never mind."

"Powers, don't worry. You did scare me. I am going to lay low. No more questions about the Burned Ladies, at least for a while. Now, would you do me a favor? Would you look at something?"

I followed her into her gloomy, but strictly clean, basement apartment.

"Janie, look," I said when she closed the door behind me. "There's a gangster war on now, between Harry and Jack, right? It's only simmering now, but someday it's going to boil over. Everybody in gangland is on edge right now."

I unbuttoned my shirt. "Don't worry, this isn't a strip show."

I flung my dress shirt to her easy chair and rolled up the sleeve of my t-shirt to reveal a deep, round scar where my arm met my shoulder.

"It's a cigarette burn," I said. "Swede Fanlund. High school initiation ritual."

"What kind of high school did you go to?"

"Catholic. And that bastard Swede was a favorite with the nuns. He brought them cookies on the holidays. Well, Swede grew up and left for Chicago years ago. Down there he picked up a gangster nickname: The Mechanic. He won't wear a suit. Work clothes only. By rumor, he was an enforcer for the O'Banions on the North

Side. But last spring he came back to Saint Paul, just as the war between Harry and Jack got nasty."

"So…"

"Swede Fanlund returned to Saint Paul because Jack Peifer brought him back. Swede will work for anybody who pays him, but he wouldn't be in town except for Jack. I doubt it's a coincidence that Swede returned to Saint Paul a few days before Sadie and Rose were burned. Swede loves to set fires. For reasons I still don't understand, Swede and his punk partner came after me on Saint Patrick's Day."

"Powers…"

"Yes?"

"Follow my logic," she said. "Papa Alt hired you to snoop on the Burned Ladies before they were murdered, right?"

I sighed.

"This is just between you and me, Powers. I can't get it out of my mind. You can't just kill people and get away with it. This is America."

"Okay, between you and me, if helps you to talk about it, prattle on."

"After Sadie and Rose were killed, two goons tried to shoot you down there in the parking lot."

"Right."

"What if Papa Alt hired them?"

"Why?"

"Because Papa Alt's ties to the Burned Ladies go deep, deeper than he wants anyone to know. He was afraid of them for some reason. He hired you to find them. A few hours after you found them, they were killed. You're the only one who knew Papa Alt was interested in them. So this Swede fellow comes after you."

"Janie, it's hard to believe the Alt family engages in murder for hire. They've got too much to lose. You're the one who found out that Jack Peifer picked up Sadie and Rose for their last appointment. That makes Jack the big suspect. And look, I'd be dead now if Jack had his way. I'd be dead if I wasn't working for Harry.

"How so?"

"Here's the difference between Jack and Harry. Jack started as a carnival barker, and he still is one. His specialties are gambling, prostitution and booze. Harry began as a shopkeeper, distributing bootleg beer, laundering money and fencing stolen objects. He branched out into insurance, or in other words a protection racket, run in cooperation with the Saint Paul police. Then he discovered a late-blooming talent for planning big-time bank robberies."

"Okay."

"Now you know as much as Goggles does, maybe more. I'm solid with Harry now. I have good reason to believe that. As long as Harry's my uncle, as long as he believes I'm a loyal man, I'm as safe as a child in a nursery."

"Like the Lindbergh baby?"

"Oh," I said, a little stung. "Smart. Very smart. I'm in good with gangland now, but things can change in a heartbeat. The boss of gangsters knows we're neighbors. He told me to shut you up. For all I know, that was an execution order. If I don't shut you up, he'll find some one who will. And I'll get my mouth shut, too. These guys are looking at long, long prison terms, or even execution. They're serious about silence."

"Okay, well," Janie said, "I've sent applications to New York. To both the Herald and the American. I'll take anything they offer. Intern, copy girl, I don't care. Once I get there, far away, and things calm down, I can sell the story of the Burned Ladies to the national magazines. A year from now, maybe, two years from now, I don't care. I'm determined, Powers. They might drive me out of town but they're not going to get away with murder."

"Janie, I'd feel better if you were back on the farm."

"I'm not a milkmaid, Powers. Believe me I've tried. I don't have milk in my veins."

Meanwhile, I had financial problems to solve. That evening I cornered Reilly down at the Green Lantern. I explained my drugstore robbery problem in vague terms and he said:

"The rube has a Ford?"

"Model A."

"I know a guy at Ford."

"Who doesn't?"

"No, I mean a right guy. See, there's only about twenty keys to a Model A."

"So?"

"You try twenty keys, you find one that fits."

"And?"

"You wait in the rube's car. You snatch his loot, he runs like a coward, you steal his car too. Filben will buy the car from you, Herb will change the plates. It's like hitting the daily double."

"How much for the keys?"

"Twenty bucks."

"Come on."

"Did I say twenty? I meant a ten-spot."

"For keys?"

When I palmed him the ten-spot, he glowed. "See, that's why I love this job. People walk in cranky, ten minutes later they're all cheer." He jammed that ten-spot into the pocket of a beer-stained apron.

"It's like being a doctor," he said, "you fix all kinds of disease."

I ordered a lunch of two pickled eggs and a short beer. As I was walking out, Melvin Passolt, Commander of the State Police, handed his suit-coat to Bess, rolled up his sleeves, selected a pool cue. His playing partner was Ralph Tallerico, aka Rico, the little bastard who took a shot at me on Saint Patrick's Day.

Holding the Commander's suit jacket, Bess passed me on her way to the coat room. She muttered: "Every cop in this town secretly wants to be a gangster."

The next night, I once again marked the drugstore at closing time. After a robbery attempt, I knew they'd change their routine. I expected maybe someone would stay late and help the clerk close up. But no, all the clerk did was park his old Ford right next to that back door. A half hour after closing, the clerk, alone, cracked open the door for a peek, then dashed to his car.

Two nights later, armed with a ring of Model A keys and my unloaded revolver, I let myself in to the drugstore clerk's jalopy. It was parked next to the door, under the spotlight.

I wrapped a red bandana around my face. Only my eyes showed between it and my fedora. The extreme fear of my first attempt had sunk somewhere deep, although I did feel an unearthly chill on that warm humid night. Was I gaining in courage? Or just in desperation?

About five minutes before ten o'clock, a lightning storm moved in from the west.

Thunder rumbled. Lightning flashed. I slumped low in the back seat. The humid air around me was condensing on the Ford's windows. Yet I dared not crack them open. Huge, ice-pellet raindrops pelted the Ford. Everything suddenly disappeared but foggy rain. Clunk clunk hailstones bounced off the roof. An explosion of thunder rattled me and the car. A crack of lightning sounded like it would take the roof off a neighbor's house. A whirlwind of dust, trash and leaves moved into the spotlight, like a tiny tornado. Lightning dueled in the clouds, lighting the car's interior as if I was on stage.

Then the storm blew over into an eerie, electric calm. Lightning flashes dueled, but far off. Rain blew sideways, then faded to a drizzle.

The pharmacy door creaked.

A rumble of thunder rattled me. I worried that the young clerk would notice that his car had fogged windows. I took the pistol out of my side pocket, lay cramped on the back seat, holding my breath.

The driver's door yanked open and I almost crapped myself when the passenger's door opened too. I could smell the kid's Camel habit and somebody's perfume. The kid rolled down the rain-spattered window to let out fetid air.

He held the passenger door open.

"Martini Lounge?" he said.

"I keep hearing about that place," said the female voice.

I had heard that voice all my life.

"They have Negro jazz," she said, "don't they?"

I looked up and saw, spilling over the front seat, the unmistakable platinum curls of my sister Mona.

I leaped out of the car and ran.

Behind me I heard the panicked animal sound of my sister screeching. In a moment, both the clerk and my sister were shouting for help into the night. Lights were flashing on in windows and on porches. My sister's blood curdling scream sounded like it came from an animal being eaten alive.

In a flash of lightning I entered a dark alley, aware of nothing but my own gasping. As I hid in that alley I worried the young clerk would play hero, start the car and try to run me down. A streetcar was trudging up at the big intersection and I ran for it. I realized that somewhere in that panicky minute, my bandana and hat had fallen off. I sat sweating, squirming, a cowering ball of nausea amid a drunks, bums, college kids and dating couples. The streetcar clanked, painfully slow, away from the Rosedale Pharmacy, so slow that I hopped off at the next stop, hid in a tavern and called a taxi to take me home.

The next morning, I took my phone off the hook in fear of a call from Mona. I visited the vet to find that Snowflake needed exploratory surgery, between $25 and $50 depending. The vet was credit wary, so I tracked down Janie at the Daily News and, shamefaced, borrowed the money from her. I left $25 at the vet, spent a few minutes petting the lethargic Snowflake.

I returned the ring of car keys to Reilly. He didn't ask and I didn't tell how I had panicked and run off. But he could read the newspapers, and could probably guess. The Daily News printed a three-paragraph story buried inside about a stickup attempt at the Rosedale Pharmacy. It was one of maybe twenty crime stories in the paper, holdups, highway robberies, burglaries. The young clerk's name was Artie Schiller. No mention was made of any woman, never mind one named Mona Powers.

The newspaper quoted Artie Schiller as saying the robber was hefty six-footer, well dressed, brandishing a machine gun. The kid told the newspapers he'd nearly wrestled the bandit's tommygun away. Detectives were to have the victim view suspect photos.

Two things I was sure of: Pope Pius lives in the Vatican and I am unknown in the Bertillion system.

At the Royal I dropped $2 on a loser at Belmont, walked home and phoned the vet. He had cut Snowflake's belly open to find a mass of peanut shells. He removed them and stitched Snowflake up. Yes, I admitted, I threw my dogs peanut treats, but Snowflake had always extracted the peanuts from the shells. Well, I half-remembered leaving a bag of peanuts out and the dogs had maybe done a feeding frenzy. Either way, Snowflake would recover, and I could pick him up in 24 hours, and should bring along an extra $10.

I didn't need a math diploma to know that making money pulling stickups was stupid and dangerous, even when you weren't running into family members. At best I would keep from starving until the cops opened a cell and tossed me in. Sure, you could buy your way out of police custody, but the minimum price was $500.

The old saying really should be changed to: Only the big crimes pay.

It made me sick to think I might be helpless in jail, Snowflake and Hula Girl hauled to the pound. At the bottom of it all, the Catholic school boy in me was ashamed of pointing a gun, even an empty one, at innocent people. And my own sister! For what?

Money?

Hadn't the nuns taught me better?

That evening I invited Harry's most trusted female, Bess, for a late night drink at the Hotel Saint Paul. We sat out on the lovely terrace overlooking Rice Park.

Since my last talk with Harry, he'd become more secretive, rarely showing up at the Green Lantern. Harry wasn't really an evil guy. He was caught in a trap of his own construction. I believe he drank hard to ease his guilt about the things he'd done to keep his empire going. Harry was whirling in the vortex and couldn't escape, like all the rest of us. He grew up an Orthodox Jew in Omaha and maybe all the rules were too much for him. He began stealing cars. The cops locked him up, and in jail he learned how to crack a safe. When they let him out he began to burgle jewelry stores. He needed to fence the jewels, and soon realized that the fences made more money and took less risk. That led him to specialize in fencing and money laundering. He moved to Saint Paul to be the junior partner of Dapper Dan Hogan, who ran the protection rackets. When Hogan was blasted apart by a car bomb, Harry inherited his tavern and his rackets.

In order the keep the dirty cash flowing, Harry began putting together bank jobs. He figured out how to control the police, keeping a few key cops fat and happy. His was a brilliant rise through the criminal ranks. The infamy of his Green Lantern Tavern spread coast to coast. But Harry himself had lately sunk into the swamps of booze and paranoia. A Harry sighting was rare, even around the Green Lantern, and he had long since quit answering his phone.

Bess drank Manhattans up, but with sipping pleasure, not drunken greed. A fat candle flickered in the late summer breeze. Over in the Federal Building, J. Edgar Hoover's boys burned the night lights. Their offices glowed as a message to us criminals that G-men never slept.

Bess was tall, willowy, flat-chested, with the strong beautiful shoulders of a born athlete. She wore a long sleeveless dress, and I had never seen her wear makeup or jewelry. Her hair was too flaming red to be natural and her flashing green eyes seemed to take in everything all the time.

I said: "Harry's sweet on you."

She laughed and took a delicate sip of her Manhattan.

"Sure," she said.

"I'm looking for work," I said.

"You and ten million others."

"I need to get to Harry when he's sober. I mean I've talked to him lately but I doubt he'd even remember. He was eye-rolling drunk. I need to get a call the minute he walks in. For serious conversation."

"Good luck. Through me?"

"I thought I'd try."

She sighed. "No man has ever bought me a drink without wanting something."

She threw one arm over the back of her chair.

"What do you want?"

"I want to mark. I don't want to be his errand boy, doing odd jobs. Those turn out messy sometimes. Harry's famous for his clean bank jobs. Nobody gets hurt, that's what I like. I just want to mark for Harry."

She closed her eyes for a long moment.

I said, "What, Bess?"

"You're a little late."

"Oh?"

"Read the papers the next few days."

"In the works then?"

She nodded.

"Who marked?" I asked.

"Ah." She held up one scolding finger. "No fair."

"Local mugs?"

"Ta ta," she said. "Nice drinking on your dime." She pushed her chair back.

CHAPTER NINE

For the next two weeks, I read the papers pretty close. Janie was writing about tax assessments and trials. Any criminals dumb enough to stand trial certainly weren't Harry's boys, so Janie was safe there. She seemed to be staying clear of the dangerous County Attorney, Michael Kinkead, or at least she didn't quote him directly. I began to hope things would cool out. Big-shot criminals were notoriously fickle. If Janie could lay low for a few months, Harry would probably forget about her.

There was plenty of other news in the papers. Out there in the flatlands angry farmers were on strike, refusing to harvest. They were blocking roads, stopping cattle and grain trucks. Gunshots were fired, farmer versus trucker. Governor Olson was convening emergency meetings.

If the farmers intended to starve the city, it wasn't working. But just in case, I bought extra bratwurst and corn flakes for the dogs, and flour and yeast for myself. I intended to learn to bake bread, an economy that might help the household budget.

Snowflake was slowly recovering his appetite, and I vowed no more unshelled peanuts for the dogs.

In the newspapers I read that Al Capone's lawyers were suing for his release from prison. Closer to home, a speakeasy called the Hollywood Inn was raided by Dakota County, on orders of its top attorney, Harold Stassen. An honest prosecutor in the neighboring county would be good for us, pushing speakeasy customers into Saint Paul.

I read that a Saint Paul cop had been in a brawl outside the Martini Lounge, and claimed he was absolutely sober when he shot himself in the leg.

And then on Friday evening September 23, I read the news Bess had primed me for. A bank in the Minnesota town of Redwood Falls had been robbed of $25,000.

The story had been re-written off the United Press wire by Janie's nemesis, Kevin "Goggles" Thornton. The robbery had all the marks of a Harry Sawyer operation. Harry used five guys for small-town banks, and six for any job in the city. In Redwood Falls, five guys had robbed the bank when it had an unusual amount of money. It had happened on a Friday. The bandits had taken hostages, making them cling to the running boards. They scattered roofing tacks behind them as they sped off. They made a clean getaway, even though the sheriff of Redwood Falls chased them in his airplane.

They had hurt nobody. Some of the clerks and tellers described the robbery as a thrilling adventure.

Janie knocked and asked to see the recovering Snowflake. Or at least that was her excuse for climbing the stairs. She gave him a rub behind the ears. He rolled over to expose his belly.

I knew the feeling.

It would have been better for both of us if I'd slammed the door in Janie's face. But I needed her friendship, and I clung to some crazy hope that she'd admire me. I've known some really awful people, but even the worst of them wanted to be admired.

Snowflake's belly was shaved, a jagged red scar where the vet had cut him open. His belly looked so sore, Janie wouldn't touch it.

"So, Michael…"

Usually she called me Powers, as if to keep me at a distance.

We stood in my kitchen, like gentle gladiators, the kitchen table separating us, cluttered with coffee cups and newspapers.

"What do you know about that thing in Redwood Falls?" she asked.

"The what?"

"Don't play dumb. The bank robbery."

"What do you care? I thought you were applying to the New York Times?"

"Not quite. And I haven't heard back. In the meantime, I can't help it, I was born curious."

She leaned over the table at me. "Come on, Michael."

"Off the record?"

"Absolutely."

"It might have been a Green Lantern job."

"How do you know that?"

"I don't. I'm guessing. First and most important, nobody was killed, nobody was wounded."

"By your kindly, bank robbing gangster friends."

"Kind? No. Robbers are much more likely to get away clean when no one gets hurt. Hell, some of these bank robberies are inside jobs. The bankers themselves hope to be robbed, because they've been dipping into the till. There's nothing that covers up embezzlement as nicely as five guys with tommyguns."

"Embezzlement?"

"Banks are coming up short left and right. Did you ever wonder how the robbers know when the cash drawers are full?"

"How?"

"Well, there's two ways. Inside dope, and careful observation. Remember the Kraft State job? Two dead bandits? There's a lot of risk for the robbers. They sometimes end up shooting it out with the whole town. For that kind of risk, they want real dough."

"So who does the careful observation?"

"We're still talking theory, right? It's the jug marker. He goes to work weeks, sometimes months before the robbery. It's a specialty. See, the tommygun guys, they're restless, fidgety, paranoid, not real bright, no patience. Half of 'em can't read or write. Balls they've got, but no brains. They make poor markers. So they team up with a guy who marks, who's patient, smart."

"So who marked this Redwood Falls job?"

"Don't know."

"Michael, I have a feeling you're describing yourself."

"Not me."

"Come on."

I put one hand in the air and the other on The Daily News.

"I swear on my honor I had nothing to do with this job. Wish I had," I said. "Be worth three or four thousand to the marker. I'd be able to pay back your vet loan with interest."

"So bank robbery, a hundred miles away, was planned at the Green Lantern?"

"I plead ignorance," I said. "All I know is I didn't do it. And we're off the record, right?"

"Just what kind of reporter were you?"

"I ran cops and fires for the Saint Paul Globe, RIP. I was just a kid, Janie. I started as a copy boy. It was the old days. Everything was different. All I did was follow the sirens and call rewrite. It was before the War. I never wrote a word, never had a byline. Whole different world now, with radio and all that, newspapers have changed."

"Did you mark this Redwood Falls bank, Michael? Just between you and me, I really want to know."

"I wish," I said. "It was my kind of job, all money, no blood."

Snowflake rolled over and licked that jagged scar on his belly.

My phone rang too early on a Saturday morning. I knew when I picked up the earpiece that it wasn't going to be friendly chat.

"It's me," said a voice, raw throated.

Pat Reilly.

"Yeah, I know," I said.

"Sea Lion. He's at home flapping his flippers. Throw him a fish."

And then Reilly hung up.

I had my choice of loaners down at Herb's, and picked a beautiful stolen 1932 Essex that had been repainted from black to forest green. They had gotten a little spray paint on the windows, but otherwise had done a perfect job. Herb swore that he only ordered the theft of insured cars, so as not to hurt the little guy. I wanted to believe him.

I drove up Summit Hill and into the pleasant suburban annex known as Mac Groveland. My chest was tight, I seemed to be choking on my own breath. Harry, I feared, was going to ask me why Janie Vetter was still above ground. I couldn't defy Harry, and I certainly couldn't hurt Janie. I pondered killing myself, but that wouldn't work either. In that case, Swede and Rico would kill Janie, and knowing Swede, they'd set her corpse on fire.

I pulled over on a street of golden-leafed trees and drank bourbon from a flask. The only way out that I could think of was to kidnap Janie, drive her somewhere far away. New Orleans? Miami?

More bourbon.

Maybe I would tell Harry that I was in love with her, that we were going to be married this Saturday, making her a loyal gangland wife.

Would he believe it?

More bourbon.

I settled on that lie, which would buy maybe three days, at best.

Montreal? Was that far away enough?

I finished the bourbon and drove on.

Harry, a manager of crime, naturally lived among the management class. His house was a stucco bungalow with a gigantic garage. His property was surrounded by hedges and fences. Sitting in the car outside his home, I pulled out my pocket pistol.

A gangland assassination.

I opened the cylinder and spun it.

Four rounds should do it.

With Harry dead, Jack would inherit the crown, king of the underworld. It was possible, I told myself, that Jack would see me as a hero. He might set me up with my own horse racing wire as reward.

But no, I knew what happened to gangland assassins. I'd hate to plug Harry, I liked the guy, but if I had to do it, you'd never see me in this town again. Janie neither.

I slipped that gun into my ankle holster. The cuffs of my tweed trousers settled over it nicely. With bourbon and firepower, I finally gathered courage.

I walked up the steps between hedges, feeling needles and pins, but forcing a smile.

Gladys sat on the back stoop, with Leona, peeling apples. Leona was the Colored maid, a squat middle-aged woman wearing an ankle-length dress. Gladys had a gray cast to her skin, and dark bobbed hair, and wore overalls. Around the women's feet were apple peelings, with the skinned fruit piled in a galvanized pan. Harry had learned how to make Apple Jack, although you had to wait until deepest winter to finish the process.

"Ladies," I said.

Gladys glared my way.

Leona kept on peeling.

"Harry in?"

Gladys huffed.

Harry's face appeared in the kitchen window and he opened the door.

"You get lost?" he asked.

"Am I late?"

"Hell yeah. Come in."

He seemed anything but the Devil Incarnate. He was like your drunken uncle, well meaning, generous, a bumbler, going to fat. He waved me past the pile of apple peels and into the kitchen. He wore gray trousers and a sleeveless t-shirt and was barefoot. People said he was illiterate, but I saw on the kitchen table a spread-open copy of the Evening Dispatch.

He looked out the kitchen window like he was scanning for coppers.

"Reilly said you wanted to see me," I said. I felt a wave wash over me. Relief. And then a riptide of foolishness. Harry wasn't going to issue execution orders, I could feel it. I could also feel that pistol at my ankle, two pounds of pointless paranoia.

"I heard your old man was a math whiz," Harry said.

"Yeah," I said. "He used to do equations for fun."

"And railroad timetables."

"That's how he made his living."

"And you, Powers, I heard you got a number system for horse racing."

"Fractional times," I said.

"I don't care what it is. I heard it wins."

"Win some, lose some," I said. "It's horse racing. So who knows."

He lit a Chesterfield, blew smoke toward the ceiling. The white ceiling tiles had been spotted yellow by an explosive keg of beer. I'd been here for that gathering, years ago, before fear of wiretaps had made Harry too paranoid to party.

"Powers, I want to give you a chance. You been a good guy for me. You know when to shut your mouth, which is all the time."

"Thanks, Harry, I…"

"Powers, I need a guy. You asked to mark, you're going to mark."

"What am I marking, Harry?"

"How the fuck do I know? That's up to you. That's what I hire guys for. You think I got time to figure this stuff out?"

He cleared his throat.

"Nothing in the city limits," he said. "We honor The Deal."

"I thought you had a marker."

"You got a nose for the winner's circle, Powers. The last guy, don't piss me off. You heard about this job out in the styx?"

"I don't know," I said.

"I love that answer," Harry said. "But anybody can read the papers, right? Redwood Falls. Big, big headlines. Somebody took down the First National."

I nodded.

"The sheriff chased the boys in an aero-plane."

"I read that."

"The boys hate a surprise," Harry said.

"Ah," I said.

He shook his finger. "That punk will never mark for me again. He didn't know the sheriff was a pilot in the War."

"Sloppy," I said.

"So another one I got to put on light duty. I'm like a charity ward here. All my guys are cripples, I gotta find this boy something to do now. So you, Powers, you don't need crutches, do you?"

"I can stand on my own feet, Harry. I want to mark. If I mark that's all I'll do. No more blind errands, all right?"

"Study the bank clearings," Harry said. "Pick your target. Come to me with a number. We gotta get off on the right foot." He tapped ashes on the oil cloth that covered his kitchen table. The cloth had been burned, dozens of ash marks.

"What's your system?" Harry asked and rubbed his stubbly chin. "You got the brains, right, like for Algebra?"

"It's simpler than that, Harry. I read in the newspapers that somebody got twenty-five down in the boonies. I can double that. At least."

He took from the kitchen cabinet a white coffee cup with blue rim. Into it he poured a measure of whiskey from a flask in his pocket.

"Good thing you don't drink," he said. "The best guys I ever used were sober."

I guess he was so drunk he couldn't tell that I was lit up with a flask full of coward juice.

He gulped whiskey and barked: "What do you need?"

"A hundred dollars up front."

"Go see Papa Alt. He owns a bank, I don't."

"It's going to take a month Harry. Methodical."

"Fifty dollars."

"A hundred now, and I'll only ask half a share."

"You only get half a share unless you carry hardware."

"Harry, don't chisel me over fifty bucks. This could be the score of the decade."

"No blood, I hate blood, my old man was a butcher, it was blood drove me out of Omaha."

He turned his back on me, disappeared into the living room, and came back with a single $100 bill.

"Smallest I got," he said.

"Harry, one more thing."

"Shoot."

"You know that reporter, the red head?"

He shrugged. Did he even remember Janie?

I said: "You told me to shut her up?"

"Remind me, Powers."

A quart a day had drilled big holes in his memory.

"Kid on the Daily News. Asking around about certain ... it happened on the docks last spring. Remember? Up in smoke."

"Oh, yeah," Harry said. "You took care of her right?"

"Threw a scare into her, Harry. She knows what's what now. She's on her best behavior, believe me. I hope that's okay, just a scare, that's what you meant, right?"

"Mick, whatever works, okay? But you better hope that turkey never squawks again."

"Agreed, Harry."

"So get busy marking. I'm sending a guy to see you."

"Okay."

"He's your only contact."

"Okay."

"If you screw up, it gets nasty."

"Okay."

"And no leaks. See a tire that leaks goes flat and then what?"

"I don't know Harry. I guess you change the tire."

"Right, you change the tire and what happens to the old one? It's no good anymore, right? You take that leaky tire to the dump and bury it."

"Got it."

Harry poured a puddle of whiskey into a coffee cup.

"I know you don't drink, but toast the deal."

I raised that whiskey to my lips. It was bad stuff. It burned going down.

CHAPTER TEN

I found the richest target in Minnesota by studying the bank clearings. The newspapers foolishly printed the numbers in the business section every weekday. I suppose the point was to reassure the public that the banks were solvent. But those bank clearings were like blueprints for us jug markers.

The bank I chose occupied the whole ground floor of a brick building over in Minneapolis. It had showroom windows, like an appliance store or a car dealership. Above those windows, a red awning was printed with 3RD NORTHWEST NATIONAL BANK. The land it occupied was a small urban triangle, streetcar stop out front. Risk of traffic jams, noted. The triangle was so small that parking near the bank's entrance might be a problem.

The getaway car would have to be parked early, to get the spot in front of the building.

That might be a problem or an opportunity. I began to envision a role that would get me a full share: driver of the switch car.

It wasn't pure greed, either. The bigger your share, the fewer jobs you had to pull, and the less your risk of disaster.

I decided to do my deep thinking in the barber shop underneath the bank. I walked down the dank steps, into the basement, past the barber pole, and then I waited my turn in a stuffed chair. I deliberately arrived at the busiest time, a Friday afternoon. As the barber was cutting my hair, no clippers I insisted, scissors and take your time, I watched bank customers come and go. I could only see them from the waist down, but that was enough. I counted. It was 45 customers in twenty minutes.

All during my haircut I'd pretended to read Startling Detective Adventures. I didn't ask the barber about the bank. I didn't tip. Weeks from now, when the cops grilled him, he would never remember me.

I took the streetcar home, walked the dogs, freed the birds, and drew a map from memory. Snowflake had been walking sore and crooked since his surgery, but he was straightening out now.

I phoned Reilly and told him to send Harry's guy around. I poached a couple of eggs, and laid them on toast, the last of the grocery store bread. On the counter, rising in pans, was the first bread dough I'd ever kneaded.

A couple of hours ticked by and I was about to shovel that dough into a hot oven when a polite knock sounded at the door. I opened it to admit a dapper man of about twenty six. He was a pretty boy, dark haired, dark eyed, roughly shaven, about five-foot-six with an athlete's build.

"Larry," he said, and we shook hands.

"The white one is Snowflake," I said. "The black one is Hula Girl."

Snowflake curled his lips. Hula Girl circled him, suspicious, sniffing.

Larry squatted to pet both dogs.

His suit was first-rate, dark blue, complete with vest and perfectly knotted bright yellow tie. His shoes were polished to a gleam.

Snowflake barked, hostile.

"Don't mind him," I said. "He's getting over an operation. Had a traffic jam in his gut."

Larry looked up at me with dark wet eyes. There was something magnetic, sympathetic in them. They were like the eyes of a pleading orphan.

"Beer?" I asked.

"Beer," he agreed.

We walked into the kitchen and I produced two cold bottles of Altwasser.

"Electric refrigerator, huh?" he said and slapped it.

"Wave of the future," I said.

"What will they think of next?" he said.

I opened the beers and we clinked bottles.

"Nice view of the church," he said.

"Cathedral," I said.

"Oh, I'm not Catholic. Born a heathen. I'll die a heathen, I guess. I don't believe in the Devil, do you believe in the Devil?"

"Yup."

Larry drank from the bottle and said. "Maybe. Maybe he's just one bad gangster. But I don't believe in no afterlife."

Beer is poison for me, but I wet the tip of my tongue. A gangster won't trust you if you drink ginger ale. I planned to use most of this beer to start my next batch of bread.

"Now look," I said, and led him to the kitchen table. We both leaned on it. On it lay a Startling Detective Adventures, two fragrant pans of rising bread dough, and a full-page map I'd drawn.

He studied the map. Sipped beer. Studied the map some more.

"I don't get it," he said. "What's these arrows?"

"It's a convergence diagram."

"A what?"

"Each guy approaches from a different way. Arrow One goes in first, see? He's in there a minute or two, filling out a deposit slip, making sure it's a go. No cops happen to be inside, no armored car guards, no Fort Snelling soldiers who might want to play hero. Who are you?"

"The outside man," he said.

"Okay, you're Arrow Five."

He furrowed his brow. He stepped back. He swigged beer.

"I get this map?" he asked.

"Eventually."

"You a baker?"

"Oh," I said, "trying to learn."

"Me too. I was a baker in the joint. Proofing, right? It's all in the sense of smell."

"Yeah," I said, but knew not to probe.

Larry removed his gray fedora and fanned his face.

"Top floor apartment," I said. "Always warm."

"Good for proofing, then. The boys want to know timing."

"Too early to say. Closer to the holidays the better."

"They're restless," said Larry.

"And I'm broke. But right is right."

"Yup," he nodded. "Right is right."

He looked around.

"Nice place."

He walked to the living room windows, the ones that overlooked the city. Charles and Amelia chirped.

"Every time I see birds in a cage, I think of the joint," Larry said. "We treat birds better, though."

He shook his head. He opened his jacket, loosened the big knot of that yellow tie.

"Nice view," he said. "Couldn't live in this town. Can't stand the winters. Lot of action though. I hear tell the cops are all right."

"Most of them," I said.

"Well, bubba," he said, and put up his dukes as if we were going to box a round. He fake punched me. "Call me. We're going to take a tour some day, right?"

I let him out and then watched from the windows. The lobby door didn't for open quite a while. The I saw Larry step out of the shadows with Janie. She held mail in one hand, and with the other, shaded her eyes.

They stood in the sunshine talking, Larry leaning casual against the bricks, as if he'd grown up on this very patch of earth. Janie, almost as tall as he was, stood close to him, in trousers, a floral shirt, purse thrown over her shoulder.

Something she said made him laugh, and he touched her shoulder.

"We should break this up," I said to Snowflake, who was watching intently too. Larry began backing away, hands in his suit coat pocket, flapping that coat like a cape. Then he hopped into a flashy yellow Hupmobile that had huge whitewall tires. The engine compartment was half the length of the car. Larry powered that Hupmobile out of the parking lot on squealing tires.

"Let's go see Janie," I told Snowflake, and followed both dogs down four flights of stairs.

Janie's apartment door was at the bottom of a concrete pit, four steps leading down. I knocked on her door. Paint flecks fell to the damp steel drain in the concrete pit. Behind the rusting burglar bars of her window, her shades flashed. When she came to the door she was barefoot and had changed into white khaki shorts.

"Where you going?" I asked.

"Running."

"Running where?"

"Running. I'm gaining weight sitting at a desk all day."

"Aren't you going to invite me in?"

"No. It's a mess in there."

"Who was that guy you were talking to?"

"Powers...."

"Just curious."

She bent to pet both dogs. "Isn't he adorable? I thought all your friends were old cigar stinking gangsters."

"Thanks."

"Where do you know him from?"

"There you go with the questions."

"I'm a reporter, Powers."

"Yeah, well report this. That 'adorable' guy is a gangster."

She twisted her lips, skeptic. "He's too cute for a gangster."

"Janie," I said, and shook my head.

"We're going on a date," she said.

"No."

"Tonight," she said. "To the air show. Haven't you heard about the air show?"

"No."

"You're so old-fashioned, Powers."

"You don't know this guy.

"But you do."

"He's poison."

"Oh, come on. You're just like my dad. I'm not a nun, Powers. I'm a grown woman. I'm sure you think I'm a virgin, but I've had a few sins to tell in confession."

"Don't get involved with this guy."

"Excuse me Boss Powers, I've got to finish dressing. Sorry, dogs," she said, and with her bare feet began to nudge Hula Girl out of the doorway. She said to Snowflake: "I finally get a date with a cute guy, and your master wants to talk me out of it."

She shut us out with a click of the deadbolt.

CHAPTER ELEVEN

As disturbing as I found the meeting of Larry and Janie, I was encouraged by the prospect of joining this bank job on the level. Six guys with, say $50,000 to split. With that much cash in my dream account, I took out a sheet of paper and redrew the potato farm at Eagle River. Along the lakeshore I sketched cabins. With $8,000 I could build two or three cabins and rent them all summer, to families from Milwaukee and Chicago. Maybe I wouldn't have to turn to farming at all. What the hell do I know about growing potatoes?

Yes, summers as a resort owner on the Wisconsin lake shore. And winters? Maybe Havana. Filben had mysterious dealings there, slot machines and who knows what else. He said Havana reminded him of Chicago, only with warm sea breeze instead of a cold lake wind. And legal booze, Havana. And a million beautiful women.

Maybe someday that would all come true, but on this day, my sister Kelly picked me up in her beat-up Model A and drove us to the Mother Mercy Rest Home. She was just a kid when she married Gary, an Italian-Polish guy from Chicago, and they had two girls just entering their teens.

"Sorry I'm late," she said. "I've been hearing bad things."

"About?"

"About Auntie. Who do you think they call?"

"They can call me."

She sputtered. "They never call the man."

"How about Mona? Heard from her lately?"

Kelly rolled her eyes. "Please," she said. "I only hear from her when she's broke. How are you doing, money-wise?"

"Surviving," I said. "I'll pay your fifty back, don't worry."

"What's in the bag?"

"Bread," I said. "I'm baking."

"You?" she said.

We left the car and crossed the parking lot. A harsh north wind carried vague threats of winter. Kelly, in long gray wool dress without benefit of jacket, hugged herself. At the steps of the rest home she lit a tiny cigarette.

"I'm smoking half a cigarette at a time now," she said, and coughed. "Gary's slack season. It'll pick up, though. People don't give a shit about coal, you know, until it gets really cold. And don't get me started on the ice business. Refrigerators," she said and blew smoke. "Refrigerators are killing us."

The cigarette burned her fingers. She dropped it and said: "Ready?"

We walked over shiny, creaky floors in an overheated hallway. It was like solving a maze to find Doris's room. On a wraparound porch, at sunny windows, old people sat nodding in wheeled chairs. Most were simply staring at a sweeping lawn, and trees whose leaves had turned red-orange. A few of the old folks moaned. The whole place smelled strong of disinfectant, and faint of feces. In the interior hallways, nuns in white bustled from room to room.

"It's better than the goddamn Poorhouse," Kelly whispered. "At least the nuns keep it clean." She sniffed. "Lysol."

We turned into Doris's room, which she shared with an wrinkled Italian lady who was asleep, mouth open, every time I ever saw her. I couldn't look at these old people for long without imagining them young and vibrant. This old lady might have been brought here as a child while Minnesota was still a territory. Had she stood in the muddy streets of a frontier Saint Paul, waving to blue-clad troops going off to fight at Gettysburg?

Doris sat in her wheelchair, bundled up, in her lap the purple shawl she'd been knitting all summer. On the floor lay a battered copy of *Alice's Adventures in Wonderland*. It was squashed, like it had been run over by a wheelchair.

Doris's white-gray hair was a curly mop on her head, her cat-eye glasses crooked on her face. She fixed me with rheumy gray eyes and said: "Get me out of here."

"We would if we could, Aunt Doris," I said.

"Who are you people?"

Kelly side-glanced me as she squatted in front of Doris's wheelchair. She held our aunt's veiny, arthritic hands.

"Kelly, your niece," I said, "and Michael, your nephew."

"Then why don't you get me out of here?" Doris's lips trembled. Bubbles of spit formed. "They're trying to kill me."

"Who, Doris?" I said and squatted. "The nuns?"

"Nobody's trying to kill you," said Kelly.

"I'm just an old lady," said Doris. "Why do they electrocute me?"

"Electrocute?" I said.

"Those are treatments to help you get better," Kelly told Doris.

"They strap me down," complained Doris.

"They have to," said Kelly. "Doris, do you recognize Michael?"

"Humpty Dumpty," said Doris.

Kelly laughed. "Humpty Dumpty?"

"He told me last night."

"In your dream?" suggested Kelly.

"All your faces look the same," Doris said. "Two eyes."

"Isn't that something Humpty Dumpty said?" Kelly asked, and then bent to pick up the book. She flicked its pages, propped it next to the white porcelain water pitcher on the night stand.

"Maybe you shouldn't read that book," Kelly suggested, "if it gives you bad dreams."

Kelly wheeled Doris to her bed. The floors were tile, and waxed to a glare. The only furniture on her side of the room was a single wooden chair, her narrow bed, and that end table. Above that bed on a white-washed wall was nailed a wooden crucifix with a bronze Jesus. Kelly rustled in a drawer of that end table and found a lipstick tube. Leaning over Doris, Kelly began to redden her lips.

"When are they going to let me go?" asked Doris. Kelly finished the lipstick job and held up a small round mirror to Doris' face.

"Are you in pain?" I asked.

"I'm going to walk out of here tomorrow on my own two legs," she said. "Don't you dare wheel me."

"We'll talk to the nuns," I said.

"Her radio went out," Kelly said to me.

"Bad tubes," said Doris.

"I'm going to bring you a new radio," Kelly promised our aunt. To me she whispered: "What do these poor souls have to do all day?"

We talked to Sister Joan of Arc, who worked at a Formica counter occupied by medicine bottles and yellow slips of paper. The papers were scattered. The medicine bottles were lined up like troops on review. Sister Joan, a giant rosary fixed around her waist, was pigeon-holing pills for the patients, sorting them into a wooden matrix.

We asked about Doris's treatments. After flipping through a sheaf of paperwork, Sister Joan informed us that Doris was scheduled for another electro-shock session at the end of the week. She said this with all the emotion of a wooden block, then went back to pill sorting. In school the nuns used to say to us pupils: *Give me your undivided attention.* I wanted that from Sister Joan now.

"Tell me what it's for," I demanded.

"What, sir?"

"Electro shock?"

"Brain function, sir."

"But she's getting worse."

Sister Joan reset the tiny glasses that shielded her cool blue eyes.

"Doctor Scully, sir, is a trained specialist. He has treated many patients for depression."

"So my aunt is depressed?"

"It's the Devil's own disease," she said.

"What happens if we stop the treatments?"

"She would go into a rapid decline. We trust in the Lord, sir, and we trust in modern medicine."

"She hates the treatments," I said.

"What our residents really dislike," said Sister Joan, "is the deterioration of their mind and body. They're suffering a long and painful decline. It is part of God's plan ... although," she sighed, "you have to wonder what He was thinking."

I'd brought along a paper bag containing two loaves of bread. I realized it was a useless gift. The nuns needed a miracle, not a couple of loaves of bread. I dropped the bag on the reception desk but Kelly grabbed it as we departed.

"To hell with the nuns," she muttered. "My kids need it more than they do." She looked into the bag. "Did you burn it?"

"No, it's whole wheat," I said.

"Oh God," said Kelly, "the girls won't touch it."

On the steps of the rest home she dug a half-Viceroy from her purse, lit it and said: "A hundred a month and for what?"

She blew smoke.

"But I admit, the nuns are better than the Poorhouse. The horror stories. People laying in their own filth all day." She closed her eyes against the smoke.

"When Doris runs out of money," I said, "she might end up in the Poorhouse."

"No way," said Kelly. "I won't allow it."

"Where are you going to get $100 a month?"

"We'll see. It'll be winter, Gary will be on overtime. Beer and overtime, it's the only pleasure he gets out of life anymore. He worries about the girls so much it's driving him nuts. Any luck on a job?"

"You're kidding, right?"

"Do you ever wish she would die?" Kelly said and snuffed her cigarette underneath scuffed shoes. "I mean come on now, be honest."

"Well, I'd …"

"I mean what good is her life? Laying there moaning. In pain. Electric shocks? Hallucinations? Humpty Dumpty? Give me a break. The poor thing. They strap her to a table and electrocute her? What kind of thing is that? Mumbo-jumbo if you ask me. They can't really do anything for her. She's never going to get better."

Two orderlies dressed in white bumped out the big dark doors and lit cigarettes.

"The thing is," I said, "nobody ever came back from the grave. That's why we hang on so desperately. As Doris says, once you're dead, you're dead a long time."

"I'd rather see her die peacefully then suffer in the Poorhouse," Kelly said. "Some things are worse than death. Besides, there's Heaven, right?"

She shot me a cynical look.

"Yeah, Heaven," I said. "Kelly, if you need bread that bad I'll bake you some, white bread, so the girls will eat it."

"We're taking the kids out of Saint Barbara," she said. "Can't afford to be Catholic these days."

She led the way to the car.

"I dread it," she said over her shoulder. "The things going on in the public schools, I'm telling you. Girls getting pregnant left and right."

I made a date to talk with Father McCarthy O'Sullivan, and met him at our favorite speakeasy. It was a brick storefront with a big, hidden back yard in the swellest part of the city. The speakeasy didn't have a formal name, but everybody called it the Barking Dog. The front half was the Portland Pet Shop, puppies in the window, scrabbling in nests of shredded newspaper. The beer garden was enclosed by a rectangular brick wall, eight feet high. Unable to import German beer, they faked it, serving local brew in steins.

I hadn't seen Father Mack since my disastrous bet on the Derby. He was a busy guy, the Cathedral Provost officially, but more like bodyguard and babysitter for a frail and somewhat loony Archbishop.

Father Mack ordered pigs' knuckles and sauerkraut. My meal was pickled eggs and ginger ale. We sat at a rough picnic bench. It was the end of beer garden season, and as the sun disappeared behind the brick wall, I wished I'd worn more than a sport coat. Father Mack, with 250 pounds of insulation, didn't seem bothered.

We ate and talked horse racing awhile, and then I switched the conversation to my Aunt Doris.

"She's at Mother Mercy, failing pretty bad, Father, and I was wondering if there was any kind of, I don't know, pay-in-the-future plan."

He gnawed that pigs' knuckle, turning it into almost pure bone.

I said, "It's $100 a month to keep her there. I don't want her with all the Protestants in the Poorhouse. The raging maniacs they have in there, they terrorize the old people. I want Doris to have a Catholic end, Father. She's got property, a farm in Wisconsin, and her bills will be paid, I promise."

Father Mack drank beer, wiped his lips with a paper napkin.

"I'll swear in a court of law this isn't Altwasser," he said. He pushed the stein toward me. I sipped and shrugged.

"It's all swill to me," I said. "I heard this place is switching to Hamm's, exclusive. It's not about the beer, Father, the beer is all the same, it's about politics and loyalty. The breweries are cutthroat now, they can see the future, all beer legal."

I pushed the stein back at him.

"About the nuns at Mother Mercy, Father."

"I don't have much influence there," he said. "The nuns tend to be territorial."

"No chance?"

"Small chance, I suppose," he said.

"I'll sign anything I have to sign."

"We'll see," he said. "The nuns are pinchpennies. They have to be, I suppose."

We lit our pipes and watched the smoke rise into the darkening sky. Father Mack ordered another stein of beer. The temptation to join him was offset by the twinge of pain in my toe. Just thinking about beer can rouse the gout monster.

Through the tavern door walked Myrtle and Andrew, her new beau. She wore a blue, spangled dress that hid her pudgy legs. Andrew was tall, boyish and gawky, in leather jacket and open shirt. Maybe Myrtle spotted me. They sat on the far side of the beer garden.

"He owns a speakeasy," I told Father Mack.

"Inspecting the competition, I suppose."

"You know him, Father?"

"Aye. And he's quite a bit younger than your heathen friend, there."

"Myrtle," I said, "she's a thief and a loose woman. But there's something good in her."

"Mary Magdalene," said Father Mack. "Whom Jesus loved."

"You think Jesus had a thing for Mary Magdalene, Father?"

"Quite likely."

He puffed his pipe. "Every man is a man after all."

He sat back.

"I'm quite pleased at the political turn of events, Michael.

Things look promising. The Irish are back in charge of our city. A
Labor man no less."

I didn't want to contemplate any of that, especially my role in it.
After I had unwittingly delivered "Pop Anderson" to his assassins,
the escape of the Barker-Karpis gang became a hot issue in the
mayoral campaign. William Mahoney, the eventual winner,
campaigned as a reformer. He kept bringing up the murder of a
helpless old man, hinting that the Saint Paul Police had allowed
Barker and Karpis to escape.

I was off in contemplation when Father Mack brought me back:
"And what happened to your young lady?"
"Janie? Oh we're not romantic, Father."
I drained my ginger ale.
"Neighbors," I said.
"Indeed," said Father Mack.
Indeed, that's the Irish way of saying: Bullshit.

I was about to challenge his skepticism when a shock-thud
echoed in the beer garden. It was followed by another thud and
then the double doors gave way. Through that breach charged
uniformed policemen, one blowing a whistle, one shouting, another
carrying a shotgun. As I turned toward the front door, it too filled
with coppers. The drinkers screamed and stood up, but there was
nowhere to run. The whistle cop kept blowing. In the doorway
stood all 350 pounds of Inspector James Crumley. Behind him,
wielding an axe, was the snarling Bulldog McMullen.

In the pet shop, dogs were howling. An excited babble rose to a
roar among the beer garden patrons. The jungfrau who had served
us stood near Father Mack, trembling.

"Stand up," commanded the Bulldog, "turn your backs, and put
your hands on the wall, everybody."

"Don't make us get rough, now," warned Crumley.

He walked into the middle of the garden, and then turned on his toes like the world's fattest ballet dancer.

Flasks fell to the dirt floor. People, no fools, hid wallets and purses, hurried to pocket their watches and jewelry. Every police raid was also a shakedown. Bulldog McMullen, resplendent in gray suit, fedora, red tie, poked a woman and then a man with the axe handle. Gradually the patrons faced the wall and were frisked by the men in blue.

"Dirty cop," shouted one woman.

Father Mack and I and the jungfrau watched from our corner. No uniform cop dared approach the priest, and the two detectives ignored us. No way was I going to put my hands on the wall, or turn my back to a Saint Paul cop.

"Into the wagons with them," said Crumley. A wry smile played at the corners of his jowls. His seersucker suit looked loose on him, as if he'd sweated off a few ounces of gut fat over the summer. "Don't trip on the way out, folks," Crumley said. "We can't afford no lawsuits against the city, now."

As the coppers led people out the wrecked doorway, Crumley said: "I take it you was only drinking sacramental wine, Father, you can go."

Crumley glared at me. "You, bum, we got a place in the dungeon for guys like you."

McMullen led the jungfrau away.

"I suppose it's still legal to drink in Ireland," said Crumley.

"What of it?" asked Father Mack.

"Well it's the law, now," Crumley said. "Volstead, he was no Irishman, see? That's what I'm getting at."

"Make sense will you, Crumley?" I said.

"You know Powers, when you're under arrest you ought to shut up. Any scumbag lawyer will tell you that."

"If you're taking this man in," said Father Mack, "you're taking me in too. I'll stand no exception for the Roman Collar."

"Well ain't that noble, Father," said the Bulldog.

"Happy Oktoberfest," Crumley shouted as a group of young drinkers was pushed toward the paddy wagons.

Crumley stepped up close to Father Mack.

"There's a new chief, see. This is what a reformed Irish mayor brings to town. The Irish should know better than to try these reforms, now. We don't like politicians messing in department affairs. These two," he said to the Bulldog, "go in our car."

When we got outside to the twilit street, one paddy wagon closed its doors on frightened passengers. Other people, separated into male and female, were loaded into the remaining two wagons. Up the block, Myrtle and Andrew sauntered away, lit by lamps in the window of a dry cleaners.

We sat in the Dodge squad car, which stank of cigars and urine. Father Mack's head nearly scraped the roof.

"You didn't have to stick up for me," I told Father Mack.

As reply, he snorted. I focused on the man's huge hands. He had killed a man in the ring in Ireland, or so they said. Killed a man and turned to the priesthood in guilt. By reputation he had a quicksilver temper. I wondered whether he might take swing at either of the detectives.

McMullen got in behind the wheel and Crumley squeezed his elephantine form into the passenger seat.

"This is what happens when you elect a Communist mayor," said Crumley, looking at us through the rearview mirror. "When Big Joe Ryan was chief, this tavern had protection, now."

"Years," said McMullen. "I drank here myself sometimes."

"Father," Crumley said, "I heard you was stumping for that Commie now, and this is what you get."

Bulldog said: "Can we fine the Church, Jim?"

Crumley shook his massive head.

"How about the other one?" Bulldog said.

"Oh he pays."

"He owes me a quart of whiskey, as I recall," said the Bulldog.

I turned my pockets inside out. "You find money on me you're welcome to it."

"I guess it's jail for Powers then," said Crumley.

Father Mack pulled out his wallet.

"Oh no, Father," said Crumley, "it would be a sin to take money off a Catholic priest, now."

"A friend of the Archbishop is a friend of ours," said McMullen. "Right Jim?"

"Oh definitely. Powers, I thought you had given up the sauce, now."

"I was drinking ginger ale," I said.

"Heard that one before," said the Bulldog. "Have you heard that one before Jim?"

"Ten dollars to the Police Retirement Fund," said Crumley.

"Or we bury you in the catacombs with the rest of the heathens," said the Bulldog.

Father Mack passed me two five dollar bills.

"I won't say no," said McMullen, taking the money I handed over the seatback.

"Turn a blind eye," said Crumley.

CHAPTER TWELVE

I saw Harry on the steps of the police station, talking to Big Joe Ryan. The deposed chief towered over everybody I've ever known, except maybe Father Mack. Joe Ryan wore a brown pin-striped suit of tailor-shop fit and quality. The trouser cuffs extended to just the right length, draped over black hunting boots. Ryan looked forbidding and soft at the same time. He had a massive beer belly, was half bald, had a sagging double chin and wore school-teacher's eyeglasses. I pretended not to notice Ryan or Harry, and walked around the block.

I stopped at Blind Benny's newsstand.

"What do you know, Benny?" I said.

Benny's chapped lips barely moved in reply. When he made change for a little kid, Benny's print-blackened hands worked into a filthy apron.

"Speakeasy raids!" he shouted to passersby. "Dozens arrested! We got the names!"

Harry rounded the corner. He didn't notice me. He bought a Baby Ruth candy bar, a copy of Field and Stream, and a pack of Chesterfields. He was tapping that pack on his wrist when I sidled over and said: "Just the saloon-keeper I wanted to see."

His dark eyes radiated hung-over misery and lonesome sadness. He wore a yellow shirt and a puffy gray sweater. He stuck a Chesterfield into his lips, lit it with a gold lighter that was inscribed: *Charley.*

"Got to get something straight," I said.

"So you stalk me?"

"You're hard to get hold of."

"I hope the G-men feel the same way."

Together we walked down a shadowy alley.

I said, "Harry I..."

He cut me off, nicotine-stained finger to his lips. He pointed his cigarette toward the sky. "Careful," he said, "the federals are listening from aero-planes now."

He led me out of the alley to a gleaming Packard convertible. It was like he was competing with Jack Peifer for the title of man with the most deluxe car. Jack's was olive and came with a Japanese driver. Harry drove himself in a cream-colored convertible.

He got in behind the wheel and unlocked the passenger door for me. He pitched the cigarette into a pile of leaves at the edge of the parking lot.

In the Packard I got a heavy whiff of alcohol. Which would give out first, I wondered, his liver or his brain?

"So Harry, I need to know if I can get on the level."

"Are you kidding?"

He reached down into his sweater for another cigarette, thought better of it.

"See," I said, "there's a parking problem."

Harry's fingers tapped the steering wheel.

"Harry, have you ever seen this place?"

"I don't go over there."

"You never go to Minneapolis?"

"Are you kidding me? You can't trust nobody over there."

"Well," I said, "the bank sits on a triangle. One side is a streetcar stop. So there's exactly five good parking spaces, and they're always taken."

He hacked through a cigarette cough.

"The solution," I said, "is park the getaway car first thing in the morning. Then you deliver the gang in a switch car when it's time for the job."

"And you would be the delivery boy."

"Right."

"And for this you want to be made level?"

"Right."

He shook his head. "This gang's different. They don't want the sixth guy."

"I understand Harry, they want the minimum. But for this job, six is the minimum."

"Double park in front of the bank," he suggested.

"On the streetcar tracks?"

Harry sighed.

"Harry, I'm marking and this is how I mark. If the boys want another bank, fine, but this is where the money is. Harry, it's like they're minting it over there."

"Five and a half guys, maybe."

"Level," I said. "I've got expenses."

"They don't need you inside the place. You're not carrying hardware, you're not level. Take it from me, five and a half and you'll be lucky."

"You'll be twice my Uncle if you make it six men."

"So you're dealing behind their backs now?"

"Whatever it takes, Harry, I'm dead broke."

"Look, half a share, plus a bonus if you get over fifty out of that joint. And I tell you what, at that price, I got another job for you."

"Okay."

"School my little friend."

"Who, Reilly?"

"Teach him to mark."

"Why? I'm the marker."

"What is it with you fucking Irishmen?" said Harry. "Extra bones in the skull? Is that it?"

I left Harry for the offices of another bone-headed Irishman, Tom Filben. I knocked at the warehouse door behind his so-called radio shop, no answer. I found him at his other haunt, the Lowry Terrace Cafe, enjoying a full British high tea with beautifully dressed older women. Tommy's hair was freshly oiled and combed, his Palm Beach suit spotless and pressed. I stood behind a potted palm and waved for his attention. He excused himself to his female companions. We crossed the hallway and into a bar which, given the early hour, had quite a few patrons. In the back, near the phone booths, we huddled and Tom waved off the bartender.

He walked gimpy, but had given up his cane.

"You're limping better," I said.

"Time heals and the doctor takes the fee," he said. "What can I do you out of?"

"Money," I said.

"Goes without saying."

"Minnesota driver's license."

"Ka-ching," said Tom.

"Two cars, two plates."

"Now you're talking."

"Both cars big enough to fit six guys."

"Sounds like quite a picnic. Will there be pie and ice cream?"

"Both cars checked over good at Herb's."

"Icing on the cake," said Filben.

"Who you got there, Ladies' Altar Society?"

"Antiques," he said. "My wife's gang. They're as vicious as any hunters who ever stalked a rhino."

"We've got to talk about credit."

"Oh boy."

"No date set yet."

"Do I look like Papa Alt? I'm not running a bank, Mick."

"Save it, Tommy. You've got enough cash to buy this hotel."

"I won't have a dime after Roosevelt."

"What's he got to do with it?"

"He'll bankrupt the nation. See that's why I'm investing in Cuba. Cuba, me lad, has a future, unlike the Land of the Free and the Home of the Brave. Do you think America is in bad shape now? Ninety percent of the money coming to this city is off the boot. I'll be begging on street corners if they put Franklin the Commie in the White House."

"Even with a Commie in the White House," I said, "banks will have money."

"You ought to see what Prohibition has done for Havana. A mere ferry ride from dry Florida, it's a wonderland of booze, babes and baccarat."

"Okay, but we're not in Cuba now, Tommy, and there's money to be made here."

"Thirty days," said Filben, "and then I come looking for you." He shot the cuffs of his pink shirt. "Not personally of course. I'll send my representatives."

CHAPTER THIRTEEN

I liked Pat Reilly, everybody did, but I hated teaching him the trade. The fewer jug markers in town, the better for me. But the more I thought it over, the less I objected. For one thing, Reilly owned a vehicle, and I didn't. For another, I was pretty sure Reilly wouldn't learn much. Marking banks is like handicapping horse races. There are many factors and angles, and it takes a head for math and organization. I was a good handicapper, and Reilly was hopeless. I figured Reilly had been nagging Harry for a promotion, and this was Harry's way to shut him up. Nobody, not even Harry who loved him, took Pat Reilly seriously.

We drove Reilly's truck to Minneapolis on a rainy chill October day. The truck was a Ford flatbed, meant to move beer barrels at night, underneath a canvas that was now rolled up and flapping behind us.

Reilly wore a white dress shirt and leather vest. His shirt pocket was stuffed with a full pack of Luckies. He hadn't shaved or brushed his teeth. He worked impatient through traffic, jamming the stick-shift left and right.

"Take it easy, we'll get there," I said.

He grunted.

"Remember this traffic," I said. "Factor that in."

Big drops spattered the windshield, his erratic wiper only smearing the rain. Spikes of cold water whipped in via the cracked-open windows.

"Suppose its rainy on job day," I said.

"So?"

"So new wipers on the getaway car. New tires. You got five, six guys in here, the windows are going to fog. You put a towel in the car for that."

Reilly bleated the horn.

"Absolutely no horn tooting," I said. "You want less attention. Less."

But I was pleased to confirm my suspicion that Reilly would never be promoted to marker.

When we arrived at the bank there was, as expected, no parking. We were only a few blocks from Minneapolis' downtown.

"Around the corner is good," I told Pat. "Out of sight is better."

He parked, yanked the emergency brake, lit a Lucky.

"You know my wife," he said. "What do you think of her?"

"What do I think of Babe?"

"Yeah, what do you think of her?'

"Pat, what kind of question is that?"

"You think she could run a high class joint, you know, hostess? Like Peifer's old lady. Standing at the front door, giving guys a boner?"

"So you're thinking about running a nightclub?"

"Yeah, who isn't?"

"Me, I'm not."

"What are you thinking of? Everybody's thinking of something, right?"

"Oh," I sighed, "vacation cottages in Wisconsin."

"Serious?"

"Yeah."

"Not a tavern? I mean, think of it, the country goes wet, joints open on every street corner."

"And that's the problem. Competition."

"That's why I need a sexy hostess, slot machines, dancing girls. I take a cue from Filben, the smartest guy I know. He's years ahead of us all, that Irish prick. He's leasing slot machines now. Not selling, but leasing them out to taverns."

"Ah… Filben."

"How come I can't think up stuff like that? Filben is what do you call them, a visionist. He's visionistic."

"So you figure you mark a bank, use that money to start a nightclub. Is that what you're thinking?"

"Basically yeah. Like Peifer. I mean who's he? He ain't the brainiest guy. Goddamn turkey farmer. But I tell you, my joint will have no whore-types. Sexy is one thing, whores is another. No. Babe won't allow no whore-types on the property."

Babe had been a notorious sporting girl, $5 a night last I heard. Never tread on another man's illusions, I told myself.

"Let's mark, buddy," I said.

I went in first. It was a strange bank, triangle shaped, one wall almost entirely plate glass windows. In the history of bank robberies, this might be the most visible. On the sidewalk, people walked by in a steady stream. A streetcar stop, service every five minutes, was right outside the glassy front doors.

I was sure I was marking for the gang that had pulled the Redwood Falls job. They were daring and fast, out with the cash in ten minutes, and willing to take big risks. Hick banks were okay, but if you wanted the maximum haul, a city bank was the answer.

I stood in the bank lobby like a bewildered customer. Men and women waited in lines at tellers' cages or filled out deposit slips at marble counters. Everyone was well-dressed, not a bum in sight, and no guard, either. All this sunlight and glass had fooled these bankers into thinking they were safe from robbers.

I joined the longest line and shuffled forward, looking around while trying to be not too obvious about it. It took almost ten minutes to get to the lady with the bobbed hair and the red dress behind brass bars.

I cleared my throat. "I would like to open a Christmas Club, please."

I pushed a driver's license under the bars. It had been issued to Patrick O. Butter by Filben's joker at Motor Vehicles.

"Oh, we don't need that for a Christmas Club," she said, and pushed the license back. Great. I'd wasted ten bucks on it.

"Denomination?" she said.

"Fifty cents," I said.

She was married, big diamond ring to prove it. I wondered if that ring would end up in the gang's get bag. Some gangs took stuff like that, but I hoped we wouldn't. The smarter gangs just robbed the banks, and let the people be. It would read good in the newspaper the next day, the gentlemen bandits, who winked at the clerks and tellers while robbing the fat cats.

The teller handed me a book of ticket stubs. It depicted a cartoon snowman and sprig of holly. In red and white letters it said: SAVING FOR CHRISTMAS, 1933.

"First payment is not until December," she said. "Unless you want to start now."

Whatever was least memorable.

"Um, I'll wait," I said.

"The Club will be paid up and ready a year from now, on the Monday after Thanksgiving," she said.

I pocketed the ticket book inside my sport coat and said: "Thank you ma'am, have a nice day."

"Next!" she said.

I walked to the counter, took out some deposit slips, used the chained pen to make nonsense marks and generally stalled for a better look around. When I could stall no more I walked out to find Reilly in the truck, rain beating on the roof. He was sipping from a cardboard cup of coffee, windows steamed up.

"Your turn, go," I said. "Where'd you get that coffee?"

He pointed out the foggy windows.

"I'll be there," I said.

I crossed the street to a breakfast joint named Folkers, a long counter is all it was, a few dark booths in the back. I sat on a stool. There were two old farmers at the other end, that was it for customers. When the waitress approached I said: "Adam and Eve on a raft."

The waitress scratched her head. Dandruff fell to her black-and-white dress.

"Sorry," she said.

"They don't know how to poach eggs?"

"Ran out of eggs this morning. There's a farmers' strike, you know. What are they doing with all them eggs? I don't know. But they ain't getting through. Oatmeal?"

"Not for me," I said. "Toast and coffee?"

"Sure," she said. "And you're lucky, we're almost out of butter." She looked at those old farmers and muttered: "Farmers on strike. What the hell is happening in this country?"

I sure didn't know. I took my time over toast and coffee. I drew rough diagrams of what I'd seen in the bank. I glanced through the diner's foggy windows, you could see the bank good from here. Somebody would be sitting here some afternoon and would get a monster surprise.

When I finished breakfast and map-making, I left fifteen cents on the brass cash register and walked out into a rainstorm that was easing to a drizzle.

Reilly sat in the truck, smoking a Lucky.

"So," I said. "Shoot."

"Can't be done," said Reilly. "Too public. Are you kidding? It's like robbing a greenhouse."

"Look," I said, "in a way, it's safer to take a city bank. Rob a bank in the country, and every goddamn farmer runs for his shotgun, and there's a shootout. Kraft State Bank, remember?

Disaster. Here, only the cops have guns and have you seen a cop since we pulled up?"

"No."

"Yes you have, you just didn't notice. Cop stopped in for a shoeshine, right across the street."

"Uniform?"

"Detective," I said.

"All right."

"What did you notice inside?"

"No bank guard."

"Good. Keep going."

"I don't know."

"How were the customers dressed?"

"Normal."

"Pat, the robbers want to dress like customers. It buys them time and gives them the element of surprise. In the country, the gang wears overalls. In the city, they wear suits. See? You've got to look around and notice things."

"The vault was open."

"As it always is during banking hours. But that's only the outer door. The inner door is under a combination lock. Right now you should be drawing maps and making notes. Everything you saw."

"You got a pencil and paper?"

"You didn't bring your own?"

We ended our days' work by driving the getaway route, down Hennepin until it entered Saint Paul and was renamed Larpenteur. We scribbled down the landmarks at every tenth of a mile. Gas station here, steel warehouse there.

"Keep it simple," I advised. "Remember, this car will be full of armed felons who are jumpy as hell."

One turn was all it took to get into Como Park. We passed the rain-emptied golf course and arrived at the zoo, where the gang would switch cars. We stopped just outside the buffalo pen.

"Here, see," I said. "Buffalo. You can't mistake it."

On the other side of a wire fence, a buffalo bull swished his tail and took a leak. The buffalo knew how to mark, Pat Reilly didn't.

I spent the evening on notes and maps. The easiest one to draw was the fake map, marking the roads from Saint Paul down to Hot Springs, Arkansas. Hot Springs was a notorious gangster town, almost as bad as Saint Paul. The fake-out map would be left in the getaway car, to throw off the cops. All the genuine maps and notes would be burned.

I had finished my mapmaking and was kneading dough when Hula Girl and Snowflake set to barking. I dusted flour off my hands and walked to the city view windows, where both dogs scrabbled onto their platform. In the glow of street lights I saw Janie and Larry in the parking lot. He was revving up his yellow Hupmobile. She leaned in to kiss him. He peeled out of the lot and raced toward downtown, like there was a demon chasing him.

I looked at the clock and it was just past eleven. I soft-footed it down the stairs. A quarter in my fingers, I reached through the burglar bars to tap on Janie's window.

She didn't answer.

I knocked on her door. Then I began pounding, then shouting her name. The light went on in the apartment above. Mrs. Holy Reardon, the landlady, peeked through blinds. Finally Janie came to the door, opened it a crack. She was in bathrobe, with dripping wet hair.

"Powers, go away, it's late."

"You're going to let me in."

"No way."

I bulled in, shouldering the door open, flinging her backward. She looked frightened. Above her head, the hot water pipes were crackling with the first heat of winter. She tied her bathrobe tighter and said:

"What is wrong with you, Powers?"

"Your choice of men."

"Powers, if I didn't know better I'd say you're jealous."

I glared.

"It's none of your business," she said.

"It's my fault."

"What do you mean, fault?"

"I had him to my apartment."

"What exactly is wrong with him?"

"Can't you tell?"

"He seems perfectly nice to me."

"Janie," I sat on her couch uninvited. "I'm forced now to tell you a gangland secret. But you can never print it, or even hint that you know it."

She ran her hand through her wet red hair.

"You know why the newspapers never tell the truth about this town? Because any reporter who wrote the truth would end up dead the next day. You know why Goggles writes the kind of crap that he does? Because gangland finds it amusing. Harry Sawyer, Jack Peifer, Big Joe Ryan and Irish Kinkead run this town, under the approving gaze of that pillar of the establishment, Papa Alt. For muscle, they can hire any of a hundred desperados who would kill their grandmas if somebody paid them. Remember when those two thugs hunted me down on Saint Patrick's Day? So what I'm about to tell you, you either keep secret, or we both die. Okay?"

"Okay, I'm scared. Once again you've scared me. Speak your piece."

"Larry is a level gangster. If you tell him I told you that, he will kill me and maybe you, do you understand?"

"He told me all about it."

"He told you what?"

"He used to run boot."

"There's more to it. Are you sleeping with this guy?"

"You have some nerve."

"Because if this is a serious romance…"

"Powers, I am going to call the police."

"The Saint Paul Police? Surely you're joking."

"Believe me I'll call them."

"With what phone?"

She stood, staring at me, hands on her hips.

"Janie, there's a bank deal coming up. You know two people who'll be involved."

"Deal, what kind of deal?"

"Dump this guy. Get a job in Chicago. Go on a long vacation. Go back to the dairy farm in what's that town?"

"Waunakee. I'm never going back to Waunakee, Powers, I'd rather die."

"You just might. Try California or how about Florida, somewhere, anywhere but here."

She retreated to the far end of her one-room apartment. At the kitchen table were the remainders of a booze party. If she was drunk she hid it well. Her bed was behind a screen, and she retreated there. All I could see of her was pale feet and ankles.

"I'm getting dressed, okay? Stay where you are."

I paced on her woven rug.

"I kind of like him, Powers," she called over the screen. "He's not a bad guy like you say."

"You wanted to know what gangster life is like, well you might find out first hand. I guarantee you won't like it. Once you get in, you start to know stuff, and if you know stuff, you'll never get out alive. Two words: Sadie and Rose."

"Powers," she said over the screen. "You asked me to pull back and stop asking questions about Sadie and Rose. So for the time being, I've dropped that subject. Now you're telling who I can and can't date?"

She appeared in striped overalls and white t-shirt. "Get thee to a nunnery, is that it, Powers?"

"What does that mean?"

"It's Shakespeare."

"What does this have to do with Shakespeare?"

She moved two cocktail glasses from table to sink.

"He's like you," she said. "He doesn't drink that much."

She looked at her feet, then up at me and said: "What bank deal?"

"You don't want to know. I'm trying to keep you out of it. You're not as bright as you think you are, even if you did graduate from college."

"And so your advice, Swami Powers?"

"Tell him you like him but you're focused on your career, you can't get serious, you're waiting for a call from the Chicago Tribune. Dump him easy. If he gets crazy, skip town. I'm dead serious here, skip town. Take vacation time. He'll soon be gone or in jail."

"Oh, you're hysterical, Powers. I don't know if it's all that drastic."

"Look, I am not really a level guy, okay? You know the only guys who get to be level? Guys who have proven themselves by putting a bullet through somebody. That's a level guy. Larry is involved in this bank deal as a level guy, meaning somehow sometime, he left a body somewhere. At least one. Most of these guys, once they've got a notch on their gun, they keep shooting."

"I don't believe you." She looked up at me, hurt in her eyes. "I can't believe you."

"Janie, I'm certain."

"Okay okay okay quit harping."

"You can't live in two worlds, Janie. You've got to pick one and God help you, you're a college girl, you don't belong in mine."

She held the door open as an invitation for me to exit.

I stood outside her apartment, in the shadows of the dim lobby light, and smoked my pipe. Upstairs I saw my two dogs in the window and they made me feel desperate to save my home here. I'd had a rootless youth. I would do whatever it took to stay put. Maybe I would just settle in and mark a bank every year. Just one a year, and that would earn enough money. Just bank jobs. No blood, no guilt.

I smoked and watched, down at the bottom of the hill, the busy busy busy little city, a thousand cars, a hundred criminal plots, and just as many crooked cops, judges, and politicians. Down on Fort Road, a cop was writing up a driver, but the ticket would never make it to court. Even a simple traffic stop had been turned into a system of bribery.

Smoking a pipe is like bootlegging. It starts out fresh and tasty, and ends up nasty at the bottom.

I walked upstairs and took out that chrome pistol, ivory handles, the one Peifer had given me. I had unloaded it for my drugstore robbery, now I inserted four brassy cartridges, letting the hammer rest on an empty chamber. I aimed at the closet door and said, "Don't make me do it, Larry."

CHAPTER FOURTEEN

Life's a competition, so I didn't tell Pat Reilly about my next marking trips. I had schooled him enough to appease Harry, but didn't give away too many trade secrets. Using a DeSoto borrowed from Filben, I drove the getaway route from zoo to bank and back again, eight miles, fifteen to seventeen minutes. There were no train crossings, that you have to be sure of, it's disaster if a slow freight blocks the getaway.

The guy at the bottom of any organization usually has a grudge, so I softened up the bank's janitor, a youngish guy named Everett. He was a bit of a dolt. He was tall, thin-faced, with a wispy mustache. He wore a mismatched suit and loose tie as if he aspired to be a banker. I made it my business to sit next to him at Don's Coney Dog during his lunch break. I said I was new to Minneapolis. I asked where a fellow could wet his lips with honest-to-god brewery beer. Not that home-brew swill, but Altwasser, direct from Papa's barrels. Everett directed me to two of his favorite speakeasies. I slipped him a buck and shook his hand. Buy yourself a couple of rounds, I said.

I couldn't find information about every employee, but the bankers' association helpfully listed the names of the executives. The big cheese was Vice President and Treasurer R.C. Teuscher. Head cashier was A.L. Enerson, in charge of that vault. I looked this up in the Minneapolis library with the intent of further snooping. Where did they sit exactly? Were any of them ex-Marines, former boxers, football players? I was determined to mark the perfect job, become the best in the trade, the guy Harry would recommend for any future heist. No surprises. That's how you rose in reputation as a jug marker.

When I got home to my zoo of barking dogs and chirping birds, the phone was ringing.

"I'm thinking about you, sport."

"I guess Myrtle's horny," I said.

"That's right," she said.

"I've got animal problems right now," I said.

"I've got an animal problem myself."

"Give me twenty minutes."

"Nineteen," said Myrtle. "And bring gin."

I walked the dogs, fed them, and covered the birdcage. "Moving day," I told Charles and Amelia. Walking clumsy with a cumbersome cage in my hand, I descended four flights and pushed out into parking lot. I never knew when I might have the use of a car again, and I didn't want these birds in the apartment forever. Dogs I could take care of, but about birds I knew nothing.

So I had the cage in my hands and a pint of gin in my back pocket when I kicked at the dark wood of Myrtle's apartment door. She opened it and said: "Oh. Parakeets?"

"Come on," I said. "They'll cheer you up."

In a sunny corner sat a sewing table, once the platform for Flyboy's cage. Myrtle cleared it of Chinese figurines and I set Charles and Amelia's cage down and lifted the cover.

The birds squawked and fluttered.

"I don't know," said Myrtle.

"Time to get over Flyboy," I said.

She'd been smoking a cigarette in a long ivory holder. Now she set it in an ashtray, stood back, hands on hips, and stared at the birds. She wore a black kimono with red dragons, but was otherwise naked. She took one step toward the cage and looked in with wonder, like a child.

"Are you my little babies now?" she asked.

Charles fluttered his yellow-green wings.

"Ah," said Myrtle and picked up her cigarette holder. "Flyboy loved me. Flyboy perched on my shoulder."

"Give 'em a chance," I said.

At least, I thought, she'll have to keep that shade raised, now that she has birds near the window. I held up, like a trophy fish, a small bottle of Gordon's London Gin.

"A Collins would be nice," she said. "You know how to make 'em."

I walked into the kitchen to assemble the drinks, but had to wash glasses first. Even though Myrtle didn't cook, she did drink, and the glasses piled up.

"I thought you had a maid come in," I called out.

"The bitch quit me," Myrtle said. "I had to slap her."

"Before or after she quit?"

Myrtle didn't answer. I made her a Gin Collins heavy and myself a club soda with lime. I carried the drinks through her elaborately furnished living room and into her dark bedroom. An outline of her was visible on the bed, face down.

"I've been a bad girl," she said.

I set the drinks on her dresser, amid a scattering of jewelry, and gilt-framed photos of the Professor, all reflected in an oval mirror.

"Spank me," she said.

"What did you do this time?"

She rolled over and accepted the drink I held out. She sucked about half of it up the straw. "I like to be interrogated."

She held out the drink and I placed it on the dresser.

"All right, roll over," I said.

She lay flat on the bed, plump ass upward.

"Did you steal something, young woman?"

"No officer."

I patted her butt.

"And if I did I would share it with you, officer. You're so handsome I can't resist."

I slapped her butt a little harder.

"What did you steal, young lady?"

"Ow, you hurt me."

I rested my hand on the warm moist skin of her back.

"What did you steal?"

"I'm not telling."

I smacked her a little softer.

"Ow. Okay. I stole a man from his wife."

"So that's it. You know what the punishment is?"

I rolled her over. Her eyes were wet with some emotion, and I really never understood where it came from.

She sighed.

She spread her legs.

A look of peace and pleasure took over her face.

"You can't get away with this," she said. "I'll call the police."

"You're kidding," I said. "The Saint Paul police?

I never met a woman who made love as ferociously as Myrtle. I never met a woman who was so utterly done with you after the uncoupling. She lay naked on her side, sweaty, finishing that Collins, reaching out to lift the shade for a look out at Grand Avenue.

I was re-introducing clothes to my own sweaty body, one hand on the dresser for balance. Staring at me were pictures of the love of Myrtle's life, Professor Banks. In one photo it was Christmas, at some lodge, moose heads and a big fireplace. The other picture showed him and Myrtle at a riverside picnic in full summer. Professor Banks, a high school dropout, looked like an actual college professor, with full, gray beard and high forehead.

"So really, how's life with Andrew?"

"Eh," she said. "He pays the rent."

"So he's sort of like a job."

"Life is like a crappy job," Myrtle said, "the pay's lousy, the boss is a jerk, and at the end of the day, everybody gets fired."

"The other night at the Barking Dog. Crumley let you and Andrew walk."

"Aren't you the clever observer."

"Did you pay Crumley off?"

"Don't need to. Andrew's my get out of jail free card."

"Okay, give, Myrtle."

"Andrew is Papa Alt's boy. His adopted son, almost. The son he wishes he had instead of his drippy kid, Richard. It's Papa Alt's money behind the Martini Lounge."

She pulled on the shade to let it rise.

"See, the Martini Lounge is like, a vision of the future. A tryout for the new age, you might say. America, wet again, and drinking at Papa's."

"Papa Alt's dream of the future?"

"Everybody talks about Big Ryan but every sewer underneath this rotten town leads to Papa Alt's beer cellar. He's the ultimate. Mahoney, the reformer? He's reforming this town to Papa Alt's liking. Sure, Mahoney is a union man. But see, the secret is, Papa Alt don't mind the unions. He figures the unions keep the workers from getting too wild, like a Communist overthrow. Which he's afraid of. He genuinely thinks this, Andrew told me. He thinks we're heading like Bolshevik Russia."

She flopped on her back, naked.

"Give me some of the good stuff, will you?"

From a gold earring box on her dresser I pulled a limp cigarette. She sat up on the edge of the bed, let me put the joint in her lips. I lit it. Her feet searched for slippers and nudged them from the under the bed. She sat on the rumpled edge of the bed, naked except for the slippers, sunlight streaming in behind her. She blew fragrant smoke at me.

"You ought to try it," she said. "Might improve your crappy attitude."

"Not me, I'm dopey enough."

"I been to that mansion twice now, can you believe it? The house that Altwasser built. Papa detests me, but because of Andrew, he'll put up with me. See, Papa hates Andrew's wife too. I think he's what you call a man who hates women, Papa Alt."

She closed her eyes. Hands in her lap, she sat like an Egyptian queen, a plump body underneath a pyramid of hair. Sacrificial smoke rose past her face.

"What do you do for fun, anyway, Mick? You don't smoke dope, and you don't drink that much."

"I play the ponies and make love to fascinating women."

She laughed. "You Irishmen sure can shovel it."

"What's Papa Alt's end game then?"

"Simple. When beer comes back, it's Altwasser owns the whole Northwest. He'll vanquish his rivals, the Hamms and the Bremers. Not a bottle of Schmidt's or Hamm's to be seen between here and Seattle. Plus, in every neighborhood, a fancy cocktail lounge. All bankrolled, see, and committed to pour only Altwasser. Plus, there's rail cars full of new pipes at the brewery. If I didn't know better, I'd say Papa's planning on building a distillery. So that's why he dotes on Andrew. Right now Harry Sawyer runs Papa's beer, but Harry's no businessman. Harry's a bootlegger, a drunk and a low-class gangster. When bootlegging dies, so does Harry. Andrew is the fair-haired boy. Andrew is going to lead the revolution."

"And you'll have Andrew by the privates."

She sputtered. "He'll dump me and his wife both and marry an Alt. There's plenty of Alt cousins. They breed like German rabbits."

"I didn't know you were a fortune teller."

"No need to guess at the future if you can see the past. Men dump you like last week's trash. The one goddamn exception is my Professor, locked up in Waupun for the next twenty years."

She lay back, wet her fingers, extinguished the joint.

"I can't figure you, sport," she said. "You've been dumped, hard. What, for a Navy man? Don't it make you bitter at the whole goddamned human race? The treachery. The lies. Constant."

I said, "I'm thinking about this thing that happened at the end of last winter. In a blizzard. They found two women burnt in a car down on the levee. Remember?"

Myrtle rolled over and stared out the window.

"You don't like to be naked, do you?"

"Not especially," I said.

"I mean you get dressed as soon as you're finished. You don't like to loll. See, men, they're no good at lolling."

"I assumed it was gangsters behind the incineration murder of Sadie and Rose. But what if it went deeper?"

"Keep chewing, sport, you'll gag it down eventually."

"I mean, it was Papa Alt who engaged me to investigate those women. Suppose it was him who wanted them dead? Suppose he was afraid that if Rose laid the trail, the federal hound dogs would follow it to the Alt mansion. I mean, Uncle Sam put Capone in prison on a tax dodge, Leon Gleckman's on his way and maybe Papa Alt is next."

"Maybe," said Myrtle. "And maybe I'm in line for the Congressional Medal of Honor."

I lay beside her, me clothed, her naked. I planted a kiss on her luscious lips. I stared into her deep soulful eyes. There seemed to be no bottom to them, you could fall in there and float happily in a dark warm pool. What lovely soul was trapped inside Myrtle's hard shell?

"Don't look at me sincere," said Myrtle. "It rouses my tender feelings."

CHAPTER FIFTEEN

"What's this?" asked McAmbly.

"A new miracle food," I said. "They call it bread." I dropped a paper bag on his counter. "It's made from flour, yeast, water and salt."

"You baked this?" he said, peering into the bag.

"I heard kids will eat it if it's spread with, let's say, peanut butter."

"You're a baker now?"

"Surprisingly easy," I said. "The yeast does all the work."

McAmbly pushed his cap back on his head.

"Am I a charity case all of a sudden?"

"How's Maureen?"

"She's at Mayo right now." His face, already red, grew scarlet. "They don't know nothing, these doctors."

"How is she?"

"They think it's kidneys."

"Can they help her?"

He held up one hand. "Look, ah, I'm so aggravated."

"Okay, let me know if I can help, give you a ride down to Rochester, anything."

"I appreciate, Mick. Come around. What do you need?"

I walked around the counter and into the Identification Unit. The heart of it was a curtained photo studio, surrounded by measuring devices that resembled medieval torture machines. The heart of the Bertillion system was to identify criminals by nine critical measurements, of head, fingers, forearms, earlobes. Names were of limited value. Every criminal had a dozen names.

"Guy who calls himself Larry," I said.

"That narrows it down to a million," said McAmbly.

I noted the absence of beer bottles.

"You off the brew?"

"Me?" said Billy. "Need to economize." He hefted his gut. "On the money and the weight."

"Larry might be from Oklahoma? Slight twang."

"Knock yourself out," he said.

He paused in the doorway: "Fingerprints are going to ruin me, Mick. I'm a dinosaur when fingerprints come in."

I walked to his filing cabinets, pulled out a drawer and began flipping through cards.

"One other thing," I said over my shoulder. "Minneapolis. What's the afternoon shift change? Same as here?"

"Far as I know."

"Three o'clock then."

McAmbly didn't answer. He was bent over the counter, studying something closely, pencil in hand.

"How you doing on the horses?" he said absently.

"Staying away," I said. "No gambling money. Kind of broke right now."

"Join the club," he said.

I flipped through card after card.

"I got a meeting with Dahill," McAmbly said. "You okay here?"

I mumbled a reply.

"Bread," he said. "Powers, you're turning into a housewife. Can you mop floors? Because if you can, I might have to marry you."

He left me alone with the cards. It was stuffy in that office, so I removed my suit coat and dressed a wooden chair with it. After about twenty minutes of card flipping, I lucked across a picture of Larry: full face and profile. Bit of a sneer. Last name, Barton, first name Harry, supposedly. Stapled to it was an extradition order, issued by a judge in Oklahoma. This was issued in March in the name of Lawrence DuVol aka Harry Barton.

The charge: murder of a peace officer, first degree.

I sat back in the chair. My coat fell to the dusty floor, and my pipe clattered out of the pocket. Sunlight filtered through dirty windows. I realized I had sweated up my shirt.

It was hard to figure this Larry, charming and handsome, as a cop-killer. Perhaps they had the wrong man. More likely, I was trying to fool myself.

I was staring at the card, thinking of stealing it and presenting it to Janie, when McAmbly pushed in through the pebbled glass door.

"You find somebody?" McAmbly asked.

"Oh yeah," I said. "Bad hombre."

He looked over my shoulder.

"Saint Paul," he said, "where extradition orders go to die."

I rode the streetcar around the Loop and got off at Wabasha and Fourth, the nexus of power in Saint Paul. From a suite in the hotel Saint Paul, rum runner Leon Gleckman had ruled this city all through the Roaring Twenties. Indictments for tax evasion had crippled him, giving rise to a power struggle between Harry Sawyer and Jack Peifer. Just down the street was the massive Hamm building, the beer family's venture into real estate. Across from it, the Bremer family, which brewed Schmidt's, operated its Commercial State Bank. In between the two, an entire block, was the Alt Arcade, rented to haberdashers, a pool hall, a travel agent, a dancing academy, a busy and truly bland Swedish smorgasbord, and the Alt family's River State Bank. All in all, this prime piece of downtown had been built with the profits of illegal beer.

Across from all this stood the mighty Federal Building, where agents were supposedly charged with preventing the sale of beer. The building was a Germanic castle that looked like it belonged in Munich. I walked in and bought stamps at the Post Office. I didn't need stamps, but that was my excuse for being there. In this town you don't want to be seen visiting G-Men. I sneaked out the side door of the Post Office, climbed to the castle's second floor and asked to see the Duke, Agent Roland Heater.

He was eating a ham sandwich on white bread and drinking from a bottle of GR-8 Root Beer.

"Hell do you want?" he asked, chewing.

"Make you a trade."

"I'll give you Babe Ruth for Jimmy Foxx and two season tickets," he said.

"I didn't know the Federal Government had a sense of humor."

"Then you don't know your Federal Government," Heater said. "We're hilarious when we get going."

He lay his sandwich delicate on its wax paper package.

"My time is valuable, Powers."

"Lunch at your desk. As a taxpayer, I applaud you."

"Very nice, now what?"

"You remember the Burned Ladies? Or, as you G-men see it, the case of the Buick that was stolen, driven across state lines in violation of Federal law, and then burned?"

"Okay."

"I was sent to spy on those women the day before they died."

"Were you?"

"Yes, and it's your job to ask who sent me."

Heater sipped root beer.

I said: "The same man who brews that root beer as a front for the Altwasser beer operation."

"The Department of Justice is not in the business of enforcing the Volstead Act. That's two floors up. Take the elevator, not the stairs. It's slippery around here."

"In the case of the Burned Ladies, we're talking about interstate transport of a motor vehicle in furtherance of a crime."

"Where'd you get your law degree, Powers? Hokus-Pokus College?"

"You see, Heater, Papa Alt is an empire builder. He has a grand plan. He's handing big stacks of money to the Roosevelt campaign. He's training his troops for the Wet Revolution. The other day I was in a speakeasy that happened to be raided. They served Hamm's in steins. They used to serve Altwasser, but they switched. A week after they switched, they got raided. Did you ever notice, Heater, that joints that serve Altwasser never get raided?"

He grunted.

"Papa Alt's dream is Altwasser Nation, the entire Northwest, from here to Seattle."

"Why are you telling me this?"

"I figure you might be interested to know who's running this town."

He smirked.

"See, Heater, I assumed Papa Alt hired me because he was afraid of kidnapping. But maybe what he really feared was exposure by a prostitute who knew too much. That would be Rose Perry. Her husband Bobby Perry robbed the Denver Mint. The money was laundered by Papa Alt's bank. So now years later, Rose is desperate for cash, has a big mouth, drinks too much and just happens to know who laundered the Denver Mint cash. Her unfortunate friend Sadie was just along for the ride. So if my theory is correct, Papa Alt had reason to fear Rose Perry."

Heater shrugged.

"The Denver Mint," I said. "That was Federal, I take it."

He quietly belched, fist in front of his lips.

"Maybe," I said, "Papa Alt is too chummy with certain presidential candidates. Maybe he's too big to be tackled by the Division of Justice."

Heater stood up, paced in front of the Stars and Stripes and said: "Sure, Powers. I can see myself dragging a respected millionaire into court and saying: Some washed-up bootlegger suspects this fine old fellow of setting two prostitutes on fire. Other evidence behind this vague accusation? Absolutely none, your honor."

"Just keep it in mind, Heater. In this town, everything leads back to that great benefactor of mankind, Papa Alt.

"Save that fairy tale for your memoirs, Powers." He stared at me. "That's it? That's what you've got?"

"I'm wrapping this town up for you, Heater."

"How about Judge Crater, do you know what happened to him?"

"See I might need something from you, Agent Heater. I'm working on a guy. Bad hombre. From out of town. I think I can put the finger on him."

"For what?"

"Bank robbery, murder."

"Neither of which are Federal. Kidnapping, now you're talking. Thanks to Congress and the Lindbergh Law, the snatch racket is about to be busted nationwide. Bring me a kidnapper and I'll put him in Leavenworth."

"Exactly what the hell do you people do up here?"

"Waste our time listening to characters like you. You got a name?"

"Michael Patrick Powers."

"No, a name for your bad hombre."

"Several," I said.

"Jenny," Heater shouted. In the next room, a typewriter stopped clacking.

I turned in my hard wooden chair and saw a young, scrawny woman, dark blonde hair, ponytail, mustard-colored dress. She stood at attention in the doorway.

"Name?" Heater asked me.

"Larry DuVol."

Jenny shook her head.

"AKA Harry Barton," I said.

She gave a slower shake of the head.

"Jenny can't help you, Powers, so neither can I."

I rode directly to Janie's apartment and rapped rude on the door. She said through it: "I'm not home to you, Powers. Not now and not ever. If you bother me any more I'll call the police."

"I've got Crumley's number," I said. "Maybe you want to call him direct. Good luck."

"I'm not home to you anymore," she called through the door.

I puffed up with resentment. Didn't she realized that I had made a gangland bargain that had saved her life? Couldn't she figure out that the bargain put me at risk too? But my Aunt Doris told me long ago: Michael, we're a proud species, far too proud for gratitude.

I climbed the stairs, brooded, smoked my pipe, and fell into a restless sleep. In the morning I took the dogs for a frosty walk along the Mississippi, down on the levee where the Burned Ladies had met their fate. It was only last spring. I remembered Sadie's nervous hands lighting a cigarette. Cold, skinny Sadie wolfing down spaghetti and meatballs, never knowing it was her last meal. Maybe Rose Perry was a blackmailer, I don't know, but Sadie was just a hard luck girl along for the ride. Her crimes were not so different from mine. She had nothing to sell the legitimate world, and needed to make a buck however she could.

What we had here, in these days of despair and desperation, was a society that knew the value of money but not justice or mercy. If Snowflake had belonged to a guy who couldn't borrow $50, he'd have been put down with a bullet to his head. If Maureen McAmbly's dad was unemployed, she'd be headed for the grave instead of Mayo Clinic. If Sadie and Rose had been the wives of prosperous men, their killers would be in Stillwater Prison. Sadie and Rose, like the hobos in the rail yards, and the bums camped along the Mississippi, had committed the ultimate American crime. They were broke.

At the railroad tracks I turned my back to Martinucci's, where Sadie had eaten that last meal. I beheld the magnificent new City Hall. It was a gleaming art deco tower, although with the same rotten politicians inside. I got the dogs home, fed them their dinner and then sat with them, looking over the busy city.

"Should I do it, Snowflake?" I asked.

He sneezed. Hula Girl, noncommittal, rolled over to get her belly scratched.

I had my answer. From my top dresser drawer I took a set of brass knuckles. They had been constantly in my pocket when I "rode the boot" from the Canadian border, but I hadn't hefted them in nearly five years. Installed on my left fist, they felt good. I smacked my right palm. Among gangsters I wasn't much of a tough guy. Among soft civilians, though, I could play the role.

Just after 5 p.m., I slipped out to the Selby stop and hopped aboard a streetcar. I got off on Robert Street, at the cluster of newspapers and their financial angels, the department stores.

The Daily News city room was unoccupied except for a library clerk. There's nothing deader than a newsroom after deadline. I remembered all the smells: ink, glue, tobacco smoke, darkroom chemicals, dust and sweat. Striding out of his corner office was Major Hoople, the editor who, according to Janie, rarely went home.

Major Hoople's true name was Leonard Walker, and he had been a real major in the War. He was tall, lanky, gray-haired, and very expensively dressed, with red suspenders over starched white shirt. He looked nothing like the comic strip character he'd been nicknamed for. His driver's license might have been issued in Minnesota but his drawl said Carolina.

I followed Major Walker out through the pressroom, silent now with all editions on the streets. Walker glanced at me, couldn't place me in his mental filing system. He sauntered over to where a dirty green Daily News truck was backing up to the dock. I tapped him on the shoulder.

Spectacles lay heavy on his long horsy face. His blue-gray eyes flamed with irritation. His hair was gray, greased, parted in the middle.

"I don't know you, do I?" he asked and stepped back.

Behind him two men in blue work clothes rolled a barrel of ink toward the huge press. That barrel thundered over the concrete floor.

"Harry," I said, "sent me."

The editor blinked.

"Harry who?"

"Harry," I said. "That Harry."

He looked around, took two steps into the printing plant, and beckoned with a long gray finger.

"Follow me," he said.

His office was in one corner of the newsroom. We passed one very old man who was fussing at a row of dusty green filing cabinets. One very young man was moving a stack of newspapers with a steel hand truck. That was it. Rows of empty reporters' desks, and the copy desk horseshoe, were scattered with all manner of paper, glue pots, typewriters, ashtrays, telephones, yellowed newspapers, notebooks.

Walker unlocked his office, pocketed the ring of keys, flicked on the overhead light, and circled to the back of his desk.

I sat in the chair facing him. To school children, rube subscribers, and civic organizations, Walker was the crusading editor of a mighty organ of journalistic justice. But I knew him as a secret friend of Filben, Jack Peifer, Irish Kinkead, and Big Ryan. Walker got a slice of the slot machine profits at a certain nightclub, which was owned by Filben and Peifer, although you'd never find the paperwork to prove it. Walker lived on Summit Hill. His three daughters attended private schools. Their angelic, gold-framed photos graced his desk. His gangland connections, however genteel, guaranteed that certain subjects, if they appeared in the Daily News at all, would be handled lightly.

Walker played with a gray porkpie hat that sat on his desk. A beautiful gray suit coat hung from a wooden coat hook behind him. His view was a city through gilded glass.

"You are mister…?" Walker asked.

"Mister mister," I said. "There's somebody on your payroll who shouldn't be there."

"Oh really?"

"Really. Miss Janie Vetter."

He pushed back his chair. I thought maybe he was going to lunge over the desk at me. I slipped my hand into my coat pocket and worked into the brass knuckles. Then I folded both hands in my lap, the brass gleaming in the harsh overhead light.

"Who the hell are you to march into my office…"

"No marching involved, Major" I said. "Harry wants her gone."

"Janie?"

I nodded. "Janie."

He picked up the phone, I thought maybe to call the cops.

"Come on, Walker, you know how this town works."

He flashed the hook on his candlestick phone and said, "What's the number?"

"Harry?" I said. "Emerson 2020."

I sat back. I rubbed the brass knuckles with the fingers of my right hand. It was Walker who was sweating, greasy beads on his forehead.

Walker went through the operator, held the phone about a

minute without speaking.

"No answer," Walker said.

"Would I give you his number if I was lying? Harry sent me. He wants this favor."

Walker stood up.

"Look," I said, "we're not asking that you ruin the kid's life. She's a nice kid. She's just in an awkward place right now. You attend all the editors' booze fests, excuse me, conventions. You must know somebody in Chicago who needs a girl reporter. You can arrange that, can't you? She'd take a job in Chicago in a heartbeat."

"That's all Harry wants?" Walker said, hands in his pockets.

"Get her out of town. Don't dare misunderstand me, now. No harm must come to her. Not a hair of her head is to be mussed. If she gets hurt, you get hurt. We're serious about that. She's just another kid reporter. You can replace her with any one of dozens of desperate grads."

"May I ask what she did?"

"No you may not."

"I'm going to speak to Harry himself before I do anything."

"Go right ahead."

"The game in this town," he said, and shook his head.

"You're one of the players as I understand it."

"Do we have any more business?" he asked.

"Nope."

"Then please get the hell out of my office."

CHAPTER SIXTEEN

On a Friday, three days before Halloween, I rode down to the Green Lantern to work an angle with Harry. It had already snowed twice, depressing this early. I told myself: I don't know if I can take another winter. How come a guy my age hasn't even *visited* Cuba? The beaches, the palm trees, the warm breezes, the beautiful ladies. And the horse racing at Oriente was fantastic, I'd heard, especially if you knew the right touts. Filben had slot machine connections in Cuba, and had hinted that he could use a fella like me in Havana.

Someday.

With Filben it was always someday.

I slipped in by the back door, hung my tan corduroy jacket in the coatroom and said to Bess: "Let's get married and take off for Havana."

She looked up from a seating chart she was drawing.

"Don't tempt me," she said.

"Is it the warm beaches that tempt you, or the thought of spending time with me?"

She looked askance.

"Why are you giving me that look?" I asked.

"Hero," she said, "go have a drink. It'll calm your imagination."

"I can dream, can't I?" I said, and blew her a kiss.

Harry's maintenance guy Jinks was painting the hallway blue. I had to slither around paint buckets and drop cloths to get to the inner sanctum. A door, cracked open, revealed the absence of

Harry.

"Where's the man?" I asked Jinks.

"Here I am," he said under a painters hat. "You're looking at him."

Jinks was a Colored man of maybe 50 with a square handsome face, a sly almost hidden smile, and white stubble instead of a beard.

"I could use a hand," he said. "You good with a paint brush?"

"Lousy," I said.

"Of course," he said.

I heard the toilet flush and Harry pushed out of the men's room.

"You," Harry said.

"Got an idea," I said.

"I thought I smelled something."

He passed me and barged into the office. His desk had been pushed toward the safe, the floor draped in paint-spattered canvas. He closed the door behind him.

"Drying out," he said. "They'll be redecorating while I'm gone."

"The water cure?"

"Hell, I don't know. What's up?"

"How about a Halloween party? You know." I inclined my head. "Over there."

"Watch what you say in here."

That told me Harry knew exactly what I was proposing: a takedown of the Third Northwestern Bank on Halloween.

"I know Monday isn't the best day, but imagine, Harry. Masks. Would anybody notice a bunch of guys in masks on Halloween?"

"No soap," he said. "The boys pick the date. Anything else?"

I looked him over. He didn't seem his usual slovenly self. His shirt was wrinkled, but tucked in. Trousers clean and pressed. No tie, I'd never seen him wear a tie, but his shirt was buttoned right up to the neck. This was the first time all year I'd seen him sober.

"Good luck on the cure, Harry," I said.

On the way out I stopped at Bess's table. She was studying that chart.

"Seating for the masked ball?" I asked.

"Costume farce," she said. "We'll be jammed tomorrow night. I take it you'll be disguised as a gangster?"

"Very funny," I said. "You should team up with Eddie Cantor."

I said into her ear: "The cure?"

She rolled her green eyes.

"You don't think it will work?" I asked.

She said: "What he really wants is for Jinks to tear up the office. Wiretap. He's convinced J. Edgar wants his scalp."

For the rest of the day, I marked. I drove the route twice around, from Como Park to the bank. There was only one traffic light, at Snelling and Larpenteur. I marked that on the map. Don't worry about your turn, I would tell the boys, until you pass the light.

Once parked on Hennepin Avenue, I bought an apple at the fruit stand across from the bank. I munched thoughtfully while staring at the target. Next to the fruit stand was a shoeshine chair, and I sat down at exactly 2:40 by my pocket watch. As the bootblack worked my oxfords to a gleam, I imagined the gang, four going in, dressed like bankers, and Larry standing outside with a tommygun.

Larry was a wanted murderer, I couldn't block that thought entirely. It sent a gurgling warning through my gut. I reassured myself: These boys knew what they were doing or Harry wouldn't be their Uncle. It was 2:52 when I stepped down from the shoeshine stand, tipped the bootblack, and imagined the boys driving away clean with the loot. The Redwood Falls job, I reminded myself, took less than ten minutes, getaway perfect.

And nobody hurt.

In the twelve minutes I had sat at the shoeshine stand, two streetcars stopped in front of the bank. A steady stream of pedestrians flowed into the bank, but no cops, on foot or by car.

Minneapolis Police shift change. Twenty golden minutes on a Friday. Perfect, perfect timing.

Just after three o'clock I met Everett in a dark "soda tavern" two blocks down Hennepin Avenue. Both of us got plain ginger ales, without intoxicating additives. He'd taken the day off with a miserable cold, and carried a blue bandana in one hand.

"It's a stupid holiday," sniffled Everett.

"Yeah," I said just to agree with him.

He hadn't shaved in maybe three days, a dark blond stubble shadowing his face.

"Stupid kids throwing stupid eggs at the stupid windows," he said.

"Must be a nasty cleanup job for you," I said.

"Too bad," he said. "I lost a hunnert twenty bucks."

"Lost it?"

"That's all I had," he said.

"How'd you lose it?"

"Stocks and bonds," he said. He shook his head. "Money. Money money money. That's all peoples cares about, now that it's got scarce."

I handed him twenty bucks under the table. Holding the map low to the bar, I showed him my work-up of the bank's interior. Following his finger, I marked with an X the three places where alarm switches were hidden in the floor. Everett said the employees had been trained to step on the alarm and keep it down for three seconds. This would trigger a buzzer in the police station, but would be soundless in the bank.

He sniffled, his nose enflamed like it was sunburnt.

The bank sent false alarms maybe two, three times a month, Everett said. The cops were getting lazy about responding.

"You're sure," I asked Everett, "there's no armed guard?"

"The big-shots laid him off."

He sneezed.

"Cut my hours too."

I slipped him another twenty. I asked: "Only these three alarms, you're sure?"

"I helped put 'em in. Drilled out the holes."

"Can you get at the wires, pull the wires?"

"Maybe," he said.

"That would be a $100 job," I suggested.

He blew his nose into the bandana.

"Could you do it with two days notice?"

"For a hundred," he said. "I can try."

When I pulled in to my apartment's lot, Reilly's truck was parked in my allotted space. Out of its passenger side got a long, lanky blond fellow. Reilly backed the truck out. The lanky fellow's face appeared at my frosty passenger window.

When he got in beside me, he was so long-legged his knees stuck up nearly to his chin. He had strange eyes: watery, pale, spooky, something missing, a world out of focus.

He stuck out a strong hand.

"Verne," he said.

"Mick," I said.

His handshake was like a frontal assault.

"I'm the wheelman," he said.

"Okay."

"Let's see the route."

He finally let my crushed hand go. I dug the route map out of the glove compartment, and silently, he studied it. His blond hair was greased, neat, shaved on the side. His lips were compressed, as if he was holding back something, impatience maybe or anger.

He handed me the map.

"Let's go," he said.

As I drove he was so silent I could hear his raspy breathing. It seemed like he had something caught in his throat.

Our first stop was Herb's Garage, across from the Selby Streetcar Tunnel. The cars we planned to use were parked in the darkest end of the garage, alongside a cinderblock wall. One was a Lincoln, dark blue. The other was a lighter shade, a green Chevy.

Verne seemed only interested in the Lincoln. He patted it on the hood. He walked around it. "Armored?" he asked. He tapped but received a hollow answer.

"Let me get a flashlight from Herb," I said.

Verne waited in the dark. If he were a wanted man, which I assumed, he'd limit his contact with people. But he didn't understand that Herb was one of us. For more than a decade, Herb had profitably shut his mouth whenever a badge snooped around.

Herb was crouched in the lube pit. He was one of those rare bosses who would rather be working than bossing. I stepped down the greasy metal steps. Herb was a mustached guy, wide and strong. The grease that encased his hands seemed permanent, like a tattoo. He had gone mostly bald, with a scabby scalp he was always knocking against the undercarriage of cars. He was down there bleeding brake lines, illuminated by a hanging light. When he saw me he wiped his greasy hands down his overalls.

I asked him: "Lights, brakes, sparkplugs, all check out?"

"Who knows?" he said. "Crap shoot. You turn the key. Think of Dapper Danny. He turned the key. Goodbye legs."

He hung the light off the car's dripping axle.

"You're worried?" he said. "Leave it running."

"I can't, it won't work, not on this job. It's got to be parked a long time."

"Then maybe, fresh starters. Improve your chances. Still, no guarantee. It's a gamble. You're a gambler. Right?"

He turned his back on me. Drip drip drip, oil down the drain.

If Verne was going to play it strong and silent, so was I. Without any conversation, I drove him to the Como Zoo, a ten minute ride. I parked outside the buffalo pen. A big bull rolled in the dead grass, snorting, while the rest of the herd looked on.

"Switch cars, right here," I said.

Verne reached into the top of his flannel shirt, pulled out a toothpick, jammed it between his yellowed teeth.

"Buffalo pen," I said. "Can't mistake it. One turn off the git road, here you are."

"All right," Verne said.

We motored up to Larpenteur, made a left turn and drove into Minneapolis, where the road was renamed Hennepin. I parked on a side street so Verne could study the bank.

"The Lincoln will be parked right there," I said, "in that one space in back of the streetcar stop. I will drop you boys off in the Chevy. Maybe you'll want to start that Lincoln before you rush the bank, leave it running."

"Maybe," said Verne, chewing the toothpick into splinters.

"What do you think?"

"I don't think, partner, it gets in the way."

"Seen enough?" I asked.

"What do you hear about me?"

"Absolutely nothing."

"Right answer," he said. "Drive."

Halloween is an annoyance when your dogs see every trick-or-treater as a threat. Few kids climbed four levels for candy, but just to be sure, after sunset I took Snowflake and Hula Girl to the rooftop.

Up there, Mr. Holy Reardon had built a square deck surrounded by picket fence on a flat tar roof. For reasons I could never figure, of thirteen tenants, I was the only one who seemed to use it. Mr.

Reardon had installed a tiny coal stove converted to a barbecue. I fired up charcoals, and roasted the last of the fall corn.

I sat in a lawn chair wrapped in a thick coat, my back turned to the brilliant-lit Cathedral and the west wind. Before me, the city glowed like a great Halloween party. Its mask of mild weather would fall, maybe tonight, and reveal its frosty face. Winter was the truth in Minnesota, summer just a beautiful lie.

Snowflake and Hula Girl had little in common, aside from being canines in my care. But one thing they agreed upon: the most entertaining thing they could eat was corn on the cob. Hula Girl with her missing teeth was less efficient at nipping off kernels, but made up for that in jaw speed. His highness Snowflake ate with royal dignity. When we had eaten every kernel of the corn, I threw the cobs atop the dying embers and sat enjoying the aroma.

Down there in the city, they had just topped off Saint Paul's tallest skyscraper. Thirty stories it rose, crowned with a big red numeral 1. That numeral could be seen miles around, advertising the First National Bank. It would have been a very rich target, except for The Deal, decades-old, and still honored by Big Ryan. All banks within the city limits of Saint Paul were to be held safe and sacred. This way, Saint Paul's bankers, including Papa Alt, enjoyed a competitive advantage: lower insurance rates, less salary paid out for guards. No wonder the city's bankers were in no hurry for gangster reform.

I entertained a vision of tomorrow morning, All Saints Day November 1st, and imagined a moving truck pulling up to Janie's basement apartment. Good luck in Chicago, kid, I murmured. I lit my pipe and fell into some sort of reverie. Dogs. Could you get dogs into Cuba? No way, even in my dream state, could I imagine leaving them behind. They're too innocent, too beautiful. Never in their perfect lives have they committed a crime.

The slamming of a car door down there got me to my feet and peering over the unpainted picket fence. I saw Larry's Hupmobile idling in the parking lot. Janie walked around its back end, dressed in sparkling white, a fairy godmother. She slipped in and the long yellow gangster-mobile squealed out of the lot.

I gave the dogs a relief walk on the lawn, and then drove for the Green Lantern. There were 275,000 souls in Saint Paul and half of them seemed to be parked down on Wabasha. I left my borrowed Ford at the police station in a lane reserved for squad cars. If they towed it, Filben would retrieve it, no harm done. I sauntered across the street to the Green Lantern, knocked at the rear door.

Bess, green mask over her eyes, opened the door. Her red hair gave her away. She wore a strapless gown showing off those sexy shoulders. I slipped into her coatroom.

"Who are you supposed to be?" she said.

"A desperate horseplayer," I said.

"Is there any other kind? Mick, it's costume only."

"Who are you?"

She reached down and parted her gown, showing leg up to the panties. "Sally Rand. You get the fan dance if you stay until midnight."

I looked into the tavern, smoky, loud and crowded with costumed posers. Behind the bar, Reilly wore the gray baseball flannels of the Saint Paul Saints, sweat under the armpits.

"Larry DuVol," I whispered in Bess's ear. "You know him?"

Bess shrugged. "Even without the disguises, I don't know half the characters in here nowadays."

"Kind of a small guy, very handsome, oily black hair, maybe twenty five, okie accent, little scar above his lips. Might have come in here with a young, chunky red-head, dressed like Snow White."

"Mick, you know I'm just a dumb dame."

"Yeah, and I'm President Hoover."

"Come on, Bess, let me in to look around."

It was so smoky in the Blue Room that my eyes watered. I had to dodge through a maze of costumed revelers, including one dressed like a skeleton.

"You're a dead man," the skeleton man growled as I squeezed past him.

I knew that voice.

Somebody bumped me from behind. Somebody spilled a drink on my shoes.

"Swede Fanlund," I said to the skeleton.

He stuck out a bone hand.

"Shaky Powers," he said. "I got somebody you want to meet. Hey, where is she?"

I could see those cold hazel eyes through the slits of his cloth skull. "Around here somewhere," he said, then whistled and raised his bone hand. Out of the smoky crowd appeared a woman dressed as a man. She wore a dark, double breasted suit and a fedora. A red bandana covered her face.

But not her identity.

Platinum curls spilled from underneath that fedora.

"I believe you two know each other," said Fanlund.

Mona removed her fedora and shook her bright locks free.

"My long lost brother Michael," she said.

"Lost?" said Swede, "he don't look lost to me."

"He's going bald," she said, and rubbed my head. "Here, here's your hat back. I came disguised as a stickup man. But you know what? I don't think I've got what it takes."

She handed me the fedora I had lost at the Rosedale stickup. The hat blocker had written MPOWERS on the leather band inside.

Mona unmasked herself, waving the red bandana with a satisfied grin. "This is yours too, I take it."

She dropped the bandana into the fedora, which I, stunned, held upside down like I was begging for coins.

"C-can I see you outside?" I stammered. "Family business."

Swede's skeleton lips kissed the top of her head.

"Don't be too long," he said. "I hate to get drunk alone."

I followed Mona across the crowded barroom, and pushed behind her out the cold steel door.

"How are you?" she said, grin on her face, hands on her hips.

"Peaches and cream," I said. "What are you doing with that gangster?"

"Douglas?"

"He's too old for you."

"Well, you know I was going with this younger guy but he got spooked by a nighttime stickup. You might have read about it in the papers."

There was nothing to do with that fedora but put it on my head. The bandana I thrust into a trouser pocket.

"Poor Artie, he got nervous and quit his job," Mona said.

"Listen," I said, but the big brother tone wasn't going to work. I could tell by her mocking smile that I was a fool in her eyes. So I changed course.

"Aunt Doris was asking for you," I lied.

"I hate hospitals," Mona said. She wrinkled her nose. "That smell."

"Someday we have to talk about the potato farm," I said. "How to split it up."

"I've seen a lawyer," she said.

"You have? What's he say?"

"He's my lawyer, hire your own," she said. "Speaking of lawyers, have you heard from Peggy? Has she filed the final papers?"

I shrugged.

"You haven't heard from her at all? She went off and left you like that? What a crock! I'd track her down if I were you."

"What for?"

"I heard she took you for every dime, that bitch. She'd better not show her face around me. I'd crack her a good one. You can't treat the Powers clan like that."

"Peggy's a good person."

"How can you say that? She screwed you over. You know what I'd do? If you're afraid to track her down yourself, hire a private detective. I'm sure they have private eye over there. They speak English in Hawaii, right?"

"I'll consider it."

Mona shook her head and sputtered. "Good person."

"We had ten warm years," I said, "and two years when it all went as cold as a Saint Paul winter. That's 5-to-1. Those are good odds."

"Huh," she said. "Nice family. My brother the bootlegger and Catholic stickup man. And my sister married to a truck driver who never comes home. And our aunt babbling in an old folks home. Don't worry, Mikey. Your secret's safe with me. I won't tell a soul. Not even Kelly."

She shook her head. "Mom had a photo of you in, what are those altar boy things?"

"Cassock and surplice," I said.

"She had that picture on the night table when she died. She always said you were the cutest altar boy she had seen. Mommy's little angel."

"All right, cut it out."

"Her only son, the lovey-dovey favorite. Not me. She had no use for me. I don't know what I did to that woman but she ..."

"Mona!"

"What?"

"Stop!"

She bowed. "Yes oh mighty big brother."

She turned for the steel door.

"Next time you rob somebody," she said, "get the money and keep your hat on."

I watched Mona walk back into the Lantern, and stood in the

glassy alcove of the dark Town Talk Diner. I felt like I was alone in the world, a man in a suit when everyone else was disguised. A fellow dressed like a cop walked past, arms linked with a woman dressed like a prostitute, complete with fox-fur stole and red turban.

Or was it really a cop and a prostitute?

Saint Paul was all a game of masks and disguises, and Halloween was the one day we admitted it. I walked down Wabasha, hat low over my eyes. Down to the blocks that bootleg beer built, I walked past the Hamm, Bremer and Alt buildings. Into the courtyard of the Hotel Saint Paul I went. Across the street, costumed revelers were drinking and howling in Rice Park. Up in the second floor of the Federal Building, Special Agent Roland Heater, working late, stood in shadow at the giant window.

Working on what, this late on Halloween?

CHAPTER SEVENTEEN

On All Saints Day, a Holy Day of Obligation, I attended Mass in the Cathedral. I sat in the back pews, alone, feeling unworthy of being near anything holy. I prayed that I would return home to see a moving van at Janie's. I prayed that in the coming bank robbery, no one would be hurt, not the tellers, the customers or the gangsters either. Just as Mass let out, I dropped a nickel for Mom and one for Dad, and lit each a votive candle. Staring into that flame I'd lit for Dad, known to the world as James Powers, I told his ghost I understood, no hard feelings. He'd been a sick man, and not a reliable provider. He'd been too proud to take a better-paying rough-neck union job, like brakeman or fireman. He'd wanted to work with his mind, with his math, while dressed in a respectable suit. Had he belonged to the Railway Brotherhood, he would have been paid for his sick leaves. We wouldn't have needed help from Aunt Doris, bags of groceries left on the back porch, bills mysteriously paid, while Dad lay in a darkened room.

What exactly his illnesses were, the doctors couldn't say.

Candle flames flickered in cold drafts as worshippers pushed out the heavy wooden doors behind me. I followed the crowd, then crossed the street to my apartment building. My prayer for Janie had gone unanswered. No moving van, no suitcases on the sidewalk.

I debated sending a brass knuckle Letter to the Editor. I made up my mind that failing all else, I would bully Janie down to

McAmbly's office and show her Larry's Bertillion file.

On All Saints Day, and every other day that week, I knocked when Janie was home, but she refused to answer.

On Veteran's Day, a Friday, I woke up twitchy with nerves. The bank was marked, when were the boys going to go? One, I needed the money and two, once the job was done, Larry would blow town, leaving Janie behind. I looked forward to both events, but the timing was now out of my hands. The bank would be closed on the Friday after Thanksgiving, so the boys went next Friday or not until December. That seemed a long, long time away. I didn't know if I could take all these weeks of worry.

I fed the dogs, made a scant pot of coffee in my French press and borrowed Mrs. Strutz's Pioneer Press from the hallway. The big news: The nation had decided to dump President Hoover for Franklin Roosevelt. One headline said:

NATION ATWITTER WITH TALK
OF PLANS TO BRING BACK BEER

A smaller one said:

FIVE BOOTS ESCAPE WITH 300 GALLONS OF LIQUOR
AFTER GUN BATTLE WITH FEDS IN ST. PAUL

Where was the sense in it? Are we going to bring back beer, or are we going to kill people over a barrel of rotgut?

I turned to the funnies.

A few minutes later I returned Mrs. Strutz's newspaper to her doorway. From the back of my bedroom closet I pulled my tan Army dress shirt. It had a three-striped green chevron on its short sleeves. Yes, sir! Buck Sergeant Powers reporting for duty. I wore it only on Veteran's Day now. My heroic service in the War had been limited to Fort Dix, driving a truck in the quartermaster corps. My duty was trucking ammo, cigarettes and tinned corned beef up to the Brooklyn docks under armed escort. It was perfect training for my future as a bootleg driver.

Maybe it was to fight off attacks of nerves or to shed some weight, but I had decided to run myself back into Army shape. I had made a running date with Father Mack, so after breakfast I leashed the dogs and waited in the parking lot for him to arrive in his modest black Plymouth.

We rode out to Fort Snelling and parked in the woodsy riverbank underneath it. On the way we had stopped to buy red poppies from a one-armed American Legionnaire. Father Mack pinned his poppy to his tattered gray gym shirt, and I fixed mine over the nametag that said SGT. POWERS. We let the dogs out of the car and they scrambled toward the river.

We two-legged creatures had to be more careful climbing down the rocky cliff face.

The trees were almost bare, the sky brilliant, the forest floor layered in mud and gold-orange leaves. I in my Army boots and Father Mack in his boxing shoes ran along the riverbank, easy going. The dogs, like scouts, stayed a few yards ahead of us. On one side of us rose the sandstone riverbank. Ice scrims formed at the sandy edge of the flowing river.

Two miles up the riverbank, we rested, catching our breath at a picnic table. The dogs, hardly panting, nosed through the charred remnants of a beach fire.

"It's no use at all," said Father Mack, black curly head bent in exhaustion. "But we must try our best."

Snowflake, white legs planted, lapped the brown water of the Mississippi.

"Thirteen years since I cashed out, Father."

"Aye," he said.

He pulled that sweat-stained gym shirt over his head and

revealed the body of a fine athlete going to fat. His right eye, crushed in some Irish bare-knuckle fight, fluttered.

"Still waiting for that War bonus," I said.

"I imagine," he said.

"A nation that turned on its own veterans," I said. "Sweeping them out of Washington like they were stray dogs."

"Thus ever from governments," he said.

"Actually, I wouldn't treat my dogs the way Herbert Hoover treated those veterans, Father. MacArthur and Eisenhower have a lot to answer for."

"Roosevelt's your man then."

"Roosevelt will be the death of me, Father. You know how I've made my living."

On the opposite bank, on the brilliant north horizon, rose the smokestacks of Henry Ford's auto assembly factory. I walked to the river to oversee Hula Girl, swimming like a black crocodile in the chill water. I called her away from the strong currents.

"The economy picks up, I might catch on there, Father. At Ford. Good wages."

"Thanks to the unions. Only because of the unions."

I threw a pebble into the river.

"Now that Roosevelt's in, Father, what's going to happen to all these people in the bootleg game? Do you have any idea how many people depend on that? Most of them will never get legitimate jobs, not the way this country's going. They have no choice but to do desperate things."

Father Mack shed his shoes, big bare feet sinking into the cold sands of the river's edge.

"Would it be okay for a Catholic, Father, to rob from the rich if he gave to the poor?"

Father Mack's smile was one of those that conceals a secret. Hands in his pockets, he turned from me and splashed barefoot along the river. Snowflake and Hula Girl followed him. After a moment, so did I. He threw his gray sweatshirt thrown over his shoulder, like a wandering hobo.

"I hear the Devil talking," he said when I caught up to him. "From the dawn of eternity, he has been attempting to strike a bargain with God."

Father Mack shook his head.

"People come to the priest requesting permission to sin, or forgiveness afterwards. The first thing sin seeks is authority."

"I'm not sure what you mean, Father."

"Murder for example. What is a state execution, but murder with authority? Murder is evil, and evil seeks the cloak of authority. It must cloak itself in reason. Mass murder, theft and rape seeks such authority, and then calls itself war. Do you know why there are no mirrors in Hell, Michael?"

"No, I don't, Father."

"Satan cannot tolerate reflection."

I let him and the dogs go on, sat on a rock, watched the river, my reflection rippling in it.

"Are there rivers in Hell, Father?" I asked, but he didn't seem to hear me. "You know, places where a condemned man could cool off?"

He stepped over a fallen tree limb. The dogs happily leaped it. Staring at the Ford plant on the opposite bank, I had to admit I hadn't tried my utmost to get a legitimate job. Men more determined had gotten into line ahead of me. Back when there were jobs available, I had not pestered my brother-in-law to get me in at Koppers, because I really didn't want to drive a coal truck. For twelve years I had been comfortable in my bootlegging world, and did not care to scramble and scratch for a living. There may be no mirrors in Hell, but I caught a rippling reflection of myself in the Mississippi. Mick Powers, happy-go-lucky rum runner turned accessory to murder, and now become a grim, desperate bank robber. It was not the image I wanted to see.

I double-timed to catch up with Father Mack and we climbed the steep trail. At the top, we stopped at the Plymouth to catch our breath. I toweled off the muddy dogs. Kneeling in the dirt I looked up at Father Mack, and tried to lighten my mood with a joke.

"So I guess you don't believe in Robin Hood, do you Father?"

"The man was a bloody thief," said Father Mack, "and worse, a British Protestant."

Harry rarely used the phone, so I was surprised by his call.

"Powers," he barked, and I knew his voice from that one word. Pat Reilly had nicknamed Harry The Sea Lion because of that distinctive bark.

"This is he," I said.

"Under the bridge," he barked. "Tonight."

"What time?"

"Just be there. Bring your maps and figures."

He hung up. I figured he'd called from the Jung Sanitarium in Wisconsin, where he felt safe. A doctor over there gave him B12 shots, put him twice a day in the steam baths and made him swim in the pool. He'd taken the cure five or six times, and come home to immediately resume boozing.

It was getting dark before six, and early that evening I took the streetcar to the Loop and walked over the Wabasha Bridge, ears stinging in the blustery winds. From the crest of the bridge, Saint Paul looked magnificent in lights, topped by its twin overseers, Capitol and Cathedral.

A spiral concrete staircase led from the lamp-lit bridge to the darkness underneath. There it smelled of river mud and oily water. The only light came from the tiny windows of a clapboard boathouse on stilts. Around those stilts, parked at odd angles in the mud, were automobiles, most of them expensive. From inside the boathouse came the muffled sounds of men, arguing, gambling, drinking. As I approached the boathouse I saw, underneath it, in among the stilts, one tiny orange glow.

This is how guys get rubbed out, my sensible self said, but my greedy self forced me to walk on. I was useful to Harry, and that was a license to live. I approached the glowing cigarette, cleared my throat and said: "Harry sent me."

"Something happen to your car?"

"It's in the garage," I lied.

When he drew on the cigarette and made it glow, I recognized Alvin Karpis. He pitched his cigarette into the river.

"I told you," Karpis said. "This is the guy."

As my eyes adjusted to the dim light I could make out Fred Barker, aka Little Shorty, a man no bigger than a racetrack jockey. He was dressed in long tweed coat and flat cap. In the scant reflection of the bridge lights, I caught a gleam of his gold teeth. Everything seemed to be wrapped in some shade of gray, everything but Fred Barker's teeth.

I was surprised because the two bank robbers I'd met, Larry and Verne, were not known members of the Barker-Karpis gang. I'd thought Larry and Verne were just two of Harry's boys.

"Harry vouches," lisped Karpis.

"I don't know," said Fred, a huge lump in his jaw.

"This guy drove an old bastard across the river," said Karpis.

"I know, I know," said Fred.

Karpis snapped his fingers.

I drew the bank diagram from my pocket and handed it to Karpis. I followed the two of them up the rickety stairs to the boathouse deck. I could hear the roll of the dice, and the cursing and groans that followed. Karpis and Fred stepped into a spotlight.

Karpis was bareheaded, hair slicked back and greasy, and wore a leather jacket with corduroy cuffs. He was taller than Fred by about five inches, but even skinnier. He dug out a pair of specs and hooked them over his ears.

"How many times have you been inside?" Karpis asked.

"About six."

"About six or six?"

"Six," I said. "I'm in the Christmas Club."

Karpis' face twisted into something that was neither a snarl nor a smile. I saw now where he had gotten that nickname, Creepy. It was those cold, lizard eyes. The man was all observation and not an ounce of feeling. Even the eyes of a dog are only the eyes of an opportunist. These eyes were pure predator.

"He's got the alarms marked," Karpis said to Fred.

Fred grunted.

"How did you figure the alarms?" Karpis asked.

"Bribed the janitor."

"So the janitor knows you?" Karpis asked.

"He doesn't know who I am."

"But he could pick you out of a show-up."

"I wore a ski mask, met him in a dark alley," I lied.

"I guess it ain't a problem," said Fred. "Not if he's telling us the truth."

"Are you?" Karpis asked. "Telling the truth?"

I looked into the lizard's eyes and nodded.

"How about the tellers and loan officers? Can any of them make you?"

I said: "I walk in, pay my Christmas Club, walk out. Account's under a name opened with fake I.D. A thousand people go in there every day."

Karpis folded the map, slipped it into a jacket pocket.

"No guard?"

"They laid him off."

"No heroes?"

"Not among the big suits. The tellers are mostly women. I asked the janitor if he could cut the alarm wires, and first he said he could, then he lost his nerve."

Karpis gave Fred a look I could not interpret, but it was those two against me, for sure.

"When it's over," Karpis said, "we'll be leaving town but you'll be here. You'll be our eyes and ears. We'll give you the name of a guy who can get us the dope. We'll be reading the papers. But anything you hear, we want to know."

"What's my part?" I asked.

"He just told you," said Fred.

"I mean of the rake."

Fred turned on me.

"You got nerve," he said. "You're not level with us and you're not going to be. You're a lousy marker, that's all."

"I'm a good marker, that's a good map."

"You'll get yours," said Karpis. "Depends on how it goes. If you've marked it right, you'll get paid right."

"That's it," said Fred. "All we want is success."

He leaned over the rail, spitting tobacco juice down on boats that were covered with canvas. He gave Karpis another you-and-me look, and walked down the stairs into the darkness.

"Where's he going?"

Karpis lit a Chesterfield and offered me one. I lit it out of obligation. The smoke burned my throat.

"What do we call you?"

"Mick," I said.

"I'm Ray," said Karpis. With Fred downstairs, Karpis let me in to the inner lizard sanctum.

"Big score," he said.

"Just sitting there, waiting," I said and blew smoke.

I hoped I didn't sound as rattled as I was. I had to fend off thoughts of the bloody demise of Pop Anderson, a cold and brutal execution. I might not have marked this job if I had known that Karpis and Barker were in the crew. But I was in now, like it or not. I reminded myself these were the boys who pulled off the Redwood Falls job. They preferred to rob a bank smooth, professional and bloodless. Barker and Karpis dealt death to snitches, but bank clerks and customers were always unharmed. Shaken, maybe, but unharmed.

"This will be a bigger haul than Redwood Falls," I probed. "I guess you read about that one in the papers."

Karpis did not take the bait. He smoked. He looked me over. He said nothing for what seemed like a long time and then: "Redwood what? Never been there."

A car drove up, bouncing headlights in the muddy potholed road. It was a Buick, like the one that had been burned with Sadie and Rose inside. I followed Karpis off the wooden deck, down the rickety stairs.

"Eight mighty cylinders," said Karpis and slapped the Buick's hood.

Karpis let himself into the passenger seat, while I sat alone in the rear. Fred drove reckless through downtown, across Seven Corners, and up the steep riverbank toward the mansion district. Karpis seemed to enjoy the dangerous driving, hanging on through the turns. He grinned like a schoolboy on his first wild ride, Fred shifting and braking like a madman. When we made a hard, squealing turn on Dale, I had a sick premonition of where we were headed.

Fred pulled up in the parking lot behind Paula's apartment building and cut the lights. We sat there for a moment, engine ticking. Fred opened the door, spit his chaw to the asphalt, and stepped out. Karpis opened the door for me.

My legs felt like lead, my stomach held a thundering riot as we climbed stairs toward Paula's apartment. It had been eight months since I'd fast-talked my way into Paula's place posing as a magazine salesman. Once she recognized me, Fred and Karpis would know I wasn't on the level. As Fred rang the bell I stifled the impulse to run.

Fred looked down the hall and said: "Where is that whore?"

He fumbled for his key ring. "Maybe she's in the shower." He cursed, inserted the key, pushed open the door.

"Honey!" he shouted.

He flung open his arms, turned to Karpis and said: "Ten o'clock at night."

He removed his overcoat to reveal a rumpled Army surplus sweater. He tossed the coat onto the couch and said, "I guess we get our own drinks."

We followed him into the dining room, where the china closet was half filled with dishes and half filled with bottles of booze.

In steady hands he poured water glasses of bourbon for the three of us, and we lifted a toast.

"To the Third Northwestern," he said. "That's the name right? To the Third Northwestern, and all its wealthy depositors."

We clicked glasses.

"Mmmm," said Fred. "I hope they've got insurance."

We set the drinks down on lace cloth that covered the dining room table, underneath a crystal chandelier. The apartment was much as I remembered, only with more furniture. A pink bag of golf clubs leaned against the wall, although nobody would be playing golf around here for months.

Karpis brought out the map, smoothed it out on the dining room table. I tried to think of an excuse to leave, and kept envisioning Paula's return, and my final bloody moments, shot in the head right here in this room.

My hands shook as I drank and Fred noticed.

"I don't know about this guy," he said to Karpis.

But Karpis, busy marking the map with a pencil, paid him no attention. He put L on the outside. V just inside the door. J in the middle. From this I deduced that he and Fred were the sweepers, the guys who got the money. Larry was the outside man, on the lookout for coppers. Verne was the inside man, blocking any escapes. J, whoever that was, would be the floater, the extra man for crowd control.

I drank but could not steady my hands.

"You got, what's that, palsy?" Fred said.

"He's a little excited, that's all," said Karpis.

"Two tommies…" said Karpis, but was interrupted by footsteps in the hall. A key turned in the lock. I looked toward the alley windows, imagined leaping through.

Paula entered, overwhelmed in furs. Like her boyfriend, she was the size of a child. Flip blond hairdo, mink coat, high heels, that was just about all I could see, except for her eyes. She was cross-eyed drunk.

As Fred glared murder at her, she stumbled over a hassock and fell into the living room. With a flash of flailing skinny legs in runny stockings, she rolled over.

"Hello boys," she said from the floor.

Fred turned away from her. Karpis and I followed his lead.

Paula stumbled to her feet, rushed past us, and tore into the bathroom, puking before she got the door closed.

Karpis looked at Fred.

Fred shook his head, then both went back to examining the map.

"Payroll day, shift change, and there's a noon delivery by armored car," Karpis said, looking to me for confirmation.

"To supply cash for the payday checks," I said.

Paula's outrageous drunkenness gave me confidence that she wouldn't recognize me. I recovered my courage and said: "Average crowd in there at this time on Friday is ten employees and twenty customers. Floor alarms marked. Keep the crowd in this corner here, everybody, and you'll be safe. I got the name of the cashier, he sits here, he's got the combination to the vault."

Karpis and Fred looked over the map in silence. Karpis scratched at his stubbly chin. Fred glanced toward the bathroom. When Paula careened into the hallway, she stood holding the walls like they might fall on her. She had shed the furs and now wore a puke-stained dress. Her bobbed hair was a ratty mess. A string of pearls had twisted like a noose around her neck.

"This here's Mick," said Fred. "Mick, meet Paula."

I shook her delicate, cold, tiny hand. No recognition flickered in her eyes. Her pupils were huge, a pair of eclipsed moons.

She banged into the golf clubs, knocked them to a spill, didn't seem to notice. She retreated to the couch, flopped on it and said, "Oh boy. Hold still will ya?"

I showed Fred and Karpis a hand-copied duplicate of the getaway map, with landmarks, the one traffic light, big arrow for the turn into Como Park.

"Buffalo pen. No mistaking it. Chevy parked here. Off you go."

Paula belched, staggered off the couch.

"I'm not drunk yet," she said, and reached into the china closet for bourbon. Gripping the bottle by the neck, she stared at me, eyes swimming and said, "Who the fuck are you?"

I stammered.

Fred snatched the bottle from her, nasty snarl on his face.

"Where's my magazines?" she said.

"Go sleep it off," Fred said.

Paula backed into the living room, fell to the floor sitting, dress up past her knees, a flash of yellow panties.

"We're keeping these maps, right?" Karpis said.

"They're yours," I said, "they're finished."

"How will you be getting home?" said Karpis.

"It's a walk from here," I said.

Paula lay back on the Persian rug, groaned and fell asleep, mouth open, snoring.

"Poor bitch," said Fred, "she gets wretched lonely for me. She's okay when we're together."

He nudged her ribs with the pointy tip of his cowboy boot.

"She's a fun gal sober," he said.

CHAPTER EIGHTEEN

After Thanksgiving dinner, Kelly and I were having a smoke, exiled to the porch. Kelly would not smoke her Viceroys around the girls, and Gary hated the smell of all tobacco. The porch was chilly, heated only by sunlight filtering through the branches of towering bare oaks.

"Tried to quit last year, but I gained weight," Kelly said, and tapped the burning cigarette against a gold-tinted tin ashtray.

"I saw Mona on Halloween," I said.

"Oh, yeah? What was her costume? Not a nun, I hope."

"She was dancing with a thug twice her age."

Kelly blew smoke. "Funny how all of her boyfriends... Oh, never mind. When I was her age, Veronica was practically in kindergarten and Elizabeth..."

"You ever have any regrets?"

"About?"

"You know." I looked through the windows into the dining room, where her husband and daughters were clearing the table of platters and dishes. "Choices you made."

"Jeesh," she said.

"You wanted to be a doctor," I said. "Remember? You told me that at Eagle River one summer."

"Well, the nuns took care of that. You know they sent me down to interview at nursing school in Chicago. Catholic vocations, that's what they were after. I was only a teenager, but even then I couldn't imagine myself a virgin in white, a rosary hanging from my waist."

In a way, Kelly was like our mom, who had dreamed of traveling the world, but settled for marriage and family in her hometown. My mother, Jean Young , became Mrs. James Powers at age 20, her journalist's ambitions pared down to a single article in the Saint Paul Dispatch, a bylined travel piece about Manhattan. It was her only published work. She kept that newspaper clipping in a scrapbook, along with pressed flowers and pictures of her three children.

"How about you?" Kelly asked.

"My regrets?" I said. "Where do I start? I guess with Peggy, I should have seen it coming. That's my fault. Maybe she would have been satisfied with an adoption, I don't know. We didn't talk enough about it, that's for sure."

"Peggy was unhappy at the end," Kelly said. "I could tell. She never said anything, but she had that…"

"Tic, yeah, I know. I didn't think … We only see what we want to see, I guess."

Kelly smashed her cigarette out, set the ashtray next to a Ouija board that lay on the table. She stood and stared out the storm windows.

"There's one thing I'll never regret though," she said. "I'll never be sorry for having my children. When Veronica was born, that's when I knew. That's when I started to believe again. God had put me on this Earth for a reason."

"I wish I could say that," I said, and sucked on the pipe but it had gone cold. It was a tiny Dublin half-bent, and I tucked it into my suit-jacket pocket.

"There's another one, though, a regret," I said. "See, there's this guy downtown named Harry. You probably don't know who he is…"

"Are you kidding? Everybody knows who he is."

"Okay then. Last spring, well, see, maybe you remember, it was in all the papers, two women burned up in a car down on the levee. You remember?"

"Sure."

"Well, I was shadowing them at the time. A certain rich guy had hired me to watch them. When the women were burnt up, the cops shrugged it off. I began asking questions. Then on Saint Patrick's Day, a couple of gunmen tried to take me out."

Kelly tried to stare right through me, as if to see whether I was sane.

"You're not kidding, are you?" she said.

"No. So that's how I ended up with Harry. If you're with Harry, you're safe from everybody but Harry. But of course then you've got to do Harry a favor now and then. And it so happens that doing him a favor, I became a witness to a crime. A serious crime. So what it comes down to, I'm a guy who could run his mouth and put Harry in prison. And not just Harry, a lot of other gangsters too. So it's like I've chosen sides. I'm one of them now."

"One of who?"

"Harry's gang. Bootlegging's over, it's all sewn up now, you can't get into that trade without using a tommygun. I can't take a regular job, because Harry would see that as a sign of disloyalty. It would look I'm going rogue. If you don't need their money any more, you're a danger, see."

"So you're telling me..."

"I could change my name, run off to Cuba, go panning for gold in Alaska, maybe. But I could never come back. For all practical purposes, I'm stuck. I'm a bad guy. I'm a gangster now."

"Pumpkin pie and coffee," Gary shouted from the dining room.

"We'll be right in," said Kelly.

She toyed with that pack of Viceroys, spinning it on the Ouija board.

"Mick, you're not a killer are you?"

"No," I said.

"Because that's one thing…"

"I'm no assassin," I said.

"… we've got to honor that woman with our lives. She gave us so much. That quiet, private woman was our core of steel."

"I know."

"She was so proud when you graduated high school."

"I know."

"There's a lot of things she would understand, Mick, but…"

"I know. Kelly, see, it's studying banks to find out which ones have the money. That's my job, that's all it is. It's like, I'm the reincarnation of Dad. I'm making a living with math, you know, pencil and paper. Which banks have all the …"

Veronica's beautiful dark face appeared in the doorway.

"Don't you want pie?"

"In a minute, honey," Kelly said. "Uncle Mick and I are talking."

"Gangster stuff," said Veronica, lips curved into a curious smile.

"Your uncle," said Kelly, "is not a gangster, now go eat your pie."

"I hate pumpkin pie. It's fattening."

"Go!" shouted Kelly.

When Veronica retreated, Kelly said: "Jeesh. Everything's fattening, yet you can see that kid's rib bones. Oh, and she eavesdrops on everything. She thinks it's cool: Uncle Mick, the bootlegger. Elizabeth is embarrassed. She tells people you're a chauffer." She laughed, she spun the pack of Viceroys on the Ouija board.

"These kids, I'm telling you," she said, "it's something new every day."

We went quiet for a moment.

"Banks, you said?" Kelly asked.

But before we could resume that conversation, a black

Oldsmobile came cruising down the street. It stopped opposite Kelly's porch. Behind the glare of the car windows, the short, dark driver was dressed in gray suit and coat. I gasped when I recognized him.

"What's the matter?" asked Kelly, lighting up another Viceroy.

"That car, why's it stopping?"

"Him? That's Ralph. Tallerico. He's a neighbor." She stepped up to the window and waved. The driver did not respond.

"He's not in a good mood," Kelly said. "What do you expect? His wife died the other day."

That Oldsmobile crept away at maybe five miles an hour.

"His wife died?" I asked. "Of what?"

Kelly shrugged. "I don't think there was a funeral or anything like that. We don't know them that well."

"And he lives where exactly?"

"Three doors down. The gray house. Dog kennels on the side there. He's a bird hunter, Rico. Pheasants, that's what they hunt, right? The kids say he's got a shotgun collection."

"Yeah," I said.

"What's the matter with you?"

"Nothing," I said.

I began to imagine Paula waking up and remembering some half-familiar guy in her apartment. Sometime after breakfast when her head cleared she would remember me as the man who had taken money for magazines but never delivered them. A suspicious man who'd spied on her, giving a phony name. And now he showed up in some kind of shady deal with her boyfriend. This guy, what was his name, Powell, Powers, whatever, he was starting to smell like a stool pigeon.

With fear coursing through me like an electric river, I remembered seeing Swede Fanlund last week, getting out of a taxi at Herb's Garage, a block from my house. I was a little alarmed then, but talked myself down. Hell, practically all gangsters did business at Herb's.

"What," I said, "does your neighbor do for a living?"

Kelly shrugged. "I don't know. Same as you, I guess. Mystery man. I don't know where he gets his money but he dresses like Rockefeller and he sure drives a fancy car. And she, his wife?"

Kelly made the Sign of the Cross over herself. "She never worked a day in her life."

"You remember Swede Fanlund, don't you?" I asked.

"Heard of him," she said.

Swede had been notorious at Sacred Heart, but that was a boys school and Kelly had gone to Saint Barbara's. Swede Fanlund was just another Payne Avenue thug by the time Kelly enrolled in high school.

"Tall, football player, crew cut, always wears a blue workman's uniform."

"Half the guys in the neighborhood dress like that."

"So even if you'd seen him around, you might not know who he is."

"No, I think I know him."

"It was him with Mona at the Green Lantern on Halloween."

"Together?"

"Hard to tell whether they were on a date or not."

Kelly shook her head. Her face worked into a satisfied grin. "One day she's dating a banker, next day it's a bank robber." She paused as if something had just occurred to her.

"You don't suppose... nah."

She pursed her lips as if thinking about something delicious.

"You don't suppose that Mona ... No. We weren't brought up like that."

"Mona what?"

"Takes money from men?"

"Oh," I said.

"See?" Kelly said. "It kind of fits."

"Well, she's not a streetwalker. I never see her standing out there on Saint Peter Street, if that's what you mean."

"But there's other kinds, right?" Kelly said. "You know. A traveling salesman checks into a hotel, and says something to the desk clerk… or so I've heard anyway."

"I don't want to think about it," I said.

"Yeah, me neither, but…"

"Back to Swede Fanlund," I said. "He knows your neighbor Rico. You might even say they're business partners."

"I knew he had to have some kind of business, Rico. I could never figure out what it was. You assume it's bootlegging."

"How about murder for hire?"

"Get out of here," Kelly said.

I nodded.

"I never know whether to believe you," she said. "You're pulling my leg, right?"

I shook my head.

"Murder for hire? Him?"

She set the cigarette-in-ashtray on the broad, paddle-shaped arm of the deck chair. It was second-hand, all of it, her information and her furniture.

Tallerico's Oldsmobile, having idled this whole time, lurched past his driveway and turned toward Payne Avenue. That convinced me. Rico hadn't been driving home, he was stalking me.

I began to put together an unnerving idea. If Paula did remember me, Barker and Karpis would come to certain conclusions. The Third Northwestern Bank was marked and the gang already had my maps. They really didn't need me any more. They could get Reilly or some other dumb kid to park the Lincoln and the switch car. If Barker and Karpis saw me as both a risk and an expense, and if the robbery was scheduled for next week, my life expectancy could be counted in hours. Very likely, I thought, my murder would be farmed out to Swede and Rico.

I would meet the fate of Sadie and Rose, or Pop Anderson. Would they light me up, or dump me in a muddy lake?

"You have that look in your eyes," Kelly said. "You always were such a day-dreamer. Come on, let's eat pie and go see Aunt Doris."

"Saint Barbara," Kelly said.

She was driving the family's hiccupping, rusted model A. Only five years old, it was a rolling pile of scrap. Gary sat beside her, fuming. On his rare days off, Gary didn't want to drive anywhere, least of all to an old age home.

"Don't start," Gary said. "Saint Barbara's Academy? We're yanking them out of there. Two hundred fifty bucks tuition, are you kidding me?"

"No I mean the saint herself," Kelly said. "Saint Barbara. Patron saint of sudden death."

"You mean against sudden death," I said.

"For or against," Kelly said. "Either way. So I'm praying to her." The girls sat on either side of me in the rear seat, and Kelly lowered her voice. "I'm praying to Saint Barbara for a merciful end for … you know who."

"Do you mind stopping at my apartment?"

My nieces, captives, groaned.

"I've got to check on the dogs," I insisted.

"You and those dogs," Kelly said.

"It's the carburetor," said Gary, "that's what's making that gasping sound. Hear it? What else could it be?"

At the Cathedral Apartments they let me out, the car spewing blue exhaust, and I hustled upstairs. I had my own patron saint to evoke against sudden death, and it was a chrome-shiny five-shot Colt revolver. I slipped it into my overcoat pocket, threw each dog a shelled peanut, filled their water bowls, and clambered down the stairs.

As we drove for the Mother Mercy home I turned in the seat now and then, checking for Rico's Oldsmobile, or anyone following us. I asked myself, was I paranoid now? Tallerico was their neighbor. So what if he drove slowly along his own goddamn street?

As Kelly parked at Mother Mercy, in front of the shrine to the Virgin, the jalopy quit with a death rattle. Gary herded his daughters, reluctant, up the broad wooden steps. He had insisted that they wear their Catholic school uniforms, to reassure Aunt Doris that there really was a Heaven.

We walked across the porch, closed for the cold season, and down the antiseptic halls. Veronica and Elizabeth hung back, giving themselves space to make for a run for it. I poked my head into Doris' room. She was sleeping, only her face peeking out from the covers. Her roommate had died, and the nuns had moved that bed out, so Doris was here alone, in this one-window room, with its severe furniture.

"Girls…" Kelly said.

Veronica, fourteen, was tall like her mother and dark like her father, and seemed almost grown up. Elizabeth, just turned eleven, was still a little girl. In the genetic lottery, she had won the Irish Sweepstakes, fair of complexion and blond. Veronica sometimes boasted to classmates about having a bootlegger uncle. But to Elizabeth I was a disgrace: shady Uncle Mick. He might tell funny stories, and the grown-ups said he brought the best booze to family parties, but …

With a sour look on her face, Elizabeth carried a platter wrapped in aluminum foil. She dropped it on the dinner tray that hovered like a crane above Doris's snoring form.

Veronica sat on the bed that had until recently held a dying Italian lady, and began flipping through a detective magazine.

Our presence stirred Doris. She flinched, twisted onto her side, fumbled for her eyeglasses, fixed them on her face and yawned.

"Happy Thanksgiving, Aunt Doris," muttered Elizabeth.

"Yeah," added Veronica, busy scanning lurid tales of violent men and reckless women.

Elizabeth lifted the aluminum foil from the platter, revealing a jumbled holiday dinner.

"Now, we know you hate sweet potatoes," said Kelly.

"And dark meat," said Gary. "It's all breast meat we brought you."

"And cranberries," Kelly said. "Not too sweet, just as you like them."

"Oh," said Doris and sat up to inspect the platter. "I'm not hungry. Is it really Thanksgiving?"

Elizabeth sat and adjusted her knee socks. Veronica unwrapped fork and knife from a napkin. Gary, a burly guy with coal-blackened hands, fluffed Doris's pillow, leaving dark handprints. Kelly's spoonful of cranberry was spurned by Doris, whose lips took a bitter turn.

"Get me out of here," Doris demanded.

"Someday Auntie dear," Kelly said. "But first you've got to eat something. Open the hangar. Here comes the airplane."

Doris clamped her false teeth shut.

When Kelly put down the spoon, Doris said: "Teddy Roosevelt. Now there was a man. He gave those bastards hell."

"Language, Aunt Doris," Kelly said.

The girls giggled, Veronica hiding her face behind the magazine.

I said to Gary: "What do you know about Ralph Tallerico?"

"The guy with the hunting dogs," said Gary. "Baying day and night. Every time a squirrel hops a branch, the dogs howl."

"He-man hunter," I said.

"Yeah," Gary said and laughed. "Can you believe it? Little squirt of a guy. I guess the little guy has to prove himself."

"So recently, his wife died?" I asked.

"Yeah," Gary said. "One day she's pushing a shopping cart

down to Essenmeyers, next day she's pushing up daisies. I didn't see nothing about it in the papers."

"Sudden death," I said.

"She should have prayed to Saint Barbara," Veronica said.

Gary shrugged. "We come, we go, what are you going to do?"

I looked out Doris's window at a frosty lawn. I imagined a cemetery stretching out to eternity.

"No kids?" I said. "Tallerico?"

"No," whispered Gary. "Unhappy marriage."

"Oh?"

"Black eyes," Gary said. "Bruises. She kept to herself a lot."

"Lu Tallerico?" Kelly put in. "Poor thing. I heard she was throttled to death."

"Humpty Dumpty!" Doris shouted.

My nieces looked alarmed. Their mother circled her ear with a forefinger to tell them: don't worry your aunt is just crazy.

"I met him in Wonderland," Doris said.

Elizabeth snatched her coat. "Mom, can I wait outside?"

"You wait right here with your aunt."

Elizabeth's shoulders sagged and her lips curled. She plunked down on a plain wood chair, sat grumpy, with a ragged cloth coat over her lap.

"Tallerico," I said. "Have you seen him lately with his friend the Swede?"

"Who?" Gary said.

"Tall, bald guy, really pale, maybe wearing a blue workman's uniform?"

"Eat, Aunt Doris, please," Kelly said. She tilted cranberry sauce into Doris's mouth and said to me: "Gary doesn't know these Catholic hoodlums. He went to Protestant school."

"Public school," corrected Gary.

"Same thing," said Kelly.

"See my parents couldn't afford the extortion," Gary said. "I mean, the tuition."

"Times have changed," Kelly said. "The public schools are a nightmare now. Kids running wild."

"I've seen Tallerico with his hunting buddies," Gary said. "Carrying shotguns. Pheasant season, that's it. You never saw the Tallericos together as a couple, the husband and wife. I'll tell you, they ain't sociable. The Tallericos? Nobody I know has ever been in their living room."

"That's because he killed his wife," said Elizabeth.

"What?" said Kelly.

"And buried her in the basement," said Veronica.

"Says who?" asked Kelly.

"Everybody," said Elizabeth. "He choked her."

Kelly shrugged. "The kids in the neighborhood. They know everything, just ask them. But don't ask them to do their homework, that they know nothing about."

Elizabeth stuck out her tongue at her mother.

Kelly laughed and said, "I need a smoke."

We walked out onto the porch of Mother Mercy, heated only by the northern sun.

"Are those really my kids?" Kelly said, and lit a Viceroy. "Or space brats, dropped out of the sky by Martians?"

She looked through the porch windows and into the great room, where people in wheelchairs were gathered around a dying fire, staring out at an empty Thanksgiving and a winter that promised only eternal frost.

"Poor things," she said and blew smoke. "Stuck in this place for the holidays. Where are their families?"

"About the farm," I said and lit my pipe. "I'm coming into money."

"Oh?"

"Feast or famine," I said.

"I wonder if there really are men on Mars?"

"So I was thinking. Would you take $2,500 for your third of the farm?"

"You're kidding?" Kelly said.

"When it comes to money, I have no sense of humor."

"I don't know, jeez." She looked over her shoulder. "The way Doris is going, we'll have to sign the farm over to the nuns. What do you want with a frozen potato farm anyway?"

"Lake cottages," I said and puffed my pipe.

She laughed. "Boy are you dreaming."

"Good times are coming back."

"For you, apparently."

"It's a way out for me. A way out of the gangs. I could disappear for a few weeks at a time, you know, tell people I'm going to tend my property and then gradually, the roughnecks might forget about me. See, you can get $50 a week for a lake cabin. You could rent out cabins all summer."

Kelly shrugged.

"I'd ask you to go partners, Kelly, but I know you're strapped."

She crumpled an empty cigarette pack, but not before peeling off the Viceroy coupon.

"You know," I said. "Mona told me she'd hired a lawyer."

"Who's she going to sue this time?"

"Us I think."

"Let her," Kelly said. "All she'll get out of me is a rusty jalopy and an ironing board."

Kelly held up that Viceroy coupon as if showing off a winning bingo card.

"New lamp for the bedroom," she said. "Twelve more coupons." She sighed. "I love to read in bed, late at night, when the girls are sleeping and Gary is out with his friends. It's so quiet."

The girls, wrapped in their coats, appeared on the porch.

"Mother can we please go now?" pleaded Veronica.

"She ate her whole dinner," reported Elizabeth.

"Her teeth are cranberry red," chortled Veronica.

"She's talking to Humpty Dumpty again," said Elizabeth.

The more I thought it over, the more I became convinced I was over my head in danger. I knew too much about the Barker-Karpis gang, but wasn't one of them. They were bloodless bank robbers, but they'd killed people they suspected of disloyalty. Someone like me would always be a disposable outsider. They were guilty of far greater crimes than I was. Barker and Karpis knew that if the law closed in, they'd be the targets and guys like me would be small-fry informers. So I constituted a danger to the Barker-Karpis gang. They had every reason to eliminate me once I had served my purpose.

As a bonus, if they killed me, they could keep my share.

At Seven Corners Hardware, I bought a half-length two-by-four and two solid steel brackets. At home I fashioned these into a bar across the front door. At Fields' Sporting Goods I purchased an Army surplus .45 and a box of Federal ammo. The pocket revolver Jack Peifer had given me was flashy enough to scare drugstore clerks, but not capable of stopping an enraged assassin. The .45 would drop a man in his tracks. I fired it in the basement range at Fields', brought it home, cleaned it, lightly oiled it and lay it on the lamp table at the front door.

Barricaded and armed, I waited.

I considered sending the dogs to Kelly's for safety, but they were my early warning system. Selfish though it was, I decided that we would prosper or die together, the eternal contract between men and dogs. I took them out for relief at sunrise and sundown, always with both pistols in my coat pockets, and otherwise we sat and waited.

I did not see Janie, either in the apartment or coming and going. I assumed, I hoped, that the editor of the Daily News had sent her to Chicago, as he'd promised.

I only had one book in the house I hadn't read, Zane Gray's Sunset Pass. In it, a cowboy returns to a town where he'd been in trouble, defeats his enemies, wins a pretty girl. Out West! It seemed a simple life. I'd never been there but now I began to daydream of sagebrush, desert sunsets and giant cactus.

I baked a lot of bread during those barricaded days. By Thursday night, I knew the bank job wasn't going to come off this week either. I was running low on coffee and tobacco, and was out of bratwurst for the dogs. I had nothing to read except for the Pioneer Press that I borrowed every morning from Mrs. Strutz. I couldn't sleep, so I stole it at 5 a.m. and restored it, only somewhat ruffled, by 6.

No repairman seemed to be able to fix my radio, vandalized by intruders last spring, so I was cut off from music and news and thankfully, Roosevelt's speeches. Twice a day I phoned the Green Lantern, asking Reilly if Harry had returned. I considered driving out to the Jung Sanitarium to seek Harry's protection directly. But driving into the countryside was the last thing any sane man in my position would do.

The murder of Pop Anderson last spring followed a pattern that never varied. Disposal of the corpse was just as important as the rub-out. A body never found was a murder charge never brought. Swede and Rico had tried to dump the old man's corpse in a lake, but had bogged down in mud. They left him naked in a bog, burning his clothes to prevent identification. With Swede, there was not only murder, but always some kind of fire.

The key was to never let them take you for a ride, especially to a body of water. Like the hero in a Western, I might die in a shootout on Main Street. But I'd never get into a car with Rico and Swede.

I thought about stalking them and getting the jump on them. I knew where Rico lived and where Swede drank. But even if I managed the spectacular feat of assassinating the assassins, their backers were Barker and Karpis, and maybe their connections went deeper than that. Jack Peifer, I reminded myself, picked up Sadie and Rose and took them on their last date. Jack Peifer was almost certainly the guy who'd brought Swede Fanlund back to town.

Or maybe I was nuts. Maybe I was blowing up the whole thing into a zeppelin when it was only a party balloon. I had been alone all week, and wasn't making sense anymore.

On Friday morning I noticed in the newspaper ads that the Emporium was having a sale on radios. This wasn't just any sale. The merchants, desperate, were letting people take radios away with $5 down and a promise to pay $1.25 a week. Carrying my pistols in a shoulder holster and belt clip, and armed with hat and overcoat against the winter day, I brought the dogs downstairs.

They were delighted, and I was discouraged, to see Janie shoveling powdery snow off the walk.

She glared at me. She turned her back. She wore a heavy coat with a fur-lined Eskimo hood and knit mittens. She petted the dogs but would not look at me.

"Are you the janitor now?" I said.

"I'm helping the Reardons," she muttered.

"How's work?"

She glared, she straightened up tall, pushed the shovel away from me. It was a steel coal shovel and made a nasty scraping sound against the frozen concrete.

Okay, I told myself, I'd been spurned. My former friend Janie. I brought Snowflake and Hula Girl upstairs and fed them, corn flakes only. By the time I got back downstairs Janie was no longer in sight.

I rode the streetcar to the Loop. At the Emporium I inspected the sale item, a Kennedy Radio, with genuine RCA tubes. The salesman claimed it could receive both police calls and commercial stations. I handed over a five-dollar-bill, and in return got a payment book and a promise of delivery Monday. I arrived home with a load of groceries, magazines and the bulldog edition of all the Sunday papers.

The Emporium truck pulled up on Monday and delivered the Kennedy Radio, a 42-inch console that fit nicely beside the sofa. On the way out, the delivery guys laughed at my door barricade and gave each other the smart-eye.

I tuned that radio all around the dial, amazed that, one, the police really were getting radio commands from headquarters and, two, that any rube could listen in.

By Monday evening I could no longer take the isolation and risked a streetcar ride to the Green Lantern. Strangely enough, once you got inside the joint, you were safe. Last year a punk named Ventress had been shot in the parking lot, and the cops had come down hard on the shooters, not for murder, but for bringing publicity to Harry's joint. The Green Lantern was a sanctuary, as strong as any medieval cathedral.

I sidled up to Bess in the cloakroom. She was tying Christmas bows, red and green, out of spools of ribbon. The woman was never idle. I kissed her on the cheek.

"Merry Christmas," I said.

"You're pushing it," she said.

"You've got a date for New Year's?" I asked.

"I've got a date with a paycheck right here."

"I'm just another admirer in line for your attention. Say Bess," I leaned against the doorway, pretend casual. "Have you seen Swede Fanlund around?"

She nodded toward the Blue Room.

"The inner sanctum," she said. "Take your coat?"

"No," I said because it held two pistols. "I won't be long."

Bess opened the dutch doors of the Blue Room and I entered a world of smoke and blacked-out windows. One wall held six slot machines. A spoiled, bored a young flapper in furs fed one of them with nickels. In a dark corner gangsters were drinking themselves stupid in company of bleach-blond sporting girls. I was relieved to note that my sister Mona wasn't among them.

The big table hosted a poker game, and my eyes fixed on Swede: He wore a leather vest over his rough blue shirt. Most guys let the crew-cut grow out in winter, but not Swede. He didn't notice me right away. I took a chair to one side.

Reilly, invisible, sent drinks through a slot in the wall. A waitress popped up from amid the sporting blondes and began handing the drinks around.

Swede glared at me with chill, sly hazel eyes.

He looked down at his cards. He folded. Without a word to his tablemates, he pushed away, walked toward me and punched me none too softly in the back. He rapped on the dutch door and Bess opened it and then he was gone.

I waited a moment, perplexed, and then knocked for exit too.

As soon as the Blue Room door opened, I saw Rico at the coatroom, handing his overcoat to Bess. That's it, I said to myself, convinced he had been following me. I stepped backward into the doorway. Swede beckoned to Rico from the bar. Rico passed me with a nasty stare.

At the bar Rico and Swede argued, nothing I could hear. An outsider would guess that Rico, dressed executive swell, was a boss giving orders to Swede, his workman. Rico waved Swede off with disgust and marched toward the men's room.

Hands in my overcoat pockets, I approached Swede.

"I heard maybe you boys were looking for me."

Swede bit his lips. "Nah," he said. "Not me."

He was a bigger guy than me, with huge hands. The twenty years since high school had put almost no fat on him.

"Because we can settle this man to man," I said.

"Who you talking to?" Swede looked around. He pointed to his chest. "Me?"

"I don't like being stalked," I said.

"There's nobody stalking you, Powers, it's all in your…" He tapped the side of his head. " … imagination."

"Maybe, but I'm not imagining your partner. He's on my tail."

"Then settle it with him," Swede said. "We got no beef."

"You're sure?"

"Go on before you get hurt. You keep shaking the tree, a monkey's going to fall on you."

I didn't want to make Swede save face in here. I turned my back on him deliberate and slow, signaled Reilly for a drink. Swede slipped in next to me, elbows on the bar.

"Right now you're untouchable, Powers," he whispered, "but that ain't going to last."

Pat approached and Swede yelled: "Reilly, this guy's drinking on me." Then he slapped me hard on the back, very hard, and walked off.

Untouchable. I mulled that over as Pat set an icy ginger ale before me. It could only mean Harry had put the umbrella over me. I was safe at least until the bank job.

Feeling relief rolling off me like a dropped weight, I turned the ginger ale into a glass of ice cubes just as Rico walked back in. The little guy looked around for Swede. He fixed me with a hostile stare. I held my glass up in invitation.

He walked past and said, "Forget it," over his shoulder. I followed him to the dutch door of the Blue Room and he turned on me. Bess, her antenna up, backed into the cloak room.

"I've seen a little too much of you lately," I told Rico.

"Oh yeah?"

"If you don't start minding your own business it's going to go bad for you."

"What are you talking about?"

"Don't tail me, don't tag me, I don't like it."

"You've got a lot of nerve for a dumb Irish prick."

I brought my hand out of my overcoat pocket, brass knuckles.

Weeks of pent up anger and fear flashed through me. I shot him a left to the teeth and he went bash against the door, bounced sideways and slumped.

I stood over him breathing like a race horse. He was bleeding from the mouth, slumped against the door, legs twitching. Reilly and Bess took hold of my arms. "Get out of here," Reilly said, seething.

I stumbled over Rico on the way out, found myself alone in the dark parking lot.

CHAPTER NINETEEN

There were only three Fridays left until Christmas, and after that there'd be less money flowing through the bank, so I marked my calendar with Xs on December 9th, 16th and 23rd. If any cop ever asked, I would say those Xs marked my Christmas Club payments. The robbery began to get hold of my mind, and I couldn't sleep as the next Friday approached, and then passed quietly.

I stayed away from gangster haunts, especially the Green Lantern. I phoned down there, and Reilly said Harry was furious. Because of my assault on Rico, I was banned.

"Swede laughed his ass off," Reilly told me. "But Rico's vowed to kill you. He's telling everybody you'll be dead by New Year's Eve."

As December 16th approached I was getting maybe two hours of sleep at night. Blustery snowstorms buffeted my apartment windows that week and left a sparkling layer on the city streets below. On Thursday at 3 a.m. Snowflake nosed me awake to tell me there was a fresh inch of snow on the ground, and demanded to go out and play in it. Hula Girl tagged along. I stood in the parking lot shivering while Snowflake rolled in ecstasy.

The next morning the phone rang at just past 6 a.m.

"Your turn at bat," said Reilly. "Hit a homer."

Click.

I hustled down to Herb's and fired up the Lincoln. At Verne's suggestion, the back window had been removed. That made for a drafty half-hour drive to Minneapolis, where at 6:47 by my pocket watch I parked the Lincoln in that prime spot in front of the bank and behind the streetcar stop. I dropped the fake-out map to the car floor, the one that outlined a getaway to Hot Springs. I stepped on that map, rumpled it, and pushed it under the passenger seat.

"Have a laugh, coppers," I said to nobody. With a piece of tape I attached a spare ignition key to the underside of the dashboard, then got out, leaving the doors unlocked.

I took the University streetcar back to Saint Paul, arriving home after nearly an hour's excruciating stop-and-start journey. On that ride I read the morning Dispatch but could hardly concentrate, except for the story about Congress being ready to vote for beer.

Now I had five anxious hours to kill. I walked the dogs down to Seven Corners and bought a copy of the Racing Form from Blind Benny. I handicapped all nine races at Hialeah and all ten at the New Orleans Fair Grounds. Though I'd never get the bets down, I copied my predictions and odds into a notebook to check later. All this busywork brought me to lunch, for me and the dogs, of hard boiled eggs and fresh-baked bread. I was quite pleased with my new Kennedy radio, and turned the volume up high during Duke Ellington's rousing: *It Don't Mean a Thing if it Ain't Got that Swing.*

I put on my best suit, just back from the cleaners, the gray tweed. I knotted an electric blue tie, folded a matching handkerchief into the breast pocket. At 12:30 I walked down the hill to Herb's Garage and started up the Chevy. I knew where Larry DuVol lived, up on Crocus Hill, two blocks from the luxury digs of Fred Barker's girl Paula. I phoned Larry from the same Rexall drugstore where I'd stalked Paula. He said give him five minutes while he made some calls, and then he appeared, like he was waiting for a streetcar, on the corner of Dale and Grand.

When I picked him up, he smelled of after-shave and drink. His hair was greased back, he wore no hat, but a thick overcoat. He was live-wired, legs bouncing, hands beating a rhythm on his thighs. He directed me to Marshall Avenue, where Verne was waiting at a streetcar stop. Verne wore an overcoat, unbuttoned, and a gray felt hat. He got into the back seat. Larry turned to him.

"You look right."

Verne grunted.

As jumpy as Larry was, Verne was as calm and quiet. Following Larry's directions, I drove four blocks and pulled into the parking lot of a luxury apartment building. A rime of overnight ice coated parking lot and sidewalk, but had already been ground off the streets by traffic. I gave thanks for this, since icy roads might have postponed the job.

We sat with the Chevy idling.

"No horn," cautioned Verne. "Wait. They know."

We sat in a cold car, with a heater that barely leaked lukewarm air. Verne lit a cigarette. Larry popped Blackjack gum into his mouth, and I refused his offer of a stick. On the dashboard stood a tiny, gold-plated magnetic crucifix. It had been put there by whoever owned this car before it was stolen, repainted and fixed with faked license plates.

Verne detached that crucifix from the dashboard, held it up to the weak winter light. He opened the passenger window and tossed it into the frozen mud.

"Superstition," he said.

He cranked up the window and filled the air with a choking nasty smoke from a cheap cigarette. Larry shoved his hands into his coat pocket and shivered.

The car idled and when the engine began to miss a bit, I eased in the choke.

"Tap it," said Verne. "Tap the gas."

I did. He listened.

"It ain't tuned," he said.

"Herb tuned it," I said.

"Bullshit," he said. "I'll settle with Herb."

Then he rolled down the window, pitched the cigarette, and we waited. Finally the back door opened. Karpis, Fred and a stranger emerged. Karpis carried a black violin case, Fred a straw suitcase and the stranger lugged a lumpy gym bag. They loaded the baggage into the trunk and then we were six well-dressed gentlemen squeezed into a chilly car.

Fred, I saw in the mirror, had an absurd set of candy-store wax teeth protruding from his lips. This, I realized, was to prevent him being identified by his gold teeth.

"What are the chances the Lincoln's towed away?" Karpis asked, but nobody had an answer.

Karpis hit me in the shoulder.

"What are the chances?" he repeated.

"Slim," I said, staring him down through the mirror.

"Dumb plan," said Karpis.

"We'll see," said Fred.

I drove the slippery side-streets toward University Avenue. The car began to get thick with smoke from four cigarettes. I had to roll open my window to keep the smoke down and the frost away. I drew that blue handkerchief out of my top pocket and took a few swipes at the windshield.

"Can't wait to get out of this here ice box of a town," said Fred.

"Soon enough," said Karpis.

Larry, stinking of cologne, chewed gum. The chubby stranger beside him stared moody and silent out the windows.

I turned across streetcar tracks and headed toward Minneapolis, through a long, dull stretch of small factories, storefronts and gritty homes.

Larry giggled. "Stick 'em up, twerps. You is about to be robbed."

"Save it," said Verne, working his hands into black leather

gloves.

"Oh, a genuine war hero," said Larry.

"Boys," said Fred. "Don't you be fighting. In an hour we'll all be fat rich."

Karpis lit a Chesterfield from the butt of one he'd smoked down.

"You really was a deputy, Miller is that right?" Larry said.

"Can it," said Verne. "You're getting stupid. You're as nervous as a girl."

"Oh fuck you," said Larry.

"I ride with men," said Miller. "And only men."

"What's that supposed to mean?" said Larry.

"Shut up!" shouted Fred.

It got quiet as we drove past the University campus and when we reached the business district, all I could hear was my own shifting and clutching, the tap-tap-tap of the engine, the rolling tires, Verne wheezing, and Larry chewing gum. I pulled up at the bank, next to the Lincoln. Two parking tickets flapped underneath its wipers.

"Be sure and pay those tickets," Karpis deadpanned.

Only Karpis got out of the Chevy. He transferred the luggage to the Lincoln's trunk and with a streetcar clanging behind me, I drove that Chevy around the block. It was 2:31 by my watch.

"You know what to do," Fred told me. "Don't let anything stop you."

All of them hustled out of the car and I zoomed off.

By plan, I was to drive the Chevy back to Como Park, where it was to serve as the "switch car."

But I had other ideas.

I drove the Chevy around the corner and tooted the horn. Pat Reilly was waiting for me, staring out the window of a dark speakeasy. I parked the car and waited for him on the sidewalk. He smelled of cheap beer when I palmed him $50. "Harry wanted you cut in," I said. "You're cut in."

I patted him on the back as he got behind the wheel of the Chevy.

"Buffalo pen, now," I said.

"I know, I know, do you think I'm an idiot?"

"Just making sure," I said, as he slammed the door. He roared away, the Chevy's rear tire nearly crushing my foot.

When you paid off Reilly, you bought something, all right. Pat was no genius, but he was loyal, and knew the value of silence. As I watched him drive away, I was sure he would park that Chevy exactly where we had arranged.

Fifty bucks was a lot of money, but worth it for me. It had taken me a while to realize it, but this gang had become the top bank robbers in the Midwest, the slickest, most successful criminals since Jesse James. Most people had never heard of the Barker-Karpis gang, but I knew, every time I read of a bloodless, big-haul bank job in Kansas or Iowa or South Dakota, there was a good chance these guys had pulled it off, and then driven back to their base in Saint Paul.

Harry was the mastermind of these jobs. Big Ryan ran the police protection, squashing all inquiries about Karpis, Barker or anyone in their gang. In all these bank jobs, no innocents had been killed, or even badly hurt.

I wanted to see this gang operate first hand.

I pushed into Folkers Diner and sat at the counter, at the fish-hook curve. From there I could see direct across the street at the Third Northwestern Bank. Folker's was dark and quiet, since it was the lull between lunch and dinner shift. A table crowded with schoolboys, way in the back, made the only noise. They gabbed, giggled, sipped loud at Cokes and ice cream sodas.

The waitress scolded them for playing hooky, and for making a mess.

I twisted on the rotating stool so that I faced directly out the

window, elbows back on the counter. I was feeling smug. I admit
there was something rotten in me that wanted to see the bank
taken down. Like many people, I hated banks and bankers, as if
they alone had caused America to go sour.

As I watched the bank robbery unfold, everything seemed to
happen very slowly. There was no such thing as time, only
impressions.

Fred, Karpis, the Dark Stranger, and Verne slipped inside the
bank. Larry DuVol stood outside, dressed like a banker, but
holding a machine gun as if he were going to war. The reflection of
the bank's window behind him prevented me from seeing anything
but shadows inside.

Out on the icy sidewalk, men and women, winter dressed, had
been waiting for the streetcar but now began to edge away from
that stop, as if Larry were a stone dropped into a pond, and they
were the ripples. Larry grinned and bowed at them, like an actor
after a wonderful performance. He pointed the machine gun
straight up and down, deadly end toward the sky. A fellow stepped
up from the barber shop underneath the bank, and shrunk back
down, like gopher into his hole. A small crowd began to assemble
at each street corner, the bold staring at Larry, the timid hiding
behind the bank's brick walls. A trucker hauling junk slowed and
blocked my vision for a moment, and when he cleared, a boy and
girl approached Larry from the crowd. They were ten, maybe
twelve years old, all bundled up, the girl in a red kerchief and the
boy wearing a hunters' cap. The boy asked Larry something and
Larry snarled. He kicked at the children, and they ran away. I could
hear the girl's screech even inside the diner.

Entire months, it seemed, had passed in less time. What was
taking these guys so long? What had gone wrong in there? The plan
was five to six minutes. The waitress walked up behind the counter,
dressed greasy in black and white, all gnarled hair and tired eyes and
red knuckles.

"Coffee, mister?" she said, then glanced out the window.

"What the heck is going on over there?"

Then she shrieked.

"My God, they're robbing the bank. He's got a tommygun."

The boys from the back of the diner clustered around the big frosty window, hands up on it, chattering.

"Mobsters!" one said.

"Neat!" cried another.

In front of the bank, Larry began to pace, like a soldier on guard duty. The sidewalk crowd, like a school of fish, moved back at his approach. Larry didn't seem to notice them much. He turned and stared into the bank's windows, hand up to his forehead like an Indian scout. A streetcar pulled up and clanged. A few riders hopped out and scattered. Other riders backed up into the car again, while some gathered at the streetcar windows and gawked. My stomach had turned so sour-sick it was making me dizzy. How in the name of God could it be taking this long?

"Come on, saps," I muttered, "you put the money in the bag and you run."

Neither the waitress nor the boys seemed to hear me. They were chatting all excited, the biggest boy shouting: "Come on, let's go over there."

The streetcar motored away. Where was Larry? I saw just a flash of him as he pushed into the bank through the revolving doors.

Something had gone horribly wrong, I felt, if the Outside Man had gone in. He was the one supposed to look out for the cops.

An eerie silence seemed to settle over me, the waitress, the boys. The streetcar left in its wake an electric flash in the trolley lines. A frigid wind snapped the bank's maroon awning. A few in the sidewalk crowd began to edge toward the bank's big plate glass windows.

A Minneapolis Police car rolled up, bounced off the curb, and jerked to a stop. The passenger door opened, and a blue-dark form began to emerge. He turned and reached into the car for a shotgun. The driver-cop, too, opened his door.

Then the bank's huge plate glass window shattered. The bark of a tommygun split the air, and its bullets zinged and whined. In an instant, the cop with the shotgun was rolling on the sidewalk, the shotgun flung to the gutter. The driver cop never made it from behind the wheel. He slumped over in his car as the tommygun barked furious and the car's horn blew and the diner's window in front of us cracked and the boys dove and the waitress screamed and I stupefied sat watching. Out of the bank's revolving doors strode Larry, as cool as if he were waltzing into a tavern. He stood over the cop on the sidewalk and blam blam blam shot rounds into the man's head, I could see the flesh and brains spatter. Larry walked around the squad car and fired through the doors and the window, jolting the driver cop with shot after shot.

Big blond Verne burst out of the bank, stepping on ice and shattered glass, his topcoat thrown open. He, too, blasted the cops and the cop car with machine gun fire. People were running for cover, ducking, lying on sidewalk and street, screaming. Horns blew. Cars and trucks pulled over.

"Wow!" shouted the schoolboy in front of me. "Look, the cops are dead."

"No they're not. They're pretending."

"Want to bet?"

Verne fired again, sweeping the street, the bullets ricocheting and whining, you could hear their power to rip through flesh, you could hear them like little rockets in the air. The Lincoln, the getaway car, sunk as one tire blew out in the rear. Fred and Karpis and the Dark Stranger ran out of the bank and hopped in, Karpis behind the wheel.

The cops' blood was now leaking onto the street and sidewalk.

Verne slipped on the ice, gunning his tommy, the bullets going everywhere, ripping through the awning and parked cars and street signs. Verne regained his footing, clambered into the Lincoln's back seat. Larry took out a pistol and emptied it at the shattered police car. He hopped into the Lincoln only when Karpis began to edge that getaway car into the traffic jam. Larry slammed the door. Driving in the wrong lane, Karpis sped off on only three good tires, the Lincoln smoking, steaming and squealing as it roared into the winter haze.

Then came a moment of pure, beautiful silence, as if nothing bad had happened, as if the dead cops were going to rise from their own puddles of blood, dust themselves off, and announce that it had been only a stage play. A frigid wind rushed through the shattered diner window. The waitress, ducked behind the counter, began crying. The schoolboys rushed across the street toward the carnage. Cars were parking in the middle of the street, drivers leaping out. People from the crowd were cautiously approaching the downed cops. Men and women inside the bank gawked out the space where plate glass used to be.

One bullet had splintered the diner's counter, about a yardstick away from my knee. Flecks of glass fell from my coat as I rose, gob-struck, from the stool. I crossed the street like I was in a dream. The driver-cop was dead behind the wheel, his hands clutching the ivory as if he could steer himself back to life. A gaggle of men and women surrounded the passenger cop, who, lying in the icy street, emitted a weak moan as they tended to him.

I wandered into the bank, pushed dead-minded through the shattered revolving door.

Bankers scurried. Clerks sobbed. A man in a suit was lying, pistol-whipped, bloody and moaning, on the floor. A man dressed as a fine executive was tending his bleeding head with a wash cloth. The teller who had taken my Christmas club payment, the lady with the big diamond engagement ring, was on her knees trembling, as if praying to the God of Survival. One man ran behind the teller's cages, slamming cash drawers. A bald man with tiny eyeglasses spat blood into a white handkerchief.

A Christmas tree, centered in the room, was hung with ornaments and aluminum icicles. Gun smoke drifted in clouds, the big room smelling strong of cordite and faint of urine. One man's empty polished shoe lay on the luxe wood floor. Deposit slips were scattered like confetti. An old lady, in black coat, head wrapped in a dark kerchief, whiskers on her chin, muttering in some harsh foreign language, sat against the wall under a shattered window.

I looked into her cloudy eyes and said: "Mother, can you stand up?"

Like a desperate monkey her hands clutched my arms as I helped her to her feet. She was much heavier than I thought and almost brought me down.

"Are you all right, Mother?"

Spittle ran down her chin.

"Did they take your money, Mother?"

She tottered off without saying anything.

I followed her out to the street. People had covered the wounded cop on the sidewalk, and the dead cop in the car, with coats. Sirens, far off, began to wail.

I followed the old lady around the corner, and she turned on me, her eyes big with fear, her hands shaking, "Are you going to rob me?"

I tipped my hat low, put my hands in my pockets and walked.

I was home, a trembling wreck, by 3:15, and let Snowflake and Hula Girl out onto the frosty lawn. A Yellow Cab pulled up and discharged Janie. She looked past me, greeted the dogs, and hustled into her dark basement room.

I trudged upstairs with the dogs and tuned the radio to police calls on the Minneapolis band. The reception was lousy but there an awful lot of chatter. The dispatcher told police to watch for a dark blue Lincoln, believed to have crossed into Saint Paul.

Exhausted, I fell into a nap. I woke up just at sundown, the radio silent. The dogs begged for dinner.

I saw the radio was turned to ON. I turned the switch back and forth, slapped the radio. "Genuine RCA tubes," I muttered. "They hardly lasted a week." I pushed the radio away from the wall, reached in, wiggled tubes, but got no sound, no glow, no nothing.

CHAPTER TWENTY

I sat up all night sipping whiskey and waiting for sleep. Not long after sunrise, I worked into my corduroy jacket and walked the dogs down to Blind Benny's newsstand. I could read the headline from across the street.

SECOND BANDIT VICTIM DIES

I dodged into the newsstand and grabbed the Minneapolis Star in shaking hands.

PATROLMEN GIVE BLOOD
IN EFFORT TO SAVE GORSKI'S LIFE

"Who the hell is Gorski?" I asked Benny.

Hunched over, coin changer belted to his waist, hands black with newsprint, Benny took a quarter from a bundled-up lady and said: "Cop."

I sat down on a milk carton.

"Minneapolis." Benny said.

Patrolman Ira Evans had been shot dead in front of the bank, I read. His partner Leo Gorski was gravely wounded, in the hospital with a temperature of 107. An innocent civilian named Oscar Erickson had been shot dead in Como Park.

"How the hell did this happen?" I muttered.

There were times in the sleepless night when I wondered whether this whole thing had actually occurred. Seeing it in the newspapers shook me all over again.

"You reading or buying?" Benny asked.

I fumbled for a dime. I had forgotten about my dogs but there they sat, loose on their leashes, obedient and staring at me.

Blind Benny barely heated that little shed, and now a shuddering chill went through me.

"You don't know what'll happen next in this town," Benny said. "Thieves and killers."

I read the Star, but meaning escaped me, broken down into isolated words: *machine gun bandits ... getaway Lincoln ... Christmas wreath salesman ... "shoes so shiny I could see myself in them..."*

"Sells papers," Benny said.

I handed him the dime.

"I'll take 'em all," I said. "Minneapolis and Saint Paul."

"Normally," Benny said. "A Saint Paul guy won't buy a Minneapolis paper."

I snatched a Journal, Pioneer Press and Daily News.

"Keep the change," I said.

"You're welcome," said Benny.

As people alighted from a streetcar he shouted: "Mayhem in Minneapolis! Blood in the streets. Killers among us! Read about it! Latest editions here."

A fellow in overalls, an old lady, and two shop girls bought newspapers. Benny said to me: "See, Powers? Death sells."

Up the hill I trudged, newspapers under my arms, eager dogs pulling on their leashes. My apartment, and the Cathedral, were atop the hill and I felt like that massive, copper-domed church was crushing me with judgment. Christmas wreath salesmen? They killed a door-to-door salesman in Como Park?

As I approached the lobby door, Janie popped out of her apartment, carrying a cheap cloth gym bag.

"Here." She handed me the bag.

She wrapped her arms around herself, having only thin cotton between her flesh and winter.

"It's from Larry," she said.

"Huh?"

"He left it last night. I haven't been very nice to you, Powers. I'm sorry for being rude. He's gone."

"Larry?"

"Home for Christmas. He's not coming back. Powers, I'm freezing do you want to come in?"

"Upstairs," I said. "Coffee. Bring your radio."

I followed the dogs and Janie up four flights. Janie walked into my kitchen to boil water for coffee. I left the newspapers on the kitchen table, took the gym bag to the bedroom, set it on my dresser, zipped it open.

Inside was a shoebox, wrapped in kraft paper, tied with a string. I tore that open. The shoebox contained a mess of bills. A few of them were blood-spattered. A note scrawled in a crazy hand said:

$3,300 more later asshole

I shoved the shoebox under the bed.

"A pair of boots?" said Janie, when I stepped into the kitchen. "Larry said he wanted to give you a pair of his boots, he wasn't going to need them anymore. I don't get it. He's nowhere near your size."

I steadied myself on the kitchen table.

"It didn't seem heavy enough for boots," Janie said.

"When did you last see him?"

"Larry? Oh," she said. "Midnight."

She ground coffee for the French press, spooned it in.

"He left something for me too," she said.

She lifted her red-striped blouse to show deep purple bruises at her ribs.

"He pushed me to the floor," she said. "He kicked me."

Rather than anger or self-pity, her voice sounded hollow with sheer disappointment.

"You were right Powers. I'd never seen him so drunk. He's different. He's awful mean when he's drunk."

She sat at the table.

"And guess what? I'm on furlough. As of January 1. Economy move, says Major Hoople."

"He fired you?"

"Furlough, he said. The Christmas ads didn't come in as they'd hoped."

"I thought you were a rising star. He didn't offer you any other job prospects?"

"Nope." Her lips formed a circle.

The kettle whistled. I poured steaming water into the French press, counted to fifty, plunged it.

"He gave me a hundred dollars. He threw it at me."

"Major Hoople?"

"No. Larry," she said. "He kicked me to the ground and threw money at me, like I was his whore."

She sputtered.

"Of course I have to keep the money now. With no job."

When I was six, seven, eight years old I used to cry over nothing. A bee landed on my arm, and I would begin sobbing. I cried when my sister Kelly was born. Were my parents going to keep her and take me to the dump? That's what my father always threatened. *I going to take you kids out to the dump.*

I cried when my toy truck lost a wheel. I sobbed and begged every morning when my mother dropped me off for kindergarten.

Michael, she would say, *you don't want people thinking you're a crybaby, do you?* I cried in third grade when Sister Charles Boromeo hit me with a ruler. I cried for the last time that summer, when our dog Skippy ran away. When I retreated sobbing into my dark bedroom, Dad poked his head in. *Keep crying and I'll give you something to cry about.*

That night as I lay in bed inconsolable, Dad walked into my bedroom and put his hands around my throat. He actually began choking the breath out of me but I wasn't afraid. I was so miserable over Skippy that I didn't want to live. My father must have been feeling very sick that night. He spoke in an ugly tone I'd never heard before or since. *The Irish don't cry,* he growled, *do you hear me?* I couldn't breathe, so I couldn't answer. He let go of my throat, pushed away from my bed, and finished me off from the half-light of the bedroom door. *If the Irish let themselves cry, they'd drown in their own tears.*

So no, I couldn't cry, but the carnage, the awful waste of human life, made me shaky and sick to my stomach. A colossal darkness came over me, and I felt I was going to spend the rest of my life in a cave.

I turned away from Janie. I crossed the apartment from Cathedral view to city view. I stood there looking out, seeing nothing. The bastard Du Vol. He had started it all. There was a plan to deal with cops should they show up. The Outside Man was to keep them pinned down with machine gun fire. The gang would take hostages on the running boards, and drive the high-powered getaway car until the cops in their jalopies fell far behind. It was a plan that had worked in job after job, until the Barker gang had taken on this madman Larry DuVol.

And the cops. What the hell. It was the shift change. They were all supposed to be back in the precinct house.

In my imagination the Barker-Karpis gang had driven all night, and were in maybe Kansas City by now. Normally, they were safe from arrest in Saint Paul, but a triple-murder, two of the victims cops, that would bring way too much heat.

Janie unplugged my console radio and set her tabletop radio atop it. When she turned to KSTP it was one bulletin after another. The man killed in Como Park had left behind a young widow. He'd been a dining car waiter, selling Christmas wreaths door-to-door in desperation, since his recent layoff. In Minneapolis, patrolman Leo Gorski was clinging to life. Funeral plans were made for patrolman Ira Evans. Saint Paul police had recovered a shot-up Lincoln automobile in Como Park, and believed the bandits were headed for Hot Springs.

Janie called me into the kitchen and poured coffee.

"Are you feeling all right?"

"Sure," I said.

"You look rotten and you smell like sour whiskey. Michael, have you got anything to eat?"

"Home-made bread. Poached eggs? Could you shut the radio off, please?"

I set a pot of water, with a splash of vinegar, on the stove to boil for the eggs. I sliced bread and plugged in the electric toaster. I tried to focus on something besides yesterday's horror.

I asked Janie: "What exactly did Major Hoople say to you?"

"Oh, just the usual lies. Wasn't his doing, he claimed. It was the economy. Blah blah blah."

I stood over the stove, staring up at the Cathedral. I could not seem to hold a thought.

"Where's home for this Larry?"

"Saint Louis?" Janie shrugged. "Maybe, I don't know, he never really said. I mean, he said a lot of things that didn't make sense, but…"

She dropped her head into her hands, and in a gloomy voice said: "I deserve this, Powers. I knew he was a bad boy. I knew it all along."

I gave her a shoulder massage. "Don't give up on the Daily

News," I said. "I know people who know Major Hoople. He can be persuaded, believe me."

"I don't know if I even want to work there anymore."

"A paycheck is a paycheck these days."

I poached the eggs, served them over buttered whole wheat toast. We ate in silence, both of us stunned, and for different reasons. After choking down breakfast, and gulping a second cup of coffee, I felt a little more together.

I said to Janie: "Can you look after the dogs for a while? And if Larry knocks, don't answer."

"Don't worry, I won't. Powers, your hands are shaking."

"Too much coffee," I said and walked into the bedroom to load my .45.

I desperately needed a reliable car. That afternoon I talked Filben into financing a used Essex Terraplane from Herb's Garage, $300. For an extra $30, Herb promised to lose the paperwork. Filben was glad to loan me the money on outrageous terms: $30 a month for 15 months. I didn't care because it was quite possible I wouldn't live to make the first payment.

I drove to the Green Lantern, no Larry, and out to the Hollyhocks. Sam Tanaka treated me like stranger. At the bar I asked bouncer Saph McKenna if Larry had been in. No.

I drove to one joint after another and by sundown, I gave up. I called Janie from the Rexall drugs near Larry's apartment, said I wouldn't be back for a while, and asked if she was okay with the dogs.

"Larry is more trouble than you know," I said. "Stay in my place. Keep the lights low. Don't go downstairs tonight."

In the Rexall I read every evening paper. The second cop, Leo Gorski, had died. The police chief of Minneapolis said arrests were imminent.

But I didn't see any cops approach Larry's apartment. I waited all night. Whoever the cops suspected, it wasn't Larry. I waited in the car, then in the drugstore to warm up, then in the Barking Dog speakeasy. I was sitting in the car again, half frozen and mostly asleep, when just after 3 a.m. sweeping headlights awoke me. They belonged to a Yellow Cab. Larry staggered out and stumbled into the apartment lobby.

I was right behind him.

He wore a raccoon coat. In the hallway, he bounced off one wall and into the other, so drunk he didn't notice me. He paused, reeling and clumsy, to insert key into lock.

I pushed into his apartment behind him. He glared at me.

"Oh!" He belched. "You."

I shut the door. The lights in this scarcely furnished apartment were all blazing, including the chandelier, which hovered over the spot where a dining table should have been. Larry walked under that chandelier, bumped his head, staggered into the bedroom.

He opened the raccoon coat and fell backward on the bed.

"Come for the rest of it, have you?" he said. "It's bonds, goddamn it, bonds, you idiot. You can't spend bonds."

He sat up.

"Whoops," he said. "Need a drink."

He stumbled into the dining room, opened a cupboard, removed a bottle of gin, and then from the icebox, extracted a pitcher of orange juice. In an empty milk bottle he mixed a giant cocktail.

I didn't want Larry to know I'd witnessed the robbery. I said: "What the hell went wrong over there?"

"Over where?" He sat on the couch swirling his milk-bottle cocktail.

"I thought you clowns were going to get away clean."

"Clowns?"

"I thought you were professionals."

"Well we all make mish-takes." He hiccupped. "The cops made

a mish-take. Is what happened." He shrugged. "Couldn't be helped."

Larry kicked off his shoes.

"Let me tell you something Joe. Joe, right? When you hire The Chopper, you don't get no choir boy. See?"

He hiccupped.

"What happened over in Como?" I asked.

"Who?"

"The switch. A civilian? What happened there? Who shot that man? Why?"

Larry waved that off, then said: "I don't know. Fred. We couldn't stop him. Nosy bastard, what's his name, Erickson? The guy deserved it, he wouldn't go away."

He removed shirt and tie to reveal a gray stinking sweat-stained t-shirt.

"Somebody turn the goddamn heat down," he growled. He lurched for the hall closet, reached in for a broom and began pounding the ceiling.

I grabbed the broom from him. He whirled on me. He reached for his shoulder holster, but it contained no gun. He spat at me, swigged from his cocktail, dropped his trousers and kicked them toward the radiator.

"Where the hell do you think you are?" he demanded. "How did you get in here, Joe?"

He took off his shirt to reveal a skinny, muscular torso, spoiled with prison tattoos. Now he was naked except for white underpants. He ran his hand through his hair.

"Got a lot of cash," he laughed. "A lot of cash. Ain't got no woman, though," he wagged his finger at me.

I felt that pistol like a weight in my coat pocket. But I was sober and frightened and I nixed any thought of plugging him. A shot in the night, somebody looks out the window, recognizes me, I'm in Stillwater for life. That sane and selfish thought kept me from drawing my pistol and drilling a hole in his head.

"Too many women," he said, "and not enough time to fuck 'em all."

"Keep your voice down," I said.

"What?"

"It's three in the morning. Do you want the cops knocking on your door?"

"I can take care of any cops," he said. "Proved that, didn't I?"

I said, "I'm getting you out of here, down to the train station and out of town."

"Oh no," he said.

"Oh yes," I said, and lied: "Harry's orders."

"Harry who?"

"Pack up," I said. "Where's your bathroom?"

He jerked his thumb and I walked into a surprisingly clean white tiled room, with a big all-wall mirror. I peed and looked at myself. Powers, how the hell are you going to wiggle out of this one? Even my reflection in the mirror looked scared.

"Okay," I said when I opened the door, but Larry was gone from the living room. The hallway door stood open. I heard knocking in the hallway, and my testicles retracted up into my belly, a puckering fear. I imagined the men in blue smothering me. With two of their brothers dead across town, the street cops would be in a savage mood.

A hard, aggressive knock sounded in the hallway. I looked out to see Larry standing at a neighbor's door.

He wore that raccoon coat, open, over briefs. In one hand he grasped that milk-bottle cocktail.

"I'm looking for a friend," he shouted to whoever opened the door.

"There's no friend of yours here." A male voice echoed in the hallway. "Get going."

The door slammed.

Larry stumbled farther down the hall as I debated whether to hustle him back here and knock him out, or simply run. He fell down the stairs and went head first through the lobby window, breaking it to shards. Indeed God protects drunks and little children, or maybe the raccoon coat saved him, because Larry picked himself up amid shattered glass, with a few nicks but little apparent damage. Waving that milk bottle, he climbed three stairs as if nothing had happened. The neighbor's door opened again and a voice said, "I'm calling the cops on you, Mister."

Larry reached into the raccoon coat and pulled out a dark revolver.

The neighbor slammed the door.

I scrambled into Larry's bedroom and looked under the bed, into his closets, his dresser drawers. I realized now that the gang had left all the bonds with him, that's why he was still in Saint Paul. His task was to launder the bonds. This was a typical Karpis move: find a sucker to take the big risks.

Now those bonds would link Larry to the robbery, and to me, and sink my chances of escaping. Frantic, I searched his room for the bonds. He stumbled into the bedroom as if he didn't see me, fell face down on the floor and started snoring.

Outside I heard car doors slam. I stood beside the window, lifted the chintz curtain and peeked out. As two cops approached the back stairs, I slipped into the hallway and out the front door.

CHAPTER TWENTY ONE

On Sunday, the police station was a riot of cops and reporters and even a man from Hearst Movietone News. The cops were a mix of Minneapolis blue uniforms and Saint Paul's green outfits, swirling around detectives and lawyers dressed in dark suits. In the lobby, Thomas Dahill, the new police chief, red faced and shouting, tried to calm the crowd of newsmen. I climbed the back stairway and pushed into the Bertillion room. McAmbly had set his peaked cap on the counter and was wiping his hair with a handkerchief.

"Ruin my goddamn weekend," he groused.

I slipped around to his side of the counter and patted him on the back.

"How's our little Maureen?"

McAmbly groaned like a sick animal.

"Operation," he said.

"Oh Jeez."

"Next week, right after Christmas." He gripped the counter. His face turned red as if were having a stroke. "It'll be a thousand bucks if we're lucky..." he made the Sign of the Cross over himself, "and she'll be two weeks in the hospital, crying in pain. Jesus, I can't take this goddamn stress sober."

"If you need a ride to Rochester..."

"Her aunt's going down with me."

Billy take help? No use to offer, I knew he wouldn't.

"What's happening downstairs?"

"Minneapolis wants him. We're keeping him. Battle royal

between the two chiefs."

Into the Bertillion room walked a short, dapper detective of about 40, wearing a brown striped suit and a gray fedora. He was as lean as a whippet and had blue, piercing eyes.

After one glance, he ignored me.

"Let's go with the other batch," he snapped at McAmbly.

Billy, like the catcher he once was, squatted to search behind the counter. He came up with a stack of Bertillion cards wrapped in a rubber band.

"What's he saying?" McAmbly asked.

"Oh he's sobering up now," said the dapper detective. "He's starting to squirm, the little bastard. Oh, he admits he done it all right. But we can't pry nothing out of him about the other louses."

The detective flipped through the cards as if dealing a poker hand.

"He claims he don't know anybody, see?" the detective said. "He come into the bank to help out the other mugs. He was supposed to stay outside with the tommygun but he comes inside, see? Then the squad car pulls up. He shoots the boys through the big window, glass shattering everywhere, he steps out to the sidewalk and finishes them off. Cold blood. The boys never got off a shot."

The dapper detective grimaced. "Oh no, this punk don't know nobody. He robbed the bank with four strangers. Ain't that something." He tapped the cards on the counter.

"We'll see," he said. "We'll see how rough it gets."

With that the dapper detective shut the pebbled glass door.

"Who's that?" I asked McAmbly.

"Lieutenant Tierney."

"Oh that's Tierney."

"Yeah," he said. "He's the Chief's main man now. It's Tierney and Chief Dahill trying to clean up after Big Ryan."

"So Tierney's on the square?"

McAmbly shrugged. "Who's on the square?"

"You are."

"Don't be so sure," he said.

But I was sure. I played first base for Sacred Heart when Billy was the catcher. A good catcher is the soul of any ball-club. You play ball with a catcher for two years, you know who he is.

"They have this guy nailed dead?"

"If only we had the death penalty. What's wrong with this state? I could name a dozen guys should be hung. And half of 'em wear uniforms."

"This guy's admitting to the two cops and the civilian too?"

"Actually," McAmbly said, "when they brought him in he was puking drunk. And while he was drunk he did give them a name. You might of heard this name before. Freddy Barker."

Light-headed, I leaned into the counter.

"The robbers shot up their own Lincoln over at the bank. The cop car had about a hundred bullet holes in it, but they hit the Lincoln too. The gang drove that Lincoln on three tires all the way to Como Park. They parked it and scrambled for the switch car. This wreath salesman, this guy Erickson, sees the Lincoln with a flat tire and pulls over to help. Barker shoots the guy..." McAmbly pointed a finger at his forehead "right in the head."

He shrugged his massive shoulders.

"So much for the Good Samaritan. What's wrong with you?"

"Oh, maybe I'm getting a cold."

"So you come in here and give it to me? I got a house, one kid after the other with a cold now, and it's Christmas. I don't have a tree yet."

He walked to the wall of dirty windows.

"The kids ain't getting much under the tree this year. I don't know, you work like a dog to make the extra coin, where does it go?"

"So this guy they're holding down in the dungeon, what's his name?"

"DuVol."

"He named Fred Barker and then he shut up?"

McAmbly shrugged.

"I don't know, ask Tierney. He's been down there for…" he checked his watch, "twelve hours now. I was home in bed, Christ. I coulda yanked that telephone right out of the wall."

He felt in his top tunic pocket. "You got a cigarette? No, you don't smoke 'em. Go on get out of here, Mickey, before I catch your cold."

I found myself at the counter of the Town Talk, ordering a grilled cheese sandwich. Across the room sat Crumley and the Bulldog, working over a dinner of beer, bratwurst and sauerkraut. I didn't more than glance their way. I feared that the next thing I would see would be handcuffs dangling from Crumley's meaty hand.

Coffee splashed into my cup and I looked up to see Lillian, a serious look on her face. "Look like you just lost your best friend," she said.

"No," I said. "My dogs are okay."

"Your dogs? Your dogs are your best friends?"

"I'll bet a thousand cops ordered a thousand sandwiches today."

"Seemed like a thousand. All to go. No tips."

She swiped my empty plate from the counter.

"You see this town if full of murderers and thieves," she said. "You can't walk down the street without passing a criminal. And what is our police doing about it? Eating sausage and drinking beer."

She walked away and said over her shoulder, "Dead policemen now, who's safe in this town?"

I shut myself into the phone booth and called the Chancery. Father Mack, reluctant, said he might have a few minutes after his

Sunday dinner with the Archbishop. I needed a distraction, but bypassed the Royal, since the races at Hialeah and Fairgrounds were about done for the day. I drove home over icy streets, fed the dogs, and sat staring out the windows at the dullness of an early winter evening.

"Might have to make a break for it, dogs," I said. "Havana."

Two hours later when I rang the Chancery doorbell Father Mack answered and led me into the library. We sat before a dying fire in a great stone fireplace, a wooden cross embedded in its stone. Father Mack offered port, which I detest, but I took a social sip anyway.

"I have a favor to ask," I said.

He sighed. "Does it ever end?"

From inside my suit-coat pocket I produced a small manila envelope.

"Billy McAmbly. His daughter is about to have an operation down at Mayo."

"Aye."

I set the envelope on a lamp table near the great globe.

"I'd like to help him out, Father, but I can't give it directly. It's twelve hundred dollars. He's got his pride. He must never know where it came from."

"Quite generous."

"He's a good Catholic, father."

The priest cleared his throat. "And as I understand it, Michael, you haven't worked in years. So I can't help but wonder, what is the source of this money?"

"Pardon?"

He spread his big hands.

"You know who I am, Father."

"It's hardly the question."

I shifted in my chair and stared at him.

"Father, excuse me, but haven't you built Saint Patrick's Pence with the help of Otto Alt?"

"Aye."

"And, correct me if I'm wrong, but isn't the source of the Alt fortune the brewing of an illegal product? So how the hell, excuse me, but why all of a sudden do you get pious on me?"

I expected an angry response, but he only shook his head. "Beer is a harmless vice."

"Why don't you just come out and say whatever's on your mind, Father. Because that's not the Irish way, is it? The Irish way is the snide remark, the dark hint, the cutting joke. Go ahead. Tell me why you refuse this simple favor to help a sick child."

"Michael, I will not be gangland's errand boy."

"Well, as I see it, Papa Alt owns a mansion but I rent an apartment, and that's the difference. His money buys him a ticket to crook's Heaven while we commoners go to Hell."

Father Mack stood, six foot six, massive in all black clothing, and stared into the fire.

"The unfortunate priest hears a lot," he said. "You must realize, Michael, that the priest hears a great deal. And because of the Seal, he can reveal not a word of it. A priest with big ears knows more than he wants to know."

I felt my hands and feet go cold.

"Father," I said, "this money comes from my Aunt Doris. I swear before God. She's very fond of Billy and she wants to help him out."

Father Mack and I stared at each other. His look began as a flare of Celtic rage. But I refused to look away and it faded to resignation.

"Don't kid yourself, Father," I said. "People have been hurt, and worse, in pursuit of Papa Alt's fortune."

I handed him the envelope and in mutual silence, let myself out. A lie told to help a sick child was better than any truth, I told myself.

I slunk along in the shadows of the Avenue of Wealthy Criminals. Known to upright citizens as Summit Avenue, this neighborhood housed in titanic architecture the glorified thieves whose land grabs had built the railroads, cleared the forests, ripped iron ore out of the soil, men who rousted the Indian tribes, then conspired to cheat the farmers of the fair value of their wheat and corn. The smell of money was wood smoke, all those oak logs burning in stone fire places, forests going up in smoke one tree at a time. No dirty coal for these people.

Below Summit Avenue is the streetcar tunnel, and a narrow icy stairway leads past my apartment to the Seven Corners. I was half way down the stairway when I saw, in the night-shadow of the tunnel, a flicker of light. I realized right away it had been a cigarette lighter, glowing inside a car. I stopped, one bare hand on the cold steel railing. I could hear the car's rough idle and smell its exhaust. The car was parked facing my apartment, its back end pointed uphill at me. Staying in the shadows, I advanced on it. I stood studying it as a streetcar clanged out of the tunnel, its headlights illuminating Swede Fanlund's blue Pontiac.

The windows were frosty but I could see two dark figures in there.

I wondered who had tipped off Swede and Rico. The way they were parked told me they expected to see me walk up from Seven Corners. Had someone in the Town Talk put me on the spot? Lillian? Crumley? Bulldog? Some sluggard cop loyal to Big Ryan? Maybe one of Harry's Green Lantern deadbeats?

By the way they were parked, it seemed they were waiting for me to take my usual route home.

I briefly thought they were stalking Janie, but now that she was unemployed and no threat to the gangsters, that seemed unlikely. Still, I couldn't leave Janie at home with Swede and Rico hovering like vultures.

And she didn't have a phone. Her basement apartment had only one entrance, down a concrete stairwell, well-lit by the glow of the lobby's lights. Any other apartment in the building, I could have gotten to by sneaking into the lobby by the back door. I thought of phoning a neighbor, but didn't want to involve Little Elmer, Mrs. Strutz or the Reardons. I did the only thing I could think of doing. I walked up the stairway and around the block. I passed through the alley behind my building, and reappeared at the edge of the parking lot, just a few shadowy steps from my Essex.

I slipped into the car. In its rearview mirror I could see the headlights of Swede's Pontiac flicker on. My Essex could outrun him. But I had another plan.

I forced myself to drive along Summit at normal speed, until I reached the circular driveway of the Commodore. The bold letters of its name burned in white lights.

The lights of safety.

The Commodore was a Harry protected joint. There'd be no gangland murders on its property.

Swede's Pontiac passed the hotel's circular driveway without a pause. I saw Rico's face glaring through the frosty passenger window. I was half relieved to know they were not stalking Janie, and half terrified that they had orders to eliminate me.

Certainly not tonight, and not at the Commodore. Maybe they were trying to figure out my patterns. Maybe my recent acquisition of a car had put a kink in their plans. I could only speculate on who had hired them, most likely Barker and Karpis, seeking to silence anybody with dangerous knowledge.

The Commodore valet took my car and I pushed, out of breath, into a lobby of crystal, marble elegance, soft lighting, a realm of safety, gentility and calm. I crossed the checkered tiles of the lobby, past a Christmas tree twelve feet tall. I signed in at the massive oak desk. A tall, hawkish clerk expressed surprise that I had no bags. I said they were probably headed for Seattle right now, as the railroad had lost them. I paid $6 upfront for a night's stay.

My room on the fifth floor was all blond wood and smelled of Christmas wreath. I phoned for Reilly at the Lantern. Bess said she'd not seen him or Harry all day. At the Reilly home, his wife Babe said: "Don't know where he is, never tells me, goodbye, whoever you are."

I called Little Elmer and asked him to feed and walk the dogs, and to use the Third Street entrance.

"Do not, Elmer please," I said, "take them into the back lot. Very important, okay? Front door only, and stay in plain sight of the road."

I wasn't afraid for Elmer. Not even Swede would harm a polio-crippled child. But he was perfectly capable of hurting or kidnapping my dogs.

I pulled out my pipe and packed it for a smoke. I looked out at the mansions and the smoking chimneys and into the great river valley, the city lights twinkling in the crisp winter air.

I smoked. As I watched the smoke rise and drift at the window, I realized only two men might help me, Jack Peifer or Harry Sawyer.

But both were on the short list of men who might have hired Swede and Rico.

I turned on the big console radio. Cab Calloway was belting them out in Chicago. The music didn't do a thing for me except jangle my nerves. I began to fight off the chill, sick notion that my time was up and nobody could help me. I called my sister Kelly.

She was listening, as I was, to Minnie the Moocher. There was talk of more radio stations someday, but for now, we were stuck with only two.

"I'm listening to the radio," she shouted, as if I couldn't tell. I had Calloway in both ears. I turned my radio down.

"I'll call back," I said.

"No don't be silly," she said. "You're coming over for Christmas, right?"

"If anything happens to me, you'll take care of Snowflake and Hula Girl, right?"

"Michael, what are you talking about?"

"Just thinking," I said.

"Oh, you're drinking again."

"Thinking, not drinking," I said.

"Are you sick? Because you didn't look good last time I saw you."

"I'm fine," I said. "It's just you know, end of the year, you start thinking of things."

"I get the Christmas blues too," she said.

"I'll feel better if you promise about the dogs."

"I promise about the dogs."

"See you for Christmas dinner," I said, and kissed the phone.

"Jeesh," she said.

When I hung up I felt dead lonesome. Gout or no gout, I needed a drink. I limped into the hallway, locked my room, rang for the elevator. The girl operator, raven-haired and wearing a crisp gray uniform, had a tiny Christmas tree set on her stool, along with a Santa Claus piggy bank for tips.

"How late does the bar stay open?" I asked.

"The Commodore does not have a bar, sir," she said with a wry smile. "The sale of alcohol is illegal, you know."

I dropped a quarter into Santa's head.

"Around behind the desk, sir, you'll find a locked door, where a sign says Management Only. Knock exactly four times. And Merry Christmas, sir."

I knocked four times and was admitted by a gangly elderly Colored man in hotel uniform, complete with brass buttons and epaulets. Up here on Summit Hill, he was just another Commodore flunky. But down on Seven Corners he was Cliff the Griff, and only out-of-towners were fool enough to shoot dice with him. I palmed him a buck and whispered: "Cliff, you never saw me."

Cliff let me into a smoky, dim-lit barroom of sleek furniture, aerodynamic, futuristic in style. I stood at the darkest end of the bar and ordered Canadian Club and ginger from a brunette barmaid dressed in pants and crisp uniform shirt.

I had that drink to my lips when I spotted her across the bar. She met my gaze and her face glowed with recognition.

I was staring into the gray-green eyes of Ma Barker.

CHAPTER TWENTY TWO

Ma Barker whispered to the woman slouched on the stool next to her. That woman was a tall, boozy-looking blonde whose 30 years on this planet had been a rough go. She had long hair, ending in a bleached flip, and topped with a red felt hat. Bright lipstick highlighted a long, pale, powdered face. She smoked an unfiltered cigarette, held in slender fingers that ended in long red nails. She kept dabbing that cigarette at a glass ashtray.

I found her appealing.

With Ma Barker's lips at her ears, this woman looked across the smoky bar at me.

She slipped off the barstool and walked around the circular bar, and I realized she was six feet tall. She rested a hand on the sleeve of my suit-coat and said, "Mrs. Jones requests the pleasure of your company."

"Mrs. Jones?" I said.

She looked at me with laughing blue eyes.

I said: "And you, I take it, are Miss Jones, her gorgeous daughter?"

"What if I am?"

"Well it would be my privilege to buy you a drink."

"Well now," she said. "A gentleman."

I followed her around the circle.

Ma Barker sat before a slug of dark liquid congealing in a low glass, an open Gideon's Bible before her on the bar. She was a nutty old lady dressed like a queen. Her hair had been sculpted with a permanent and tinted a hideous red-orange. She wore a cashmere jacket over a black dress, and was throttled by a sparkling diamond necklace.

"We meet again," I said to Ma, and shook her tiny hand. "I'm Patrick Powell."

"Oh I remember," croaked Ma.

"Well I should buy you a drink."

Ma pushed her squat glass toward the barmaid.

"Both of you," I said, and looked at the blonde.

"I have a pain no booze can touch," said the blonde, "but what the hell." She drained a fluted glass and shouted to the barmaid: "Whiskey sour."

The blonde glared at me. "How do you two know each other, or should I ask?"

"Mister Powell was in business with Arthur," said Ma.

"Oh, with Arthur," said the blonde. "Arthur. Well." She held up her empty glass in a toast. "Here's to Arthur. Wherever the hell he went off to."

Ma did not raise her glass.

"Another pint of blood?" asked the bartendress.

Ma nodded.

"What the heck is a pint of blood?" I asked.

"Vodka drowned in cherry syrup, splash of seltzer," answered the blonde. She stuck out her tongue in disgust.

"I'm Sylvia," she said and I shook her bony hand, bejeweled with a sapphire ring. "Kind of a lousy Christmas, ain't it? Stuck here so far from home."

"Where's home?"

"Wherever it's warmer. They need igloos in this town. You're not local, are you? If you were, you wouldn't be staying in this overpriced flop house."

"Chicago," I muttered.

Ma wobbled off the stool and tottered toward the restroom.

"Will you be okay, Mother?" called Sylvia.

She took the silence for a yes.

"Poor old lady can't hold her water, never mind her booze," Sylvia said. She pulled out a long Pall Mall. "Shoot me before I get to that age, will you?"

I lit her cigarette with a match, and returned the matchbook to the bar. It said GREEN LANTERN in gold script on a white background, with a depiction of a bubbly cocktail glass. Sylvia's gaze fixed on that matchbook a moment, and then reappraised me.

"What's your game, slugger?"

"Thoroughbred horses," I said.

"Oh, one of those."

"What's yours?"

She blew smoke. "Right now? Baby sitter. And I'm getting out of this racket before it becomes ass wiper. That's where I draw the line. Where do you draw the line, Patrick Powell?"

"I'm not sure what you mean."

She tapped ashes into a cut-glass ashtray imprinted, at bottom, with the gold word: COMMODORE.

"You know who this old dame is, don't kid me," said Sylvia. "Her boys lit out for the territory. Abandoned her. I'm the designated nurse, baby sitter and mother confessor. And let me tell you, I'm sick of the old bat already."

She blew smoke. "They don't want her around, and it's easy to see why."

"You wouldn't happen to know," I said, and rattled the ice in my cocktail. "Ah. Better not ask."

"You're buying. Ask."

"I was hoping to get in touch with Little Shorty."

"Who?"

"Now who's playing games?"

She put her hand on my knee, let it linger, withdrew it.

"I hear good things about Tulsa," she said. "Although they say it's a very hot town. They say you could work up a real sweat in that town."

The barmaid delivered drinks, and Sylvia raised her whiskey sour toward me.

"To more gentlemen, and fewer bums," she said.

We drank.

Sylvia looked over the shoulders of her padded jacket and said, in a husky whisper: "You know there's the brother Doc, right? Doing life at McAlester, right? Well, there's a lawyer in Tulsa can spring him for a fee."

She tapped ashes off the tip of her cigarette.

"Oh yeah," she said. "Oklahoma prisons leak like an old stove. Look, I'm not going to ask about your business, it obviously ain't horses, but I am going to give you a piece of life-saving advice. Don't get involved with the sons of this old lady. She ain't harmless and neither are they. And Doc, he's the worst of the brothers. You don't want to know him, believe me."

She swirled her drink. "There, if you take my advice, stranger, I've paid you back for this drink ten times over."

We drank in silence awhile. I felt the alcohol untangle my frazzled nerves. "We Three Kings of Orient Are" began playing over the bar's loudspeakers. An unholy thought occurred to me. The three kings all right. The three kings of Saint Paul: Harry, Jack and Big Ryan.

Hearing a commotion behind us, we turned to see Ma Barker bump into a wooden chair, and grab it to steady herself. Sylvia rolled her eyes and strode over to help. I got there a step later. One of us holding each of Ma's arms, we guided her back to the bar stool.

"My heart's giving way," complained Ma, hand to her chest.

"Mother," said Sylvia, "you're just anxious."

"I almost fell into the toilet," Ma said.

"Sit, Mother," said Sylvia, "and have another drink."

Ma settled her round rump on the barstool, and clutched her dark red drink in trembling hands. Hunched over it she muttered: "Arthur, my Arthur, he was a no good rascal."

Underneath the bar, Sylvia flirted, touching leg to leg.

Ma looked at me.

"You knew my Arthur," she said to me. "What kind of man runs out on a woman like that? A coward."

Sylvia sucked in a deep breath like it was a prayer for patience.

I didn't know what to make of Ma's proclamation. Arthur Dunlop had been murdered on order of Ma's son Fred. Had Fred fooled his mother, telling her that Arthur had run out on her? Or did Ma know the truth, and was covering up for her son? It was hard to say, but the stories that followed the Barkers here from Oklahoma painted a picture of a mother who would do or say anything to protect her sons.

Ma licked her forefinger and began paging through the Bible. Sylvia crushed the lipstick-stained butt of her Pall Mall. The Christmas music came to its scratchy end and left a dead silence, broken only by the barmaid stacking glasses.

"She just loves the Old Testament," Sylvia said to me. Then she admonished Ma: "It's the Jewish part of the Bible, Mother. Jewish!"

Ma cleared her throat and read out loud:

"Then I will teach transgressors your ways,
  so that sinners will turn back to you.
Deliver me from the guilt of bloodshed, O God,
  you who are God my Savior."

Ma sniffled, and wiped at a tear. "Sinners will turn back to you, see? God promised that right here in the Bible. My Freddy," Ma sniffed. "Four boys raised Christian, and all of them lost to the

Lord. Freddy's the only hope left."

Sylvia said: "Kate, he doesn't know your boys."

"He knows Freddy. He damn sight knows Freddy. Don't you know Freddy, Mister Powell?"

"I believe I've met him," I said.

"There," said Ma. "He knows Freddy. Herman's been gone five years now. My Doc and my Lloyd, oh my sweet Savior, they might as well have locked up my heart as put those boys in prison."

"I'd better get her to bed," muttered Sylvia.

"Because my insides are all tore up like I'd swallered razor blades," said Ma. "That's what it feels like inside me."

Sylvia kicked at my ankles.

"The boys was brought up poor," Ma said, "but they was brought up righteous and Bible believing. It's the law that's crooked."

"We honestly have to get going," said Sylvia, and collected her red purse, dropped her pack of Pall Malls in, drained her whiskey sour, leaving cherry and orange slice in the glass.

"Mother, you are getting loud," Sylvia whispered. "Finish your drink and let's go."

"My Bible," said Ma.

"Bring along your book."

Ma wagged a finger in my face. "Don't you say nothing bad about my Herman. It was the crooked cops that shot that boy, tore his face up so bad we couldn't have no proper viewing."

Sylvia raised her eyebrows. "Three vodkas," she muttered in my ear. Then to Ma she said, "You're a lightweight drinker, Mother."

"Mother's love," said Ma. "It's a curse, that's all it is. If you want to have your heart broke, Mister Powell, just raise yourself up some children. My boys has killed me twenty times over."

Ma was shaking as Sylvia, head and shoulders taller, led her toward the arched lobby. Together they looked comic, like a celery stalk and a potato.

The celery stalk doubled back to me.

"What's your room number?"

"Five oh six," I said.

"Expect a visitor," she said.

I rode the elevator up to my room. The elevator girl had gone off duty and was replaced by the cranky night clerk, reluctant to split duties between desk and lift. I tipped him a buck to send up a bottle, and another buck to seal his lips. Despite the tip, he grumped at me.

"Merry Christmas," I said.

I sat in my room, smoked my pipe and waited. There was a heavyweight bout going on in my mind. In one corner, in the light trunks, was the fear that I would soon be in prison. In the other corner, in the dark trunks, was the memory of that horrible minute when Larry and Verne had executed those wounded, helpless cops. Those lumbering heavyweights of my mind came together in a sweaty clinch and kidney punched each other.

The booze helped. I was in a boozy amnesia when a discreet tap sounded at the door. I let Sylvia in. It had been a while since I'd been in a hotel room with a female stranger.

"We're out of whiskey sour," I said.

"Whiskey anything will do."

Sylvia brushed back her hair. She had left her red beret and shoulder-padded jacket behind, and was now in frilly blouse, red skirt, elastic stockings and low heels.

"This was exactly what I've been trying to avoid," said Sylvia. "Mother getting lit up and running her mouth. She's asleep now. God knows if she ever sleeps for more than two hours at a stretch. I've had her a week and I'm worn out already."

She accepted the cocktail I'd mixed her and we stared for a moment at the city lights.

"My real name is Michael," I said.

"I understand," she said with a laugh. "My real name is Sylvia. My mother gave it to me, and I've used it ever since."

We clinked glasses.

"Tree Top, that's what they called me in high school. Because I was almost this tall in sixth grade. My whole life I've tended to slouch. You don't mind a taller woman, do you Michael? You're not intimidated, I hope."

"Enchanted," I said.

"Oh, well, mister flattery."

I embraced her for a long kiss. It did not put her in a romantic mood.

"Murdering sons of bitches," she said. "The whole bunch of them. I can't wait to get away from them."

She lay on her back on the bedspread, and casually unbuttoned her blouse.

"See they owe me, but they're shrewd. They know if they pay me in full, they'll never see me again. Freddy. He's the paymaster. He's the shrewd one."

She wiggled out of her blouse, kicked off her shoes, sipped her drink and set it on the side table.

"Don't worry, I'm a widow."

"Wasn't worried," I said, and worked out of my sport jacket and tie.

"You look worried. Somebody dogging you? You owe somebody on a bad bet?"

I crawled into bed with her, shedding clothes. She rolled over onto her stomach and I unhooked her bra and gave her a shoulder massage.

"Uh," she said. "How did I get involved with this mob?"

"I ask myself the same question."

"I went to a good Catholic school."

"So did I."

"Don't stop, Michael ,please."

I resumed my massage, dug my hands deeper into her shoulder muscles. Her pale skin had blackheads here and there and her bones were thin and light.

"Did you take rubdown lessons?"

"Not really."

I began to unbutton her skirt but she said: "Oh you can't stop now. It's going to take an hour to massage that old bitch out of my flesh and bones."

"Okay," I said, and resumed the back rub.

"I'm an easy lay," she said. "Just no rough stuff, okay?"

"Okay."

"Because I've had it with tough guys."

"Okay," I said.

"Be nice to me, Michael whatever your real name is."

"That will be easy," I said.

I rubbed her back for a while, and then realized that her silence had become sleep.

CHAPTER TWENTY THREE

"Hey, Shaky," said Reilly.

"What did you call me?"

"Shaky, that's what everybody calls you now."

"Since when?" I demanded.

"What can I do for you, Powers?"

"I've got to get square with Harry."

"He's laying low these days."

I stepped aside so Pat could sell a $2 ticket for a race at Agua Caliente.

"Best thing that ever happened to Tijuana," Pat said, as the player walked off with his ticket. "Prohibition. I don't know what them lazy Mexicans are going to do with themselfs when California goes wet."

The ticker tape chattered, spewing out prices for win, place and show. The Royal's janitor had nailed up a couple of trashy Christmas wreaths at either side of the big board. Glittering ornaments hung from the ceiling by ribbons. But nothing could change the nature of the place: cigar smoke, brief hope, and permanent despair. Reilly's contribution to the décor was a coffee can wrapped in Santa Claus paper to hold his tips.

"He's still at the Jung," Reilly admitted.

"Oh."

"Christmas gets him down. He's a Jew, you know. But don't get me wrong, not all of 'em are bad, there's good Jews. And Harry is one of the better kind. Give you the shirt off his back and his belt and tie too."

"Look, Pat, I've got a serious problem."

"So I heard."

"Harry helped me last time."

"He's inter-communication."

"He's what?"

"What do you call. He don't want to hear from nobody, especially people."

I put my hands in my trouser pockets and stared at the big chalk board. Hialeah. Could I scrape out a reprehensible living selling tout sheets to rubes at Hialeah? No, sooner or later some Saint Paul gangster would spot me in Florida.

I turned for the door.

"What, no bet?" shouted Pat. "I make a living here."

"Give me the Form," I said.

I looked over the next day's races at New Orleans Fairgrounds.

"I got a guy in New Orleans," Pat said. "Friend of Filben's, actually."

"What's he say."

"Inside rail."

"All right," I said. I looked over the first two races, at the horses with inside posts. I never bet on a horse that won its last race. Usually the winning horse has gone all out to get to the wire, and hasn't much left for its next race. So I picked losers with inside posts.

"Write me the daily double," I said, and forked over ten bucks.

"Nine bucks for the ticket, one for you. Give me the 2,3,4 over the 1,2,5."

"Good luck," said Pat, and punched the numbers into his ticket machine.

"I'll need it," I said. "That's my last tenner."

I drove my Essex from the Royal Cigar Store to the alley behind Tom Filben's radio shop. Naturally, he wasn't there. I caught up with him around the corner, in the lobby of the Saint Francis Hotel, where he was practically a resident. He was lounging in a stuffed chair near a sunny window, between potted ferns, reading a copy of Sunset magazine. The cover was a painting depicting the mountains of the West, and a cowboy on a horse.

"The man I needed to see," I said.

"California," he said, closing the magazine.

"What about it?" I asked.

"Mountains and ocean," he said.

"No Cuba? I thought you were the man for Cuba?"

"Things are getting rough on that fabled isle. Or don't you read the papers?"

"Tommy," I said, lowering my voice. "I need some blanks."

"What exactly are we talking about?"

"Courthouse, you know."

He whistled. "Those are ten dollars."

"Put it on my tab. I'll be in debt to you the rest of my life, so what the hell."

"Ten per sheet."

"Yeah, okay."

"Now?" he said. "I'm not dressed for this weather."

"It's around the damn corner, Tom."

He walked me back to his shop, where, in return for an IOU, he produced a blank Ramsey County Court document, which I filled in on a typewriter. I also borrowed from him a genuine Ramsey County Sheriff's badge.

From Tommy's shop, I drove to the Jung Sanitarium in the woods of Wisconsin. I had heartburn so bad I had to pull off in the town of Prescott and buy a blue bottle of Phillips Milk of Magnesia. I drank it while driving up the knoll where the great brick building commanded the countryside like a castle. Outside these iron gates is where I turned Pop Anderson, aka Arthur Dunlop, over to the killers Swede and Rico. And now maybe God or the Devil was putting me in the sights of those same vicious thugs. Maybe I deserved it. Maybe Swede was right, and we all get what we deserve in the end.

I parked the Essex, mounted the broad wood stairs and rang the bell.

I was wrapped up against the frost with a heavy topcoat, hat, scarf and gloves, but I shivered waiting at the glass door. A thickset, white-haired nurse appeared.

I held up the folded document

SUMMONS

PROCEEDINGS OF THE GRAND JURY

COUNTY OF RAMSEY

STATE OF MINNESOTA

"What's that?" she said. "I don't have my spectacles."

"It's a Grand Jury summons. For one of your patients. Harry Sawyer."

She looked me over.

"Our patients are not to be disturbed, sir."

She tried to close the door but my foot got in the way.

"This is a locked facility, sir."

I flashed the badge.

"I'm sorry," she said.

"No, I'm sorry, nurse. Step aside for the law!"

I shouldered in. The nurse looked behind her for help. A hallway lined with potted palms was empty. An old lady in bathrobe was the only occupant of the sun room.

"I drove out to serve this summons and I'm going to serve it. If you interfere I'll place you under arrest."

I hung the deputy's star, on a chain, around my neck and

paraded down the main hallway, looking into rooms. The nurse behind me scrambled for help. I rounded the corner into a kitchen of white tiles, then back out. I mounted a narrow dark stairway and prowled the second floor. Down the corridor, I saw Harry sitting in a sun porch, where a wood stove provided warmth that the December sun could not.

"Harry," I said.

He was napping.

"Harry," I shook his shoulder.

"Powers! What the fuck are you doing here?"

Footsteps sounded in the hallway and the white-haired nurse appeared, behind her a lanky male orderly dressed in white, and a short, square woman in a dark dress.

"This is a private facility sir," said the nurse, "and I'll have you removed, deputy or no deputy."

Harry held up a hand for peace.

"I know this bum," he said.

I curled my lips at the nurse like a dog giving warning. She looked from me to Harry, from Harry to me.

"I'll get Doctor Jung," she said.

"Don't bother," said Harry. "This man is just leaving."

I waited for the nurse, orderly and business lady to consult and retreat.

"If you need us, Mr. Sanders, ring the bell," the nurse said.

When the gaggle of them moved down the hall, I said: "Sanders, eh?"

"How did you find me?" Harry asked.

"I guessed."

"Did you bring booze?"

I shook my head.

"Then what the fuck good are you?"

"Harry, I need your services."

"You're a deputy now?"

I lifted the badge from around my neck and dropped it into my topcoat pocket.

"Filben," I said. "Sends his greetings."

"He owes me more than greetings."

Harry lifted his ass off the rattan seat and farted.

He barked: "Who sent you and what for?"

"I sent myself. Swede and Rico are right on top of me."

"Who?"

"Swede ... and ... Rico."

"I don't know those bums."

This was the point at which you were supposed to hand Harry fifty bucks.

"Harry, don't run that game on me," I said.

Around his bare swollen feet were pages of Twin Cities newspapers. He rolled them up, added them to the blazing wood fire, stirred it with a poker.

"They ain't on my payroll," Harry said. "There, is that enough for you?"

"I need protection."

"There's a war, Powers. Me against a turkey farmer named Peifer. Now, I hear those torpedoes work for the turkey man. They don't like me, I don't like them, and so I can't help you no more. Once I could do it, but things have gotten too hot. It's like a civil war out there. What do you think I'm doing in this dump? You've gotta take care of yourself now."

"No price?"

"It's a war. Soldiers gonna die."

"For Christ's sake, Harry." I sat across from him. The stove's heat got to me and I flung open my topcoat.

"You staying sober?" I asked.

"Here and there. I've got to say, Powers, I don't like it. If you can find me, so can the G-men."

"I've got sources they don't have."

"I'm going to wring that little prick's neck."

"It wasn't Reilly," I lied. "Pat would take a bullet before he'd give you up, Harry. He adores you like he was your natural born son."

Harry shot me a skeptical look. He sputtered and said, "They can't prosecute a sick man. It's in the Constitution."

"Harry, you would tell me, wouldn't you, if Barker and Karpis were on my neck?"

"Who?"

"Harry it's life and death here."

"The names don't make sense to me."

"Ray and Little Shorty."

Harry shook his head. "Powers, nobody from my side of town is after your ass. Maybe Peifer's got it in for you, I don't know. Take a vacation. I hear Hot Springs is nice this time of year."

On the icy drive back to Minnesota, I turned it all around in my head. Odds were 6-to-5 Harry was lying. But maybe, just maybe, I was nobody to the Barker-Karpis gang, only another guy on the margin, like Larry DuVol, expected to take their cut, go away and shut up. Maybe they didn't care if I lived or died.

The other possibility was Jack Peifer. If Jack found out I had marked for the Barker gang, that put me in Harry's camp, a double-crosser from Jack's point of view. A few months ago he had sent me to spy on Harry and now I was marking for Harry's gang.

If Jack had put Sadie and Rose on the spot, he'd have no qualms about ordering his thugs to leave my corpse in a ditch.

Sure, Rico had it in for me since I'd brass-knuckled him, but no hit man would target a guy under protection, not without getting an okay from Jack or Harry. So if it wasn't Harry I'd angered, it had to be Jack.

I drove to the East Side of Saint Paul, turned at the Minnesota Mining complex, and parked near my sister Kelly's house. Up and down the street, Rico's house was the only one without Christmas decorations. It was a dark, gray bungalow, snow on the roof, a long narrow driveway leading to a garage. My Essex purred, I kept it running for the heat. The more I ran it through my mind the more it seemed logical that Rico and Swede were under orders from Jack. My betrayal, my work for Harry's gang, meant I deserved to die, as Jack saw it. That was why, I figured, Sam refused to take my phone calls. I switched the odds. I made it 2 to 1 that my nemesis was Jack Peifer.

I sat watching Rico's house for a long time, but learned nothing. I shut off the Essex. Patting my coat to reassure myself I had both pistols, I crossed the street to my sister's house.

Kelly and Gary were paying off this cramped bungalow, which had a second story, with peaked, narrow bedrooms for their daughters. The girls were off at school, and Gary was out in his truck delivering coal, and my sister was home alone.

Kelly made coffee. I had recruited her into the French Press army, and her brew was thick and strong.

"How are you getting along for money?"

"I'm on a lucky streak," I lied.

"You sure can pick the horses," she said. "Amazing."

"Sometimes," I said. "Have you seen much of your neighbor, the little Italian?"

"Ralph? He's never home since his wife died. I think he's going to sell the house."

"What makes you say that?"

"Hunch," she said and slurped coffee. "He doesn't want to be in the house where she died." She shuddered. "Creepy. Intruder. Poor thing. Home invasion. Strangled in the basement. The laundry room. I can't go do laundry without thinking of it."

"Yeah, I wonder who investigated that."

"What do you mean?"

"Cops came to your door, didn't they?"

"The girls were home when the cops knocked, not me." She gave me the wise-woman eye. "You're suspicious."

I shrugged.

"So is Gary," she said. "Gary says Ralph killed her. And Gary is not prejudiced, he's half Italian."

"What does that mean?"

"Well, you know what people say about Italians. Al Capone. That kind of Italian."

She lit half a Viceroy with a kitchen match.

"He never comes home," she said.

"Who, Ralph or your husband?"

"Neither one of them," Kelly said.

On an earthen berm behind her house was a rarely used railroad track. It once led to a sawmill, but the mill went broke. I left Kelly and walked the rails one, two, three houses and stared down the bank into Rico's back yard. His wife had put a bird-feeder fountain in that tiny yard, a fountain holding an inch of snow now. Feeling again for those pistols, I worked my way down the hill. There was no way to cover the snow tracks I made. But I no longer cared. A confrontation was coming between me and Rico. I could not avoid it, although Shaky Powers, the coward inside me, wanted to. Sometimes all you need to conquer the inner coward is that first brave move. I rattled the side door of Rico's garage and opened it. No need to break, just enter. The garage was dark and cold, and spacious, without the car.

It was just possible that Rico kept weapons in his garage. If not, a search of his house was next. If I could nab his tommygun, that would cut down his firepower. Even for a criminal, tommyguns weren't easy to replace.

I stumbled around and, lighting matches, discovered a kerosene lamp and lit it. Its puny flame revealed a rusty scythe. Cans of motor oil. A cardboard box of rags. Two spare tires and a beat-up wire rim. A cob-webbed galvanized wash tub set on its side. Then I came across something I did not recognize. On a narrow shelf, near the bottom, sat a glass beaker with a glass stopper. The liquid in it seemed pale yellow.

Etched into the bottle were the words:

CON
NITRIC
ACID
HNO_3

I took a long look without touching the bottle, then killed the lamp's flame.

CHAPTER TWENTY FOUR

"They have the wrong guys," I told Janie.

"Who has the wrong guys?"

"You reporters."

"I'm currently unemployed, so I don't count as a reporter, do I, Powers?" She sipped coffee at my kitchen table, one hand petting Snowflake. *Margaret.* That was my wife's baptized name, although you used it at your peril. She looked nothing like Janie but she used to pet Snowflake just like that. Snowflake, he was always a sucker for women.

"In the bank robbery," I said. "They arrested the wrong guys."

"Who arrested the wrong guys?"

"Don't be difficult, Janie. The Minneapolis cops arrested the wrong guys and the reporters swallowed it whole."

"I can't help that."

"And I ... it's between you and me, right? We were both down on the dock that day, we both saw them take the burned corpses out of the car, and neither one of us can seem to forget it so ... do you want to know or don't you?"

"Spill."

"I was poking around in the garage of a certain Saint Paul thug. And I came across a bottle of nitric acid."

She stared over the rim of a white coffee cup.

"The guy is a professional assassin," I said.

"And you were in his garage."

"He wasn't home. Nitric acid. Those words, etched right into the bottle. Of course it's not proof of anything."

"Where does this thug live?"

"Saint Paul."

"No, I mean where exactly?"

"The East Side, but ..."

She stood up. "Take me to him. I want to lay eyes on him."

"Not a chance."

"I just want to see."

"Don't think you're going to write this up in the detective mags."

"Who the hell has nitric acid in their garage?"

"I just wanted you to know. That's all. You've been on this case for what, nine months now..."

She put her head in her hands, a sour, defeated look on her face.

"Nine months," she said.

"Some cases never get solved, Janie. Hell, in Saint Paul, most cases never get solved. You've got no witnesses and one lousy piece of circumstantial evidence."

"Nine months," she said. She walked to the Cathedral windows, braced herself. The great green-copper dome was spot-lit against the winter sky. She wore a white blouse and a long gray skirt that reached her ankles. Snowflake rubbed against her skirt. Hula Girl trotted past them both on her way to the water bowl.

"Michael," she said, "I've got problems more important than the Burned Ladies right now."

"Yeah, I know, like finding a job."

"Worse than that," she said.

"Okay," I said and reached for the French press. "Your lease is up," I said, "and you don't know whether to renew. I'm in the same boat."

"No you're not," she said. "Not in the same boat." Her back

turned on me, she muttered: "I'm pregnant."

That word took awhile to circle my brain before it knocked rudely and entered.

"I see," I said. I couldn't seem to remember why I had a coffee pot in my hand. "I don't really know what to say."

"Don't say anything," she said into the windows. I could see her reflection, crowned with all that red hair.

"The father..." I began.

She whirled on me. "I said don't say anything. Don't you listen?"

My brain finally made a connection.

"Oh," I said.

"I'm in a fix," she said.

She walked to the city view windows, barefoot over the Persian rug Myrtle had stolen especially for me. Snowflake trailed her and hopped up on the viewing platform, engaged her with his eyes, mouth open, tongue and nose sampling the air.

I walked up behind Janie, but not too close, sat on the couch, and toyed with my Blue Nile pipe.

"I shouldn't ask," I said.

"Then don't," she said.

"But marriage is out of the question?"

She shook her head.

I asked: "It's not out of the question?"

"Powers, please, you're the only one who can help me."

She flopped onto the viewing platform beside Snowflake, who stretched out into her lap.

"Oh, Snowflake," she said, "your friend Janie's been a fool."

Hula Girl hopped onto the couch next to me.

"I can't," Janie said, her eyes reddening, "I just can't."

"I see," I said. "Janie, have you been to the doctor?"

"Of course I've been to the doctor."

"Okay, well," I said. "You don't want to have this baby, is that what you're saying?"

She rushed past me and clomped down the stairs. I gathered her boots from the hallway and eased down four flights. I walked out of the lobby into shuddering cold, then knocked at her basement door. I held up the boots at her window. She opened the door only a crack.

"It's a mess in here," she said, sniffling.

I handed in the boots.

"Thank you," she said. "Go away, you'll freeze."

She shut me out.

I climbed up to my apartment, worked into my overcoat, dropped the revolver into one pocket and the automatic into the other, and led the dogs down. They scampered around the snowy parking lot. I lit my pipe and stood under the winter-bare elm and watched the dogs, and watched Janie's apartment, and watched the shadows for Swede and Rico. One dull steady light glowed in Janie's place, and once I saw her shadow at the barred windows. Just as I finished smoking my pipe, Janie emerged, coatless, hugging herself, and crossed the snowy lot.

"Do you know somebody?" she asked. "Somebody who can help me?"

I embraced her.

"Oh, don't hug me Powers. I don't feel lovable right now."

The next day, Janie took a taxi to Union Station, heading for Wisconsin and a family Christmas, promising to return in a few days.

"I love my family, but I can't stand them," she said. "You will help me, right Powers?"

When she left, I called Reilly and asked if he knew a doctor who was a right guy.

"Hey, I got seventy bucks for you," he said.

"What?"

"Your horses came in, the double. Seventy two fifty, minus the tip is seventy even."

"I'll be right down," I said.

At the Royal, Pat paid me in ones and fives, and gave me the name Dr. Napperson, and an address in South Saint Paul. I phoned and spoke with his nurse, who was evasive and rude until I mentioned the magic name: Pat Reilly. Then she booked an appointment for the day of New Years Eve.

Normally, I got my Christmas Obligation out of the way at Midnight Mass, but this Christmas Eve I sat home in fear of Swede and Rico. I phoned my sister Kelly and made a date to visit Aunt Doris. Maybe it was Janie's plight that bothered me, maybe it was guilt over three people needlessly shot in the bank robbery, maybe it was fear of Swede and Rico, but I slept jangly, and greeted Christmas Day cold, down and weary.

There was nothing under the tree.

There wasn't even a tree.

And forget about Santa Claus.

I dug into the back of my closet, past old galoshes and a jumble of sweaters, and pulled out a torn cardboard box that contained a toy electric train set. It was the only thing I had left of my old man. It was a present for graduation from eighth grade at Sacred Heart.

I shoved the couch along the floor and cleared out a dusty corner and laid the tracks and plugged the transformer in. I coupled the black locomotive to the coal car, to the dull brown box car to the silvery tank car to the red caboose. Around and around they went. I was on my knees like a child, setting the trains right after derailments, imagining myself as a conductor. In the caboose. The stove with a wood fire. A ceramic pot of coffee heating up, ham sandwiches in the icebox. My father had twice sneaked me onto a caboose for a ride with his conductor friends. We didn't go far. But I remember every dusty, bone-rattling, thrilling moment of those rides.

In the lobby of the Mother Mercy home, the nuns had placed a giant stuffed paper-mache Santa. A cave in his belly contained wrapped gifts for the old people. I never saw Aunt Doris as lively as she was that Christmas, her last in this world. When Kelly and I walked into her room, Doris brightened like a bulb.

"I thought I'd never see you two again," she said, as we stood on either side of the bed holding her hands. Tears leaked down the suffering woman's cheeks.

"My eyes have glimpsed it now," she said.

"Glimpsed what?" asked Kelly.

"Wonderland." The word whistled through Doris's false teeth.

"Oh, Aunt Doris," said Kelly, and patted her hand.

"I'm going there," said Doris.

"With Humpty Dumpty?" I asked.

"Humpty Dumpty?" said Doris. "No, I'm going with Alice."

She smiled, or was that a grimace of pain? Her bony hands felt warm, a lively sparkle lit her pale blue eyes.

The headboard of her bed was steel tubes, built in an arch, painted a chipped hospital green. Above it, nailed to the wall, was a wooden crucifix with a bronze Jesus. I happened to be looking at it when it moved. The whole building shuddered, as if an earthquake had rolled through Saint Paul.

"What was that?" asked Kelly.

For a moment I thought Aunt Doris had died and Heaven had shaken the place, taking up her soul. But then Kelly and I crowded the sparkling clean window to see a racy Auburn smashed, rear-end first, against the porch foundation. The car's wheels spun as it pulled away.

It was a gorgeous speedster, custom painted red, with white fenders. It looked more like a rocket ship than a car. As it pulled away from the porch, chrome pieces dropped from the crushed trunk. Out the driver's door popped our sister Mona.

"What the hell?" said Kelly. "Where'd she get that car?"

"The latest beau," I suggested.

Mona, dressed in green turban, three-quarter length mink stole, and fringy flapper dress, stood hands on hips, looking from porch to damaged trunk, as if trying to assess what was to blame, the car or the building. Sister Joan stepped down the porch stairs in her white habit, strode in black shoes over the snow, inspected the porch, said something to Mona, and headed inside. Except for a couple of cracked porch clapboards, all the damage was to the trunk of that beautiful, expensive car.

"Mona's here," Kelly said to our aunt.

"Where's my purse?" said Aunt Doris.

We returned to her bedside. Kelly bent to look in the cabinet, atop which were medicine bottles, an alarm clock, and a porcelain pitcher of water.

"I don't know, dear," Kelly said. "Did you have it here?"

"What?"

"Your purse?"

"Mona keeps stealing my purse," Doris claimed.

Mona strode in. Her face was red. She smelled of gin. Her platinum curls were tied back with a black ribbon.

"Did I miss something?" Mona said.

"You should have missed the building," I said. "That's what you should have missed."

"Shut up," she said. "My foot slipped on the clutch."

Her hands went to her hips. She looked from me to Kelly.

"Two against one," she said. "That's the way it's always been in this family. You two do nothing but judge me."

Kelly embraced Mona, kissed her on her lipstick-glazed lips.

"Merry Christmas, Mona," Kelly said. "We're glad to see you."

I could see Mona's face over Kelly's shoulder. Something genuine shone from Mona's eyes in that moment of love and acceptance. Something hard left her tavern flapper's face, and it softened, for that moment, into a child's.

"It's only metal, it can be fixed," Mona said.

"I know a good body shop," I said, and hugged Mona, getting a whiff of perfume, cigarette smoke and booze.

"How are you, auntie?" Mona asked, and kissed Doris on the cheek.

"Humpty Dumpty," said Doris.

"What?" Mona laughed.

"They pushed him off the wall," Doris said.

"Oh, I see," said Mona. She patted Doris' gray hair. "Has one of you got a cigarette?

"You can't smoke in here," said Kelly.

"To hell I can't," said Mona. "My nerves. I need a smoke."

Kelly's purse sat on a wooden chair, and she dipped into it, shook out a Viceroy, which I lit in Mona's lips with Sadie's lipstick tube lighter.

Doris, suddenly asleep, snored.

Mona blew smoke toward the ceiling. "Guess what, I'm getting married," she said.

"Get out of here," said Kelly. "To who?"

"What?" said Mona. "Are you surprised that somebody would marry me? Is that it?"

"Come on," said Kelly. "Be serious. You're engaged to the guy who owns that flashy car?"

"Yup."

"Holy mackerel," said Kelly, "what's he do for a living?"

"Who is this guy?" I asked.

"You know him," Mona said. "Robert."

"Robert who?" I said, but my gut was already signaling my brain.

"Pearson. You know. Serious Bobby, that's what his friends call him."

"Mona!" I said. "He's older than I am."

"So?" she blew smoke.

"When did you get engaged?" Kelly asked.

"Last night," Mona said. "At the Lowry Terrace. He asked me."

"And as a wedding present," I said. "You smashed his speedster."

Mona tapped ashes to the polished floor.

"He's got plenty," she said.

"Mick, do you know this Bobby character?" Kelly asked me. "What's he do?"

"He's a diplomat," I said, diplomatically.

Kelly raised her eyebrows. She pulled out a Viceroy and I lit it for her. "Wow," she said. "Shocker."

"We're picking out rings tomorrow," Mona said. "It's going to be a whopper. I'm not a cheap date."

Mona looked Kelly over. "You're getting too skinny," she told Kelly. "The girls are running you ragged."

"Yes they are," said Kelly.

"I'd take the paddle to the both those brats. And you," Mona said to me, "I keep hearing rumors."

"What rumors?"

"Dark secrets," she said. "You're in it up to your eyeballs, I heard."

"In what?"

"Never mind," Mona said.

She walked to the window, lifted it, tossed her cigarette out into a snow bank. Like a guilty schoolgirl, she tried to wave the smoke out of the room.

Maybe that cold draft woke Doris up because she flailed under her blankets, then tried to set up on her elbows.

"When I'm dead and gone..."

"Come on, Aunt Doris," said Kelly. "It's Christmas."

"I'll be dead a long time," Doris said, "so you two have fun with my money."

I laughed.

Then I said: "What money?"

She waved: "Oh, you know."

Kelly shrugged. Mona approached the bed, dropped to her knees, took one of Doris's hands into her own.

Looking over Mona's shoulder, I stared intently into my aunt's cloudy eyes. "You do know, Doris," I said, "that we've used all your cash to pay for your care here."

"Plenty more," she said.

Kelly glimpsed a nun passing in the hallway and stomped her cigarette under black high heels. "I wish you really did have some more money, dear," Kelly said, "because we'll soon be in hock to the nuns."

"I was always a saver," Doris said. "The crash of Oh One. I never trusted the banks after that. Teddy Roosevelt. He's the man. He saved us from the Robber Barons."

"Did you hide money at Eagle River?" Mona asked.

"Don't look for it until I'm dead. Don't give it to these damn nuns, they keep electrocuting me."

"Okay, where exactly did you hide the money?" Kelly asked.

"Oh," Doris said, "who remembers?"

"You can," Mona urged. "Try."

"Your Uncle Joe's best friend was Earl," said Doris. "They used to go fishing."

"Okay," I said.

"Earl was in love with your mom at one time," Doris said.

"Aunt Doris," Mona said. "The money. Finish about the money."

"Oh," Doris said, and closed her eyes. "Uncle Joe, your Uncle Joe … Teddy Roosevelt, you see … the railroads went bust … and your uncle … no work … Humpty Dumpty."

"Oh no," said Kelly, "not Humpty Dumpty again."

"They can't put him back together," said Doris. "He's all in little pieces."

When we figured she'd had her last moments of clarity for the day, we put Doris in a wheelchair and rolled her out to show her the Christmas tree in the lobby. We took her gift out of Santa's belly and unwrapped it: a pair of chrome dime-store cufflinks. Obviously the nuns had mixed up the residents' gifts, but Doris would not be denied those cufflinks. As we wheeled her to her room, she claimed we were trying to kill her by reckless wheelchair pushing. She said she hated being in a wheelchair and would rise from it or die. Once we got her into bed, she fell into a snoring slumber.

Out on the porch, Kelly lit a Viceroy. Mona stood, hands on hips, staring at the snowy landscape, then at the damaged speedster, then at Kelly and I.

"You *two*," said Mona. "You *two* enjoy my money. That's exactly what she said."

"She meant the three of us," said Kelly.

"Bullshit," said Mona. "I'm cut out. I know it. She hates me."

"Doris does not hate you," said Kelly.

"Have you seen the will?" Mona demanded.

"It's…" Kelly said.

"I'll get my lawyer looking into it," Mona said. "Doris can't do that to me. It's not fair."

"Are you coming over for Christmas dinner?" Kelley offered. "We've got plenty."

"Are you kidding?" Mona said. She walked to that Auburn speedster, ran a white-gloved hand over the smashed trunk.

"Next time you two hear from me," Mona said, "it'll be my attorney speaking."

How much money had Aunt Doris hidden under the floorboards or behind the walls? Maybe enough for a year of escape and survival. Once I got Janie to the doctor's, I could head out for hours of icy driving to Eagle River. It would be cold and isolated in that farmhouse, but it would be far out of range for Swede and Rico. And now I had something to do: search the house and barn to see if Doris had left us a hidden inheritance, or whether it was only another loose thought Humpty Dumpty had pried from my aunt's slipping brain.

I worried that DuVol would talk in prison, or that the Minneapolis cops would realize they had arrested the wrong guys and come looking for the robbers and their jug marker. I needed to get out of town. All I needed to do was avoid Swede and his little partner for the next six days.

CHAPTER TWENTY FIVE

On the last day of 1932 I visited Downtown Dutch at Pawn Paradise. I paid nine dollars to redeem what I'd pawned: a typewriter, my golf clubs, and a pile of chipped china that had been passed down through my mother's family. I didn't need my golf clubs or Peggy's typewriter, but I hated the fact that they were in Dutch's possession.

On a shelf behind Dutch ceramic figurines, and I focused on one of them. It looked like an egg wearing a blue suit. This ceramic egg had painted eyes, arms and legs. It was a little smaller than a baseball. I asked Dutch to hand it over the counter.

"What the hell?" I said.

Dutch flung his one good arm out in a salute.

"Perfect, Powers," he said, "for soft poiled eggs."

"Humpty Dumpty?" I said. "A Humpty Dumpty egg holder. How much?"

"Special por you," spat Dutch. "Pifty cents."

"And the regular price?"

"Twenty pive."

"I think I've got two dimes somewhere."

I held Humpty Dumpty up to the light of the grimy window. I could see the crack where this figurine had been glued, a thin line just underneath Humpty's red grinning lips. Yes, somebody had put Humpty Dumpty back together again.

"Damaged goods," I said.

"One of a kind," countered Dutch.

"A dime," I said. "I want this as a gift for my Aunt Doris. You remember Doris?"

"Powers, please. Don't pluck my harp springs. Pifteen cents and you're robbing me plind."

I drove home and carried my golf clubs, typewriter and box of china upstairs. Humpty Dumpty I slipped into the passenger door's pocket, wrapped in tissue paper, atop the gas station maps. I would take it to Aunt Doris as a New Year's present, but first I had another duty to perform.

I may be a gangster but I come from decent people. I was in debt to Filben and my sister, and it was tempting to spend that $2100 in blood money that lay in a shoebox under my bed. I didn't know what to do with it. I sat on the couch for long spells, watching the toy train go around on its tracks, wasting electricity on its miniature journey to nowhere.

After an hour of what seemed like a hypnotic spell, I wrapped up the money in three newspaper packets, $700 each. I set Peggy's typewriter on the kitchen table and banged out a note addressed to Major Walker, Editor, Saint Paul Daily News.

The note suggested that each $700 packet be used to help the families of those who'd died during the robbery of the Third Northwestern Bank. I asked that the cash be used as the foundation of three funds that the public could donate to.

I brought those packets down to Little Elmer. I said I'd pay a dollar a piece, plus taxi fare, if he delivered the packages to the Daily News. The source of the money would remain our secret, though.

"Really, mom, can I?" Elmer said, and turned at his doorway to peer into the darkness of his family's apartment.

Mom, in the shadows, hated and feared me. I understood. She didn't want this boy to grow up admiring gangsters.

"It's a good deed," I reassured the shadow of his mom. "He

might get his picture in the papers."

"Oh, Lord, I don't think so," said the mom.

"Mom!" cried Elmer. "Three dollars. And a taxi ride!"

"Mister Powers," said the mom and walked into the half light. She was a willowy woman, thirty some years old, with plain face, a prominent nose, shoulder-length mousy hair. She wore a long tattered housedress.

"I heard you gave my boy a gun," she said.

I stammered.

"I let him hold it a minute," I said. "It wasn't loaded. I guess I wasn't thinking. It will never happen again."

Elmer staggered into the hallway light, his crutches hitting the floor like drumbeats.

His mother said: "Don't you offer my boy money at any time for any reason."

"Yes ma'am."

"But you've got him all excited now, so this one time I will allow it."

"Isn't she the best mom?" said Elmer, his eyes shining.

"She sure is," I said. "I'll call a cab."

When Little Elmer returned via Yellow Cab, mission accomplished, he boasted of having been photographed by flash camera, how he'd talked with a nice lady reporter. He clomped down the hallway whistling.

Now I embarked on grim errand. I descended into the concrete well that led to Janie's door and knocked. She answered ashen faced. She was ready, though, wearing a black cloth coat over khaki trousers. She could not look me in the eye.

"No talk, Powers, please," she said.

She got into my Essex and stared ahead, like a condemned prisoner accepting her fate.

I drove in silence, except for the burble of the Essex's engine.

South Saint Paul is a blue-collar city that smells of slaughterhouse. It is built in the flatlands in a bend of the Mississippi, and its main virtue is cheap housing. Many residents work for one of the two slaughterhouses, Swift or Armour.

The better neighborhoods rise on the riverbank behind the city, farthest from the cow lots. On these sloping streets stand homes and bungalows built during the 1920s boom, and occupied by the professional classes. Among these was a much older home, of three stories, a shambling Victorian. It was clad in dark shingles, with a long driveway leading back to a five-car garage. As instructed by Reilly, I parked in the garage, killed the engine.

"Ready for this?"

Janie inhaled frosty air and said: "I guess so."

"We can put it off if you want to think it over."

"I've thought it over, Powers," she snapped.

"Okay, okay."

"I want a baby, but not like this, not this baby."

She bit her lip hard. "Once you decide to ..." she said. "... it's done forever. There's no going back. Am I hard hearted? Am I doing the wrong thing, Powers?"

"I don't know, Janie, you can't look to me for wisdom, I don't know what the right thing is anymore."

Her hand, holding the arm rest, seemed shaky. She was a strong-built girl but seemed shrunken in that black cloth coat. A green silk kerchief was tied tight into her red hair.

"It's a mortal sin, Powers. I'm paying for my sinful life."

"We're all sinners, Janie. Without sin, we're nothing."

"Well aren't you the philosopher." She let out a deep sigh and said, "You'll walk me up there?"

She flung open the door and thunk, Humpty Dumpty fell to the asphalt driveway. She bent over to retrieve it and held the figurine in her cold red hands. She unwrapped the tissue paper and Humpty

Dumpty, in three ragged pieces, fell onto her black coat.

"I'm sorry, Powers," she said, her eyes wet. She tried to assemble Humpty Dumpty, but it wouldn't hold. "I've wrecked it."

"Aw it was only a little joke gift for my aunt," I said. "She's in her second childhood, reading Alice in Wonderland."

"I'll pay for it," she said.

"We should probably be on time," I said. "If we're going to do this."

Janie nodded. We left the Essex and mounted a gray-painted wooden porch, and climbed to the third floor. There at a windowed door I tapped. The shade was lifted, then quickly let go. The door lock clicked. I held Janie's cold hand.

The woman who opened the door was of average build, with long, salt-and-pepper hair. She wore eyeglasses that were oddly tilted to one side. Her dress was gray and hung strapped from her shoulders.

"Hello dear," she said.

Janie squeaked a greeting.

The kitchen was the only normal room in the flat. A pocket door opened to a dining room that had been converted into a hospital ward: three beds, separated by medicine cabinets. The shades were pulled and the room was dark. Beyond that, behind another pocket door, was the surgery room.

"Let me take your coat dear," said the woman, who I assumed was the nurse.

I turned my back on Janie, produced three folded $50 bills Janie had given me, and slipped them to the nurse. She glanced at them, dropped them into a pocket.

"The doctor will be a little late," she said.

I embraced the trembling Janie. She sat on a bed to remove her red snow boots.

"He had an emergency," said the nurse.

There was no waiting room so we sat in the ward, the only

patients. Janie perched at the edge of the bed like she might take off running.

"Can you send some more heat up?" I called in to the nurse.

"Oh dear," the nurse said.

"Which one is it?"

"The one in the middle," she said.

I was glad for this duty. I hustled down into the dark dusty basement and opened the door of the biggest furnace. It was clad in asphalt and there was barely a glow from its bed of ashes. I trooped to the bin for a heavy shovel full of coal, tilted it into the furnace door, poked the coals with an iron rod.

When the heat was rising I climbed the stairs and now Janie had changed into a white, knee-length gown. She sat at the edge of the bed, flipping through Good Housekeeping magazine. The nurse was boiling a huge pot of water on the stove. Alongside that stove, in an alcove, was a secretary desk with paperwork stuffed into the pigeonholes. The nurse was sterilizing instruments in that boiling pot, and had laid white towels along the kitchen table.

The doctor entered whistling. He was a bald man, not quite my size, with a reddish complexion and gold-plated eyeglasses. He ignored me and said something into the nurse's ear, which caused her to nod. He removed his topcoat, hung it on a coatrack, along with his suit-coat. He snapped his blue suspenders, rolled up his shirt sleeves, and whistling, washed his hands for a long while at the sink. I approached this fellow from behind. I did not detect, as I'd feared, the smell of drink.

"She's, ah," I said quietly to the doctor, "in kind of a state."

Without looking at me he said, "They usually are."

He tucked his tie into his shirt, plucked a half-smoked cigar from its pocket, and propped it an ashtray. He removed a leather-strapped gold watch from his wrist, and set it on the secretary.

"How long will the recovery be?" I asked.

He shrugged. "A few days, in most cases."

He opened the pocket door.

"So you're the patient," he said to Janie. "Don't worry, we'll take good care of you."

The heat hadn't made its way up the pipes yet. When I took Janie's hands to wish her luck, they felt like they'd been in the icebox.

"No," she said, and gave a soul penetrating look. All I could see for a long moment was something fierce in her green eyes.

"I can't do this," she said. She turned to the doctor and said: "I'm so sorry, doctor, I can't keep this appointment."

The doctor looked past us to the nurse, who nodded. I supposed that look told the doctor she'd collected the money.

"Michael, get me out of here," Janie whispered.

As the sun set dull orange on the last day of 1932, I helped a wobbly Janie Vetter into my apartment. Although she'd had no surgery, no anesthesia, not even an aspirin, it was like bringing home a patient after a serious operation. Janie was weak, pale and trembling. I settled her on the couch, where she rolled up in blankets. She made grateful noises when I delivered an egg salad sandwich and cup of hot chocolate.

I spread out the Daily News on the coffee table. A teaser headline at the bottom of Page One led me to the inside fold, which featured a big photo of Editor Walker, dwarfing Little Elmer, on crutches. In front of them, cash was fanned out on the editor's desk. The story announced the creation of Friends of The Victims Funds. The donor, the story said, was a charitable Saint Paul banker who wished to remain anonymous.

Janie seemed to be napping, I wasn't quite sure whether she was asleep or just exhausted. I grabbed a leather leash for the gentle Snowflake, and a chain leash for the wild Hula Girl, and followed their scrambling paw-steps to the lobby.

It was pleasant in the side yard, with the oak tree still clinging to a few browned leaves, the Cathedral lit up, a mild night with a fragrant hint of wood fires drifting over from the mansions. I always leashed the dogs against the dangers of the parking lot, but here in the side yard set them free. I sat at the picnic bench and smoked my pipe. The heavy Colt .45 in my overcoat felt like a gangster insurance policy. I smoked in peace. The dogs ran from one smell to another in the snow banks, enjoying a fragrant world only they inhabit.

When a pair of headlights cut into the parking lot, I put my hand on that pistol and called the dogs. I leashed them both to the picnic bench and stepped behind the oak's trunk.

The headlights belonged to a yellow cab. From it emerged a woman alone.

The dogs yipped.

"Myrtle!" I called.

She was dolled up in a dark beaver coat with a wide black leather belt. Her head was swathed in red turban with a ruby eye.

"I seen the lights on," she said. "I've been calling and calling."

The dogs were squirming and I let them off. Myrtle, defending her beautiful coat, stepped away.

"I need a date," she said. "Don't tell me you're staying home on New Year's Eve."

I shrugged.

"Come on, sport, get dressed, you're taking me out."

She grabbed my elbow.

"No arguments," she said.

She followed me and the dogs up the stairs and I warned her: "I've got a visitor."

"Oh ho."

"She's not feeling well."

I opened the door. Janie was at the kitchen sink, washing dishes.

"Well, hello, sweetheart," said Myrtle.

Janie muttered and turned back to the sink.

"I'll be ready in a jiffy," I said, and defected to the bedroom.

Off came an Army sweater. I opened the closet and inspected both my suits. Myrtle slouched in the doorway.

"I knew you'd get into college girl's undies some day."

"She's feeling bad."

"I'll bet, after all the gin you fed her."

"She's not drunk."

"Michael Powers, you're home on New Years' Eve with a college girl. Now what do you expect people will think?"

"Not much since I'm going out on a date with you."

I held up a gray pinstripe two-piece that I had bought at Rothschild's.

"Would you accompany a man so dressed?"

"I might if he ever managed to get into it."

I managed, and Myrtle inspected the bed. If she hoped to find strands of red hair or a college girl's underwear, she was disappointed.

"What about Andrew?" I asked.

Myrtle made wry lips. "The wife gets all the holidays, don't you know the rules?"

"To where exactly would you like an escort?"

"To Harry's," she said. "And make that an armed escort."

"Ah, Myrtle."

"What?"

"Swede and Rico?"

"Swede's on the outs with Harry, and Rico's out of town."

I buttoned my jacket and Myrtle straightened the lapels.

"I never been seen with a coward and I'm not going to start now. They dare not start trouble, especially Rico, the heat's on. His wife died mysterious. One of Dahill's choir boys has been asking sharp questions."

When I stepped into the living room with Myrtle, Janie was wrapped in a blanket, making an embarrassed move for the front door.

"Will the dogs make you feel better?" I said, "you can take 'em downstairs."

"No, that's all right," said Janie. "Nice to see you again, Mrs. Eaton, and I hope you have a good New Years Eve."

Myrtle rolled her eyes as Janie slipped out the door.

"Myrtle wins," she said. "That kid's got to learn. You don't give up a good man easy."

CHAPTER TWENTY SIX

I let Myrtle out near the back door to the Green Lantern and found parking three blocks away. When I rapped on the tavern's back door, Bess let me in. Myrtle had already been swallowed up in the smoky crowd. I handed Bess my coat and she said:

"Hardware."

She held out her open hand.

I reached into my trouser pocket and handed her my nickel-plated revolver.

"All of it," she said.

"That's it," I said.

She locked that revolver in a safe, beside which stood "hardware" that wouldn't fit in. Sawed-off shotguns, carbines and tommyguns were half hidden behind a rabbit-fur coat. Beth crouched to restore order in this gun collection and then turned, surprised I was still there.

"What's the matter?" Bess asked.

"There are guys I hoped I wouldn't bump into."

"One of 'em is here. Everybody's on good behavior. Harry isn't taking any shit tonight."

"Harry's back?"

"And he doesn't want a spectacle."

"Did my uh friend turn in his hardware?"

"He did."

"And the little guy, you haven't seen him?"

"Nope."

"I love a no-nonsense woman."

"Beat it, Romeo."

Reilly and his cousin Tommy Gannon were tending bar, besieged by rubes who were penned into the main barroom, and had no hope of admittance to the Blue Room. That inner sanctum was separated by a dutch door. When the bottom half was closed, the Blue Room was open to rubes, upon appeal to Bess. When top and bottom were closed, the room was heavy with gangsters, with a strict admission policy. Bess let me in and closed the door behind me.

The Blue Room had blacked out windows and apparently, no air vents. Cigarette smoke drifted to the ceiling and descended again in a heavy fog. Small crowds gathered at slot machines along the back wall, and tough guys played poker at the big table. One of them was the Swede.

He had abandoned his workman's guise and wore a dull brown suit that might have come from the Salvation Army. I could see the little nicks and scars on his face, from a lifetime as a bruiser. He wore a fedora tilted back, and on the pinky of his right hand, a ruby-and-gold senior class ring from the Sacred Heart.

He was locked into his cards and didn't notice me. I sidled along the edge of the room to get to Myrtle. She was talking with Loretta, her friend from the Free Love Group.

"Here's my date," Myrtle said, and grabbed my arm. "Ain't he handsome?"

"He'll do in a pinch," said Loretta.

"Honey, my whole life's a pinch," said Myrtle.

Loretta's company was for hire, and I didn't know which gangster she'd come with. Loretta was like a Typhoid Mary of gossip, she could spread it to a hundred bad guys, so I pulled Myrtle away. I whispered: "That table. Front corner."

"Okay," she said looking over my shoulder.

"You know who they are?"

"What is this, a test?"

"Karpis," I said. "With the greasy hair."

"Heard of him, never met him."

"Freddy Barker, the little guy."

"Him I know."

"How about the girls?"

"Never seen 'em."

"Go over and chat Freddy up," I suggested.

"Why?"

"So I won't be so obvious when I join you."

She looked me over as if checking my sanity. "What are you, the master of strategy?"

"I did you a favor."

"When the hell was that?"

"I'm here, right? With you."

"Dating me is a favor?"

"I wanted to stay home."

She sputtered. "I shoulda left you with fancy-pants, the girly collegiate."

Myrtle sashayed over to the Barker-Karpis table, squeezing through knots of people. She pulled a cigarette out of her gold case and asked Freddy for a light.

The face of Lillian the cook appeared at the high window, and her hands shoveled platters of spaghetti-and-meatballs, cocktails and glasses of foaming beer through the pass. A player at the poker table stood and cursed. A slot machine paid out, chugging nickels as a woman screamed in delight.

I waited until Myrtle put a hand on Freddy's shoulder, then made my way over there.

Karpis was drinking a glass of milk and eating a purple, pickled egg. Beside him sat a tiny teenager, heavy with makeup, dark hair and an Irish pixie face. Her drink appeared to be a Coke. Fred was drinking a high-ball and Paula, martinis. It gave me a weak stomach to approach with Paula there, but I had to take the chance.

Myrtle grabbed my arm.

"And here's the love of my life, Michael Powers."

She giggled.

"At least for tonight," I said.

"This sweet girl is Dolores," said Myrtle, and the Irish pixie smiled. "And her man there is Ray."

"Pleased," I said, "to make your acquaintance."

"Fred and Paula," Myrtle said.

Fred grunted. Paula glanced up from her martini.

"Well, if we had room, I'd invite you to sit down," said Karpis, aka Ray.

That was our cue to leave. I said: "We need to get our drinks, don't we honey?"

"Ta-ta," said Myrtle.

We walked off, just behind Swede at his poker game. I could have reached over and strangled him. Except he would have beat me to death before I cut off his air supply. When we reached the pass-through, Myrtle shouted to Lillian for two high-balls.

I told Myrtle: "Get to Karpis. Tell him to meet me in the parking lot."

"He won't do it, are you kidding me?"

"He'll do it. Please. Myrtle."

She grimaced.

I walked out the dutch doors.

"Leaving us so soon?" teased Bess.

"Smoky in there," I said.

I walked out into the crisp dark night with only a suit-coat to ward off the cold. Harry kept the parking lot dark, and the only light came from the moon and the boarding house across the way. I waited, chewing on the end of my Dublin half-bent. I leaned against a car fender but that was so chill I began pacing.

The door opened. Karpis, in shirt sleeves despite the cold, lit a cigarette, as casual as could be.

"Thanks, Ray," I said.

"What's up?"

"I was wondering whether I had done something to piss you guys off."

Karpis blew smoke. "Look, you got the dough, didn't you? And there's more coming when things get straightened out."

"It's not the money. It's certain guys giving me the stink eye, that's all. See I figured I was with you guys so..."

"You aren't with us. You can't be with us. Don't take it personally. We go back, all of us, see? To Oklahoma. The old roughhouse days. It's a good old boys' club."

"Well, I did a right job, though. No hard feelings, against me among the boys, I take it."

"If it was hard feelings," he said, "you wouldn't be talking. At all."

"Because I feel like I did good."

Karpis twisted his lips, impatient with me, and tapped tiny sparks off his cigarette.

"Ray, all I was thinking was, the respect for you guys around here is really something and, well, if you put out the word, nobody would touch me."

He glared at me.

"A couple of words, all it would take," I said.

He clapped me on the shoulder and said: "Why don't we go back inside and have a good time."

What that meant, I could only guess. All it did was set me up for more worry. As the night went on, I drank more than I should have. I sat with Myrtle and Loretta, swapping dirty jokes. I sneaked the occasional glance at the Barker-Karpis table, and twice I saw

Paula whispering into Fred's ear. Both times it sent a bolt of fear through me. Sooner or later her martini-soaked brain was going to recall that I had stalked her in the guise of a magazine salesman.

In my imagination, Fred Barker pushed through the dutch doors and came back with a tommygun, rushing me, murder in his cold eyes.

I was on my third drink when Swede Fanlund fixed on me. He stood up from the poker table, stretched and made a show grab at his testicles. Then he stepped away from the table and nodded at me. He said something to the player on his right, a dark fat guy. The guy snickered. Swede made kissy lips at me, and walked off for the men's room.

I began ordering double high-balls.

They worked their magic. My fears began to soften, and then dissolved into warm sentiment for my fellow gangsters and molls. Liquor began to whisper its sweet lies into my brain. We gangsters weren't such a bad bunch, really. It was the cops who were the louses.

Myrtle wanted to dance so she, I and Loretta bumped our way into the main room. Loretta's date had abandoned her, but she had no trouble finding dance partners. The music was provided via radio, the Ben Pollack Orchestra, piped in from New York City. Just before midnight East Coast time, Harry Sawyer made a command appearance, stood on a chair, shouted down the crowd, and conducted as we sang Auld Lang Syne.

I kissed Myrtle. Rushing toward us on the crowded dance floor was Loretta. She hugged Myrtle and kissed her face all over. Right behind Loretta was her latest dance partner, Swede Fanlund.

We shook hands, his grip a crusher. He had the swollen, battered hands of a street fighter.

"Should old acquaintance be forgot," I said. "Let bygones be bygones."

"Do unto others," Swede said, "Because they deserve

whatever's coming to 'em."

I pulled my hand out of his grip.

"Happy New Year, Shaky," he said.

He tossed his drink down his throat, turned his glass upside-down, let the ice cubes fall on my shoes, and walked away.

"Gives me the creeps," said Myrtle. "Half the fires in this town, it's Swede playing with matches."

"He's a fabulous dancer," said Loretta.

I pushed back to the bar to get another double from Reilly. *Shaky.* That nickname was getting around and it could mean only trouble in this world of tough guys. Pat delivered my drink and I sipped it brooding. I was beginning to lose track of my drinks and the clock. At some point Loretta put her chubby arm around my shoulder.

"Mickey," she said. "Would you be pissed if Myrt and I..."
"What?"

"You know. Split. We don't need a ride or nothing."

"Go," I said.

"You're a sport, Mick."

"A sucker," I said.

"Myrtle loves you so much," she said.

"That she's leaving me flat."

"You're good for her. She can't stand anything that's good for her."

"You're bad for her?"

"We're very bad girls. We're the queens of awful."

"Go on, get out of here."

"Thank you, Mick."

"Have fun."

"We will."

"Invite me next time."

"Not a chance," said Loretta.

I was so drunk I didn't even feel bad about being left flat. It was well past midnight when a kid came around selling the bulldog edition of the Pioneer Press. I gave him a nickel for a two-cent paper, and read it at the bar.

New Years was now just another drunken night, like so many back when Peggy was my wife and drinking companion. I loved that woman, genuine. But she wanted babies and I wanted a lifelong party. When she went melancholy, I was blind to it. Our twelve-year party had turned into a permanent hangover.

I fought off nostalgia, read the newspaper not out of any real interest, but to keep myself awake for the next drink. A little item about Havana caught my attention. Soldiers in the streets, fears of a revolution. I tried to imagine it, the warm breezes, the sea air, the exotic women, all spoiled now, with riflemen patrolling the rooftops.

I staggered to the cloak room and Bess handed up my overcoat and pistol. I stumbled along the snow-banked street to my Essex, choked the engine, started it up, and drove it to the Green Lantern parking lot.

And there I waited in idle. The car warmed slowly, the booze soaking my nerves.

Shaky.

I held out my hand. It looked steady to me.

It was somewhere near two in the morning when Swede Fanlund pushed through the Green Lantern's back door.

Swede.

In my drunken state I saw the history of it, not just Swede burning me at the Sacred Heart, but the Viking rape of Ireland. Oh, I had learned it at my grandmother's knee. The invaders, one after the other. Plunder, rape, murder. The Spanish, the Normans, the Danes, the English, and worst of all, the Viking hordes. Swede the ancient and feared enemy. The Irish retreating, cowards in the hills, starving in caves as the Vikings built port cities and took their choice of colleens.

I knew Swede's route and there was no need to follow him. I let him disappear around the corner, consulted my pocket watch. In exactly seven minutes I put the Essex in gear, turned up Wabasha and crept along Saint Peter Street. Speakeasies obeyed no curfew and stayed open as long as there were customers. The lights of the bordellos and taverns along Saint Peter were bright. I measured Swede's pace and pulled over to park, a block behind.

It was him or me, and I finally admitted it. Harry's tavern was a zone of safety for tonight, but the next time I saw Swede Fanlund he might be pointing a gun down my throat. These were the first hours of 1933, and I vowed I would not spend the year cowering, looking over my shoulder for the Swede. I wanted a confrontation, and I was drunk enough to overlook its dangers.

I quietly left my auto and hustled. Swede, head lolling, swaying with drink, entered a dark alley that led to his rooming house. Hand gripping the pistol in my overcoat pocket, I followed. At the end of the alley, Swede tried to climb the concrete stairs to his apartment lobby, but banged into trash cans.

That's when he saw me.

Maybe he saw the streetlamp glint of my nickel-plated revolver, I don't know. Maybe he thought I was a Chicago gangster come to hunt him down. He kicked away the garbage cans and ran up the stairs. He slipped on the ice, then crumpled, his head making a horrific bang on the steel cellar door.

He lay there sprawled. His overcoat was thrown open. He wore no gloves. His hat was lying atop a snow bank. Little streams of blood leaked from his nostrils. He made an agonized groan. And then, with a snort, he passed out.

I looked behind me. Nobody. I looked up at the buildings around me, nobody at the windows. The alley was dark and deep and far from the noisy street. I pointed my revolver at Fanlund's head and caressed the trigger.

My hand was steady, not shaking at all.

I remembered the day long ago when he had burned me with a cigarette. That warm morning in the schoolyard seemed just as real as this frigid night. I remembered him coming after me on Saint Patrick's Day, when only my panicky driving saved me. I remembered him driving off and leaving me stranded the night of the barber shop fire. I remembered Rose, the gold crucifix dangling in her cleavage. I remembered Sadie, and that sweet kiss in a warm hotel room as a blizzard blew in from the west. Her last kiss, as it turned out, the kiss of death. I saw again that fire on the levee, I smelled that vile stink of cooked flesh and melted rubber.

I squeezed the trigger and felt the hammer pull back.

And then I changed my mind.

It would get below zero tonight.

In the morning his neighbors would find a body, and the medical examiner would conclude that he'd come home drunk, slipped, and frozen to death. It happened often enough during a Minnesota winter.

Do unto others. They get what they deserve.

I slipped my pistol back into my pocket.

I turned my back on Swede Fanlund.

A harsh wind whipped down the alley and it began to snow.

# # #

Historical Note:

AFTERMATH OF THE CRIMES

The 1932 bank robbery at Redwood Falls, Minnesota was never solved. Most historians attribute it to the Barker-Karpis gang, and it was very likely planned at Saint Paul's Green Lantern tavern.

Minneapolis patrolman Ira Evans died at the scene of the Third Northwestern Bank robbery on December 16, 1932. He and his partner responded to the call just as they were going off shift that afternoon. Both policemen were shot just after they pulled up in front of the bank, and before they could get out of their squad car. Evans was 39 years old.

Patrolman Leo Gorski lingered two days in the hospital after being shot outside the bank. His fellow officers lined up to provide blood transfusions, but on Sunday, December 18, he died, at age 34, leaving behind a wife and son.

Oscar Erickson, unemployed dining car waiter, was selling Christmas wreaths door to door when he had the misfortune to happen upon the Barker Gang. They were switching cars in Saint Paul's Como Park after the Third Northwest robbery. Erickson, believing these men were experiencing car trouble, stopped to offer help. Fred Barker pulled a pistol and shot him in the head. Erickson died the next morning. He was 29, newly married, and left behind a young widow.

Larry DuVol was convicted of robbing the Third Northwestern Bank and firing the machine gun rounds that killed officers Evans and Gorski. He was sentenced to a life term at Stillwater Prison, where the warden cited him as the most dangerous man incarcerated there. He became so disruptive he was transferred to the hospital-prison at Saint Peter, Minnesota. There he led a breakout of seven prisoners. In July, 1936, he died in a shootout with police in Oklahoma, but not before he killed another policeman, Enid patrolman Cal Palmer.

FROM THE PREVIOUS WORK:

IF THE DEAD COULD SPEAK

In *If the Dead Could Speak*, Mick Powers was assigned by wealthy brewer Papa Alt to snoop on two gangster molls, Rose Perry and Sadie Carmacher. Those women were found the next day, shot dead, their faces splashed with acid, and their bodies burned in a car.

Mick enlisted reporter Janie Vetter in trying to find out who murdered the women, but they never identified the killers with any certainty. Two of the suspects, Rico and Swede, tried to gun Mick down on St. Patrick's Day.

Mick's investigation leads him to the Barker-Karpis gang, which has just taken up residence in Saint Paul. In return for protection from the men who are gunning for him, he agreed to cause a traffic distraction that helps the Barker gang pull off a Minneapolis bank robbery.

As the story ends, Mick unwittingly delivers Ma Barker's boyfriend Pop Anderson to the hands of executioners.

Mick all the while hopes to escape gangland by clever gambles on horse racing, but loses his entire stake in the 1932 Kentucky Derby.

Next in the series,
A sample from
Mick Powers Book 3:

DEAD LIKE LAZARUS

These chapters of Dead Like Lazarus
are from an unpolished draft of the book.

DEAD LIKE LAZARUS

CHAPTER ONE

Around Saint Patrick's Day, I realized how much I missed Saint Paul. There was nothing Irish about Eagle River, nothing to celebrate on Saint Pat's except being one day closer to a mushy spring. Eagle River might have worked if I'd been a deer-hunting, muskie-fishing guy. The men up here — Finns, Germans, Norwegians, French-Indians— were decent enough, but silent and solitary. There wasn't an Irish pub or horse parlor in town, and you couldn't buy a Racing Form for fifty miles around.

Worse, the thermometer and the population of available women lingered near zero. Sitting near the drum-stove with my dogs, staring at a red barn surrounded by snow, I realized how much I missed city life. I forgot all the dangers and began to think fondly of that lively, corrupt little city where I seemed to recognize half the people on the street. I knew how to get things done in that town. In running away from Saint Paul, I had sentenced myself to solitary confinement in a snowdrift. A man alone, I discovered, is not a man at all.

So as the sun began to descend over the pine trees for another long night, I worked through the long distance operator to phone Sam Tanaka.

"A voice from the past," I said.

"Maybe it should stay in the past," he said.

"Don't hang up," I said.

"Why not?"

"First Saturday in May," I said. "At odds, I think. Looks promising."

"Speak."

"A pair at five-to-one at least."

He didn't say anything.

"Sam? Anybody talking about me there?"

"Perhaps."

"Swede and Rico?"

After a hesitation he said, "They're laying low."

"I'm thinking of making an appearance," I said.

"Up to you."

"Come on, Sam, melt the ice, will you?"

"Wait."

He left me holding the phone, long distance charges racking up, for about five minutes. I was using an old-fashioned candlestick phone, so I rested the ear-piece on the desk and petted Snowflake left handed and Hula Girl right handed. They watched intent as a white-tail buck, heavy with antlers, devoured a sapling in the snow-covered garden.

When Sam came back to the phone I let the dogs go, and they scrabbled at the windows, barking and howling at the deer. I shouted into the phone for Sam to wait as I let the dogs out. They chased the buck into the woods, and he bounded away, no contest.

"What the hell is going on?" Sam asked.

"Deer versus dogs," I said. "The deer ran away."

"I know the type," said Sam. "Look, maybe Jack is interested. More interested than I imagined. He thinks you learned something with Harry. He's intrigued. He's got the upstairs guest room, you can have it for a few days."

"Really?"

"I'm surprised too."

"I could leave tomorrow," I said.

After a pause I reconsidered.

"I really need to be sure about Swede and Rico."

"They're out of favor with Jack."

"Oh? May I ask why?"

"Why ask a question that can't be answered?"

"How's the snow cover? Should I bring my golf clubs?"

"Are you kidding?"

So the next morning I packed a suitcase, put the dogs in the back seat of my Essex Terraplane and slalomed down the snow-packed driveway. Both dogs got panting-excited about any road trip, but for me it was six dull hours of icy driving.

I was exhilarated by my first sighting of the Saintly City, its outer ring guarded by the brick fortresses of Minnesota Mining and Hamm's Brewing. Construction crews were doubling the size of the Hamm plant, and the shrewd brewers who had survived Prohibition were going to bubble up a fortune now. I was returning to a changed world: President Roosevelt had closed the banks and opened the beer halls. I didn't vote for him, but had to admit he'd made people happy.

I avoided downtown and its Loop and the tangle of autos, trucks and streetcars. I crossed the Mississippi on the easy side and drove along the river to the Hollyhocks casino.

I let the dogs out to relieve themselves on Jack's big brown lawn. The winter's snow clung only in the shadows, but the ground was frozen as hard as pavement. Sam was right, we were weeks away from golfing weather.

Sam was on an errand so Violet greeted me on the big porch. The Hollyhocks dining room didn't open until five, but behind her bustled waiters and cooks and porters, all male and either Colored or Japanese. The walls wore the cardboard remnants of a Saint Paddy's party: shamrocks, shillelaghs and leprechauns.

Violet was gangland's loveliest woman, a thin, icy, Scandinavian blonde, a former underwear model and tennis ace with blue eyes and a perky ski-jump nose. She wore a black gown that hid her figure but not her movie-star looks.

"Jack has your room made up," she said as the dogs and I followed her up the wide, carpeted staircase. The casino was dark, one woman in there, sweeping amid felt tables. In Jack's office, Suzy the Doberman stood to guard her territory but let my dogs pass with only a snort. When we reached the turret room Violet pushed open the door without stepping in. She fended off a thousand passes a year, but need not have worried about me. I was not such a fool as to rattle her husband's cage.

"Call the desk," she said, "if you need anything."

"The Master?" I said.

She pursed her lips. Her husband, feared boss in the underworld, was a source of amusement to her.

"The Master is out being masterful," she said. "Saph will send up a drink if you like."

"Maybe a little meat for the dogs?"

"Saph," she said, "will provide," and then closed the door, glad, I felt, to be rid of me.

So the dogs dined on steak and potatoes and I, road weary, took a nap in the bed. It was dark when I awoke. I crept downstairs to see the office door cracked open. I knocked, pushed, and there sat Jack, in tuxedo, at his desk.

Suzy the Doberman, that dispirited creature, barely rattled her chain as I stepped over her. I thought of suggesting that Jack let her roam free once in a while, but didn't want to renew our relationship with a lecture.

Jack extended his hand over the desk, and said, "Good."

He had the oiliest hair of any man I'd ever known, and despite his fearsome reputation, a rogue's twinkle in his blue eyes. They gave the sense that a soul was trapped in there somewhere, if shrunken to the size of a walnut.

"Sit sit sit sit sit," he said.

He crossed his arms over his shiny tux jacket.

"So."

"I'm back," I said. "Took the winter off."

"Florida?"

"Not exactly."

He waved me off. "No matter. How's Harry?"

I wobbled my hand.

"What does that mean?" asked Jack.

"We haven't talked in a while," I said.

"Oh." He kicked back in his chair. From a desk drawer he pulled a quart of Canadian Club, and poured us both a heavy drink in water glasses.

"He's a good guy, for a Jew."

"Harry? Sure, I like him."

"But … " Jack said.

I waited.

"But …? "

"Well," Jack said, "everybody's blaming everybody for that bloody mess in Minneapolis. I can't blame you for taking a powder."

I shrugged.

"Okay, well see…" Jack reached over to finger his venetian blinds, his view a bare oak tree.

"See," he said, "I can't find the boys. And I need to."

"I've been out of touch, Jack."

"But you can get in touch," he said, and turned, pointing a finger at me. "You can slip into Harry's world. I can't. Sam can't."

"So who do you need?"

"Shorty or Ray. Actually, Ray is the brains of the outfit so make it Ray. But Shorty would do. Either one. And soon. Urgent!"

"Are they back in town?"

"If they were in town, would I need you?"

"Jack, I've got to ask. Swede and Rico."

He shook his head.

"They won't be a problem."

"Both of them have it in for me, personal."

"And why is that?"

"I gave Rico the brass knuckle treatment," I said. "And Swede, he probably blames me for his fingers."

Jack looked sideways. On the long wall he had posted photos of prize fighters, baseball players and race horses. I knew he wasn't looking at them, but thinking of an answer.

"Saph will speak with them," he said.

"They don't forgive, Jack."

"Saph is the soul," he said, "of forgiveness."

Actually, Saph was the soul of back alley beatings. But Jack's assurances made me feel better. It was common for men to "wear a halo" bestowed by Harry or Jack. Always that halo cost something, but in my case the price would be cheap: I would connect Jack to Fred Barker or Alvin Karpis. It didn't seem so much to ask.

That night I ate a steak and baked potato dinner in my turret room, saved the Caesar salad for desert, and fed the dogs meat scraps. No matter Jack's assurances, I would avoid Rico and Swede. That wouldn't be easy, since I'd have to mix with low characters if I was going to find the Barker-Karpis gang.

Last I'd heard, in January, Barker and Karpis were headed for Reno. But they never stayed anywhere for long. One guy from the Barker-Karpis gang, Larry DuVol, had taken the rap for three murders the gang committed last December, during the Third Northwestern bank robbery. DuVol was the only member of the gang who was caught, and wasn't naming names. Other guys, who'd had nothing to do with that crime or with the Barker Gang, were facing trial in Minneapolis. The local cops, it seemed, had a special talent for arresting the wrong guys.

So where were Fred Barker and Alvin Karpis? It would take delicate probing to find out.

My last call for the evening was at my former apartment, top floor of an elegant brick building on the hillside between the sleazy Seven Corners and the holy Cathedral. I would have phoned, but last I'd heard Janie didn't have a telephone, so I tapped on the door. I heard her shuffling feet and the rattle of safety chain.

"Powers," I said.

She opened the door, puzzled look on her face.

"You're alive!"

"There were rumors to the contrary?"

"Certainly. Come in."

She stepped back. She was a delightful woman in her early twenties, a little chubby, with sparkling blue eyes and red hair. She wore a light blue bathrobe that may have been her father's. Or it may have been a lover's. I hadn't talked to her in three months, since I'd delivered her to a dreadful appointment.

"You've done wonders," I said, looking around my old place. She had mixed her furniture with mine. She'd been sending $40 a month to my sister, and had the sublease until January.

"How are Snowflake and Hula Girl?" she asked.

"They miss you."

"Oh, I doubt that. Coffee?"

"French pressed?" I asked.

"Of course."

I had converted her to the True Coffee Religion last summer. As she put the kettle on the stove, I stood at the window staring down at the autos and streetcars crisscrossing Seven Corners. With beer declared legal, half the storefronts had hung out signs that said

SCHMIDTS or HAMMS or ALTWASSER. Seven Corners had always been a raucous district of bordellos, pool halls, dice dens and speaks, but for more than a decade, the taverns pretended they weren't selling beer.

Janie walked to the window. "Take your coat off and stay awhile," she said.

I handed her the rumpled topcoat. A quizzical look crossed her face.

"So what's new in the news biz?" I asked.

"Oh," she said, and hung the coat in the closet "I'm getting the cops."

"Where?"

"The Daily News of course."

"You're back? I thought you got the heave-ho?"

"Major Hoople found me a spot. He says the ads are picking up. Goggles is getting promoted, a byline and everything. I'm his legman. Goggles takes the weekend off, but crime knows no holiday."

"You've had the whole winter without a job?"

She bit her lower lip. "My parents helped. I think, to be honest Powers, I think the Major has romantic feelings for me."

"Oh," I said.

"It's a little embarrassing," she said.

"In love with your boss."

"Come on, Powers, he's too old for me."

"Since you're on cops, keep your ears open," I said. "Fred Barker and Alvin Karpis."

She frowned. "Everybody's looking for them."

"Me too. I need to get one of them on the phone, that's all."

"Powers, are you mixed up again? I thought you were out? Isn't that why you skipped town?"

"You sit in an igloo for three months and see how you like it."

"He's written me."

"Larry?"

"I burned the letters."

"What did he say?"

"Never mind."

"Did he say anything about Fred or Karpis?"

"No. Never. He never mentioned them to me at all, not when we were dating, not in a letter. He never admitted anything to me."

The kettle whistled but she did not answer its call.

"He's lost his mind in prison. He thinks he's got magical powers that will spring him free."

She shook coffee grounds into a chrome-and-glass French press.

"When he gets out," she said over her shoulder, "he'll come for me."

She poured steaming water into the press. "I'm afraid Powers, I admit it. Our prisons are leaky. Guys have bribed their way out."

"He's got no money to pay bribes. I have sources, I'll check to make sure."

"Would you?"

"And you keep an ear out. Shorty, that's Fred's gangster name. Ray, that's the code name for Karpis. You're going to run cops for the Daily News? Jeez, that paper lives on cop news. You'll be hearing all kinds of stuff you can't print."

"I hope I don't hear anything about you, Powers."

"What do you mean?"

She depressed the plunger.

"Your coat weighs twenty pounds."

I shrugged. "It's a dangerous town."

"So that's why you came back. You missed the danger."

She poured coffee into cups that were leftovers from my married days, fancy with gold trim and painted with roses. I rarely let myself wonder about the woman who had left me. It was like a big, black hole in the ground, and I didn't want to walk anywhere near it. Peggy was, as far as I knew, living near Pearl Harbor. But those cups, and this apartment, brought it back to me, the days when I was a happily married, high-living rum runner.

I sipped. The coffee was bitter, like the memories.

Janie said: "I thought you wanted out of the gangster life."

"One guy, one favor, that's it."

"A favor that requires you to carry a gun?"

"Guns plural," I said. "There are people who don't care for me. Look, beer's coming back and the breweries are hiring. Maybe I can catch on at Altwasser or Hamm's. You understand, Janie. You grew up on a farm. I don't like being cooped up all winter."

"So you came back to go straight."

"Kind of," I said.

"Hmm," she said with a sly smile.

DEAD LIKE LAZARUS

CHAPTER TWO

I didn't dare enter the Green Lantern. Its creepy denizens would have ratted me out to Swede and Rico as fast as they could drink a watered-down beer. Instead I drove toward the Capitol. In its shadow lived Pat Reilly, the Green Lantern's bartender and idiot savant. He had been kicked out by his wife and was now a guest of his long-suffering mother. Mother Reilly was part-owner of a laundry, worked twelve hour days as Pat lolled around, a bachelor bum, drinking beer.

He answered, holding a can of Altwasser.

"Canned beer?" I said.

"It's the modern age, Powers."

"Can I come in?"

He belched. "Why not?"

He stepped into a living room that was tidy, except that beer cans were scattered like buoys marking danger spots in a river channel. Pat's teeth were growing fouler, stained by his Lucky habit. He extinguished a cigarette, opened the blinds to let in a sliver of sunlight.

"I thought you was in Florida?"

"Not even close."

"Well, it's been a rough winter."

"How's Harry?"

"Shitty. He's giving up. What the hell is he going to do now? The breweries are crushing him, ruining all the old bootleggers. All of a sudden, booze is legal and Harry is nobody special."

He swigged beer.

"He's giving me the Lantern."

"Giving?"

"He's drinking more than ever. Want a beer?"

"Gout," I said.

"Still?"

"Never goes away," I said.

"You poor bastard."

"Looking for somebody," I said.

"You got a Derby horse?"

"Too early to tell. Looking for somebody who used to know Harry."

"I can't see a horse."

"The Derby? It's too early Patrick. You've got to wait for the odds to settle, and let the rubes pick a favorite. When I work my figures, I'll let you know, but in the meantime, I need to see somebody."

"Who?"

"Shorty."

"Huh."

"Or Ray. Either one."

"Good luck." Pat swilled.

"Pat, you know everything, come on."

"I don't know nothing that nobody else don't know," he said, "only I don't know it sooner."

"What?"

"I'm kind of in the twilight of my career as, you know, a messenger boy, in one ear and out the other. Nothing sticks to me now because I don't listen to what I'm hearing, and I don't see nothing that don't see me first."

"Okay. Look, I know these fellas got their pictures in the Post Office. I'm not J. Edgar Hoover. I don't want to electrocute them. All I want is a phone call from Shorty or Ray."

"What's your number?"

"I'm not settled. Call Myrtle. Leave a number. I'll call back."

Pat shook his head. "That don't work. Those boys don't leave their number."

"Call Myrtle at five o'clock any night, then. I'll make it my business to be there."

"How's Myrtle?"

I shrugged. "I'm going there next."

"Who wants these guys?"

"Me."

"They owe you?"

"Nope."

"Harry's cooled down."

"Yeah."

ow that they nabbed those Minneapolis guys," he said and shook his head. "Poor saps. Rotting in jail for something they didn't do. I thought our cops were bad."

"They're all bad. Hey, there's twenty in it for you, Patrick."

"Great, I can retire."

"Plus the Derby tip."

"What about running a horse wire at the Lantern? You want to go in?"

"Don't do it. All that telegraph equipment. And the cops bust you, you go broke. Running a crooked game in this town, all you do is enrich the cops and the lawyers. Jesus, Pat just run an honest tavern. People will be drinking until the Second Coming."

"And possibly after," said Pat.

DEAD LIKE LAZARUS

CHAPTER THREE

Myrtle was as good a gangland source as Pat, or so I told myself when I knocked on her door. She stepped aside, let me in to a dark apartment that smelled of loco weed. The marijuana smoke had somehow not killed her parakeets, Charles and Amelia. They occupied one sunny corner, chirping happy in their cage, like they were on a treetop in the Amazon.

"Well, buster," said Myrtle. "I heard you were dead."

"Dead like Lazarus," I said.

"Among the goddamn living," she said with a goofy smile. "Well, come in."

"I am in."

"All the way in."

I shed my overcoat and wrapped her in my arms and kissed her a long time.

"I'm not clean," she said.

"But still adorable."

"Oh, Mick," she said. "It's been a bad winter."

She sat on her elegant mohair couch, swathed in a purple robe. She leaned forward, arms on thighs, studying me, as if she couldn't believe I had returned.

"Get some daylight in here," I said.

"Don't. Hurts the eyes."

I pulled the curtains anyway.

"Tell me, kiddo," I said.

"Shit," she said.

I sat in the chair across from her.

"Andrew left me."

I was glad to hear it. "Sorry," I said.

"What a prick," she said and lit a joint. "Don't start smoking this crap. It makes you sad."

"I'm smoking it as I breathe. Did you love him?"

"Nah," she said. "But he treated me right. Look around. Did you ever see such furniture? Persian rugs! From goddamn Persia! Look at that vase. It looks like Papa Alt's mansion in here. Except no servants."

She waved the smoke away.

"You know, Myrtle, I'm still a little sweet on you."

"Ah Mick."

"We're perfect. Two ruined statues in a weedy garden."

"Cut the poetry." She blew smoke. "Where you staying?"

"Dump downtown," I lied.

"How long you in town for?"

"Until the first Saturday in May."

She looked over her shoulder at the sunlit window.

"I'm finished, Mick. Thirty five. Look for my obit in the Dispatch."

"What are you talking about?"

"I can't walk past a store in this town but the store dicks call the cops. Chicago too, every fur shop seems to know I'm coming. So I take the train to New York last month," she blew smoke, "and they got my picture in the Macy's. I'm there ten minutes trying on furs, and these two mugs rush me out. Shove me down on the sidewalk. They'll give me a beating if they see me again. Stepped on my hand, see? Broke my pinky finger. It's crooked now."

She lay back and sputtered those heavy red lips.

"Professionally," she said, "I've had it. A thousand miles away, Mick, and they got my picture in a book."

"I made you an offer once."

"I ain't living on no farm."

I shrugged.

"Is that where you were all winter?"

"No, I was in Florida," I lied.

"Oh yeah?" She rolled over. "You don't look tan. They had a cloudy winter down there?"

"I need something."

"I told you it's my time of the month right now."

"Freddy Barker and Alvin Karpis."

"What do you want with those assholes?"

"Just a phone call."

"If I see those hillbillies I'm running the other way."

"I've put out the word that they should call here."

"Here?"

"Five o'clock, any day."

"Are you nuts giving out my phone number?"

"Myrtle, everybody knows your phone number."

She hugged herself.

I didn't want Myrtle to know I was staying at the Hollyhocks, so I fumbled. "I can't have 'em calling my hotel. Are you kidding? The switchboard operators? They eavesdrop. Hey, I'll make you dinner."

"I don't want dinner. What'd you give out my number for, Mick?"

"You must've heard something about the hillbillies."

"Yeah, well."

"Come on."

"One of the punks came on like Romeo to me. Never mind

who. Not Fred or Ray, not them. One of their errand boys. Sent me a card from California."

"Where?"

"Lost Angeles."

"When?"

"Last month."

"Where is it?"

"Lost Angeles? It's in California."

"The postcard."

"I threw it in the trash where it belongs."

I rose to walk toward the kitchen.

"It's gone, Mick."

The kitchen was gleaming clean, because Myrtle never cooked. I stepped open the trash can, saw a dead flower bouquet but no card. I backed into the living room.

"I had a dream, Mick?"

"While you were doped up?"

"While you were gone. I dreamed the Professor got out of Waupun, but he didn't know me no more. Went off with a whore to Sarasota. How do you like that?"

"But it's only a dream."

I kneeled at her side, rested my hand on her knee.

"Myrtle, the Professor's never getting out of Waupun."

Her eyes began to flood.

"I know."

"I'm here, I'm sweet on you, what's wrong with me?"

She looked up at me, teary.

"I don't know. I can't shed him, Mick, I can't, he needs me. He'd hang himself if I wasn't out here waiting for him."

I touched her cheek. "There's a beautiful girl in there. Let her out to play."

The phone rang.

"I don't want to subscribe to no magazines," she complained on the way to answer it. She raised the phone to her ear and then turned with a look of fright.

"It's for you."

DEAD LIKE LAZARUS

CHAPTER FOUR

"Shaky Powers?" said a harsh voice.

"If you want Mick Powers," I said, "ask for Mick Powers."

"I was told to ask for Shaky."

This was followed by a fit of coughing.

I waited it out, phone away from my ear.

Recovered, the voice wheezed: "We're outside."

I turned to the window.

"Who is we?"

"We'll see you out here."

He hung up. Down on the street, double parked, was an idling yellow taxicab. A tall angular figure wearing a gray suit and hat burst from the drugstore, crossed the streetcar tracks, and entered the cab.

I had never seen this guy before. I grabbed my overcoat. In one pocket was a cheap chrome revolver with a pearl handle, in another an Army Colt .45. Even carrying my arsenal, I resolved not to get into the cab.

The parakeets chirped as I kissed Myrtle and rushed the door.

Downstairs, the taxi had pulled in front of a fireplug that was surrounded by melting snow.

"Get in," said a fellow from inside.

"We'll talk out here," I said.

I stood my ground on the curb. One fellow leaned forward to pay the cabbie. Then they both got out. The tall angular fellow hacked coughing. The shorter fellow, dressed expensive, stuck out a hand like he was a greeter for the chamber of commerce.

"I'm George," he said. "Excuse Monty, he's got a cold."

George was a handsome man of average build and blond hair. He wore a cashmere topcoat, creased fedora, shoes shined to a mirror finish.

"You were expecting us, I take it?" asked George.

"Not exactly."

A puzzled look crossed his face.

"Jack didn't set us up?"

"Jack?"

"Yes, Casino Jack."

I looked toward Monty. It was obvious that George would do all the talking, and Monty would do all the coughing.

"Casino Jack?" I said.

"Yes," said George. "The nightclub man with the Japanese servants. Oh, don't play dumb, fellow."

"Maybe I know Jack but I wasn't expecting anybody."

George looked toward Monty, who shrugged.

"How do you like that?" said George. "And here we are in the age of communication."

Monty laughed. He was maybe six-three and a hundred fifty pounds of bones. He had the hawkish expression and pale face of a man who'd been sick a long time.

"May I suggest," George said, "that you telephone Jack?"

"He doesn't take calls," I said.

George scuffed his soles on the sidewalk.

"Oh, he doesn't take calls," he said. "May I suggest a visit? Are you in possession of an automobile?"

I looked from one man to the other. "Look, I don't know anything about this."

"You are known as Shaky Powers, correct?"

"Mick," I said. "Mick Powers."

"Jack volunteered your services as a tour guide."

"Tour guide?" I said.

George nodded. Monty nodded.

"What are we touring?"

"Lake properties, I was told."

I said: "Why don't you gentlemen have a cup of coffee across the street and let me make a phone call?"

The two crossed the streetcar tracks while I climbed the back stairs to Myrtle's apartment. The door was cracked open. Myrtle stood naked, except for sky blue panties, at her bay windows.

"There wouldn't be so many peeping toms," I grumbled, "if you didn't tease them."

She stood mesmerized.

"Who are those guys?" I asked.

"Never seen them."

I picked up her phone.

"They stink like Chicago to me," she said.

"You can smell 'em way up here, eh?"

"Oh, there's a train every hour."

"Very perceptive."

She crossed her arms over her breasts. "I should know those guys."

I dialed the Hollyhocks. Saph answered and shouted for Sam and a minute later Sam said: "What's up?"

"Two mugs from out of town," I said.

"So?"

"Jack sent them. But I don't know anything about it."

After a pause, Sam said in a low voice, "The Master is not quite himself lately. Let me see."

He left me holding the phone. In the drugstore across the street,

George and Monty were sitting at a window booth, hats on the table.

Sam fumbled the phone and said, "They're looking for a summer place. East of town. Near the lakes. Good fishing."

"And so?"

"Help them," Sam said. "Jack owes them. They're friends of the Italians."

"The Italians," I said.

"Find them a cottage for the summer," Sam said. "They're looking to escape the city heat."

"Okay," I said. "But remind Jack we're living in the age of communication."

Myrtle, goose-bumped arms crossed over her breasts, held a cigarette lighter in one hand and flicked it. No flame.

"Friends of the Italians," I said. "I wonder what that means?"

"I'll tell you exactly what that means," she said.

"Spill," I said.

"Starts with a C- and ends with P-O-N-E. We don't have enough troublemakers? We bring them from out of town."

"Capone's in prison, in case you haven't heard."

"Prison don't stop those guys."

I patted her butt.

"Let me go earn some money," I said.

I pulled my Essex in front of the drugstore and tapped the horn. George sat in front, cashmere coat thrown between us. Monty sat in back, drinking dark fluid from a medicine bottle.

"You're straight now?" asked George.

"All squared away."

"Not too close to town, no too far in the boonies," said George.

"I know just the place," I said.

"Now we're communicating," George said.

I drove them through the swell part of downtown. The bankers and insurance clerks were leaving for the day, the night creatures beginning their prowl of Saint Peter Street. Would boozing be half as much fun when it became legal?

As we passed the Civic Center, George asked: "Do they have much of an opera in this town?"

I said I wouldn't know.

"Well," he settled in to his seat, "we'll be here all summer. Won't we Monty?"

"Won't we what?" said Monty.

"Be here all summer?"

"Federal Building," I said, when we passed it.

"Right across from the opera house," said George. "Seems fitting. I imagine J. Edgar is an opera fan."

"Horse racing fan," I said, "or so I hear."

"Dreadful sport," said George. "I don't suppose you gamble on it."

"Occasionally," I said.

"Really," said George, "opera would be a much more enriching use of your time. He should start with something simple and understandable, shouldn't he, Monty?"

Monty coughed.

"I would recommend," George said, "the Barber of Seville. It's a simple *opera buffa* that anyone can enjoy. It's in Italian but you don't need to speak the language to enjoy it. I've taken Monty to see several performances, isn't that right Monty?"

"Very nice," said Monty. "Good singing."

"Good singing," George muttered in disgust. He tapped me on the shoulder. "The Barber of Seville, remember that now. The Barber of Seville, and you'll be an opera lover for life."

That was a silencer for maybe ten minutes until we approached the Hamm Brewery.

"Ah," said George. "Legal beer. The country has come to its

senses. Did you hear that, Monty? I said the country has come to its senses."

"I heard you," coughed Monty.

"Don't drink it myself," said George, and patted his flat belly. "I'm a cocktail man." He looked at me as if seeing me for the first time.

"How do you fit in, Powers?"

"Me?" I said.

"Your name's Powers, isn't it?"

"I do a favor here and there," I said. "I know everybody in town, pretty much."

"He knows everybody in town," George said to Monty. "Now that could be helpful, couldn't it, Monty?"

"I guess so," said Monty.

As we turned onto Highway 61, we blew past a shallow ring of suburbs and entered the countryside. It was that awful time of year, neither winter nor spring, the rich black loam either hidden by snow or turned to muck amid last year's corn stalks. Here and there stood a forlorn farmhouse, cows that had barely survived the winter, rusty trucks and muddy tractors.

However curious I was about these guys, I knew better than to ask questions.

George, turning his hat in his lap, said: "We're looking for quite a big place."

"Oh?"

"Monty's got a substantial family, and I expect we'll have visitors from Chicago."

"How many people are we talking about?"

"Six to eight, depending," George said.

We turned off at the resort town of White Bear. Its modest downtown included drugstores and cafes, a pool hall, a sweets shop, and a big market, Bloom's Cash and Carry Grocers.

"Everything you need," I said. "Right here in town."

When we rolled up to the shore, the lake was icy at the edges, but calm.

"Two popular lakes here," I said. "You're looking at White Bear. Bald Eagle's up the road."

Monty, chewing gum, said: "Fish?"

"Plenty," I said. "Walleye, muskie."

I drove them along the lakeshore and they gawked at cottages. A boardwalk featured kiddy rides, hot dog stands and taverns, all closed for the season.

"I imagine it livens up in summer," George said.

"Streetcar comes out here," I said. "Brings pretty ladies."

"Well, Monty's married. So am I. Monty's got children."

"They'll enjoy the lake," I said.

"So," George said, "you can rent us one of these cottages, right?"

"Sure you could…"

"I'm in need of an arm's length transaction, if you catch my meaning."

"I catch your meaning."

"As close to the lake as possible, as many rooms as possible."

He turned to Monty.

"What's your assessment?"

Monty coughed.

A half hour's quiet drive later, I dropped them off at the Hotel Saint Paul, the most expensive joint in town. From there I drove alone to the Hollyhocks and parked behind the garage. Sam and I began to lay out the Derby, each with our own tasks.

"So Sam."

"So Powers."

"Who's calling me Shaky?"

"I never heard of this."

He was lying. Sam has heard of everything.

"I'll bet the Swede's spreading that around," I said. "I don't like it."

We were sitting in his retreat, at the back end of the Hollyhocks garage. A mechanic's light hung from a workbench as our only illumination. Sam worked on scrap paper, I used pencil and Catholic School notebook.

"So two guys come to town," I said. "One's an opera buff, the other is a TB skeleton. They're from Chicago. They want to spend the summer at the lake."

"So?"

"I was under the impression Chicago had a lake of its own."

Sam looked up from his scrap paper, which he had stapled together into a book.

"I have something for you, Powers."

He lifted one haunch, drew his wallet out of his hip pocket and produced a fifty dollar bill.

"For you." He handed it over. "Clench your teeth and take it."

"Payday," I said. "So when were you going to tell me?"

"Tell you what?"

"About this money."

Sam sighed. "Mick, when are you going to learn to trust? The Master always comes through. The Master is far seeing. Think about it. It took him years to put together this nightclub. The cash, the slot machines and roulette wheels, the real estate, top class liquor connections, the furniture, hiring discreet help, fixing everything with the cops and politicians downtown. Do not underestimate the Master, he sees many, many moves ahead."

"Jack, sure, I get Jack. But these Chicago guys are a little spooky."

"Powers, will you work your figures, please?"

I turned to a fresh page in my notebook. I subscribed to Watch Clocker, a mail order service. Every week I got sheets of numbers, private clockings from wise guys at the race tracks. From these I extracted my own speed figures, equalized for various track conditions. There's no two racetracks run the same, that's the point. A horse can run like Man O' War over the Jamaica track, and plod like a mule at Havre De Grace.

Sam worked the class angle. A horse's first race counted for nothing with Sam. In the horse's second race, only his ability to leave the gate quickly counted. From then on, Sam kept book on who-beat-who in any race at a mile or longer. Put together, we had speed and class angles that, with luck, could extract a small fortune from the Kentucky Derby win pool.

We agreed that the likely favorite, Ladysman, had run weak times and had beaten nobody special.

"They want their money up front."

"Who are we talking about?"

"The landlords. At White Bear. We're talking maybe three hundred for the summer, at least"

"It will be provided then."

"How about providing it now?"

"You tend to annoy me, Powers."

"I'm not a banker, Sam, I need folding money."

He sighed and walked into the sunset and toward the nightclub. The Hollyhocks patrons were well into their steak dinners and Sam was free of them now, having risen above head waiter to become Jack's Man Friday. But he was no happier for the promotion. Having a wife and children in Japan hung around his neck like a stone. I wondered what kind of deal he had worked with Jack for his eventual emancipation. Sam had gotten his start in America as a waiter on the Empire Builder. Someday soon, maybe if we hit it big in the Derby, Sam would take that train to Seattle in the first leg of his journey home.

I stood with one hand on the polished fender of Jack's olive-green Packard. The circular driveway was jammed with expensive cars. The Hollyhocks drew its share of bankers and tycoons, but was a particular favorite of the legal crowd. There were more lawyers in the Hollyhocks than in any courthouse in Minnesota. The infamous criminal defender DeNoblis, known for his whiskey habit and his indiscretions, let the valet take his car while he escorted a fur-wrapped lovely, certainly not his wife, up the wide stairway. A moment later, a yellow cab pulled in and disgorged my new Chicago acquaintances.

Violet herself rushed the door to greet them.

George was accompanied by a toxic blonde and Monty was followed out of the cab by Myrtle.

Violet kissed George on the cheek. That told me he was somebody. Violet was not a kisser.

Myrtle and Monty climbed the stairs to the velvet carpet. The toxic blonde turned to take in the Mississippi sunset. George was arm-in-arm with Violet. They entered the gilded doorway, followed by the blonde. Myrtle, wrapped in silver fox fur, was having some kind of problem with her high heels. She kicked and fussed and Monty dropped to one knee to help her.

Powers, why the jealousy? I asked myself. Myrtle is loyal to no one except the Professor.

Still it made me feel rotten, and left out. When they all disappeared into the dining room I returned my attention to my horse notebook. But soon it was full dark, and Sam's work light wasn't bright enough to work by. What was keeping him?

I crossed the lawn and climbed the front porch. An older woman dressed in a shimmering wrap was laughing with a man young enough and big enough to be a college football player. I stood away from them and looked into the big windows.

There at a candle-lit, white-clothed table sat the four of them, the blonde hanging on to George's arm, Monty reading the menu, Myrtle smoking a cigarette, its end heavy with lipstick. Sam trotted up from the side of the porch and discreetly handed me a wad of money.

"Every priest has his altar boy," I said.

"Speak English, please, Powers."

"George is the golfer, Monty is the caddy."

"Now I understand."

"George escorts the high-priced peroxide blonde, wears the cashmere, does all the talking. He's the one. Monty's just tagging along. I've got a feeling about this George. He's big. Who is he, Sam?"

Sam shrugged.

"And if he really is a big shot Chicago gangster, why is he here?"

www.ingramcontent.com/pod-product-compliance
Lightning Source LLC
Chambersburg PA
CBHW020235180626
46810CB00006B/2210